WINTER
SONG

WINTER SONG

SUSAN C. MULLER

Cover design by
Najla Qamber Designs
http://www.najlaqamberdesigns.com

Interior Design and Formatting by:

emtippettsbookdesigns.com

Books By
SUSAN C. MULLER

The Secrets on Forest Bend

The Witch on Twisted Oak

Voodoo on Bayou Lafonte

Circle of Redemption

Redeeming Santa

Winter Song

Spring Shadow

Summer Storm

Autumn Secrets

For my parents who instilled in me the joy of reading.

Eleanor Elisabeth Jackson Curry
Stanford Bernie Curry

I miss you every day.

CHAPTER ONE

SLEET BEAT AGAINST the roof of the car in a syncopated rhythm with the windshield wipers, creating a tune only winter could sing. Bitter night air seeped inside through the rusted floorboard. The driver shivered, yet never lowered his guard, watching from the darkened lot.

Waiting for his target to appear.

Cars zipped by his secluded spot, but not the one he expected. His heart rate kicked up with each minute that passed. Could she have slipped by him, unnoticed? Scooted around the corner when he wasn't paying attention?

Impossible. He'd hardly blinked for the last half-hour.

An industrial-sized dumpster hid his car from curious eyes, but obstructed his view. He strained forward against the seat belt as if an extra two inches of visibility would make a difference.

Maybe if I took the belt off. His hand rested on the cold metal. No, there wouldn't be time to fasten it again. No driving infractions. A good rule he followed faithfully.

When her red BMW rounded the corner, she was speeding, but he'd been warned to expect that. His heart settled into a steady rhythm. *Tha-thump. Tha-thump.*

"Here she is," he called over his shoulder, the tremble in his voice betraying his excitement. "It's showtime." He switched on his lights and slipped into traffic, two car-lengths behind her.

His eyes flicked from the road to her car and back, constantly measuring distance, speed, witnesses. He crept up beside her. Two more feet and he'd be perfectly positioned.

The back window lowered with a soft *whirr.*

Without warning, she swerved into the next lane. *What the hell?*

He tried to copy her move, but his front wheel hit a patch of ice. The car fishtailed, forcing him to ease off the gas.

Had she seen the ice, was that why she'd switched lanes? Or had she spotted him? The open window? The barrel of the gun?

By the time he regained control of the car, it was too late. An SUV had pulled out of a parking lot and filled in the gap between them. Bile burned the back of his throat at the prospect of failure.

"What're you doing? We can still catch her." His back-seat passenger beat on the headrest. "You said it had to be tonight."

"Maybe, but not here. We'll have to wait until she's on her way home. Close that window before someone notices. " An open window in the middle of a sleet storm was an invitation to be remembered. He'd picked the shooter for his skill and intelligence, neither of which he was demonstrating tonight.

"This is where we planned for. We haven't scouted anywhere else." The whiney voice from the back seat caused the driver to clench his teeth.

"We've got an hour, we'll scout it now. As long as we complete the job tonight, what difference does it make which side of the freeway we're on?" He rolled his shoulders, trying to relax, but his muscles refused to cooperate. Working with a partner made every step more challenging.

One foolish mistake ten years ago and he was still dealing with the consequences.

"What the fuck is Bellaire PD doing in the middle of our crime scene?" Detective Noah Daugherty jumped out of the car and let his partner worry about parking.

A gust of frigid air slapped him in the face. He trudged down the icy street, resentment oozing from every pour. With the neighboring PD here, he'd have to play nice, pretend he cared what they thought. All the while, the evidence would be growing colder.

To hell with that. He was through pretending while bad guys got away. All he wanted was to keep busy and solve cases. Screw making friends.

He jammed his hands deep into his pockets and studied the dynamics of the group in front of him. In seconds, he knew who was in charge and who were the toadies.

"Good evening, officers. I'm Noah Daugherty, HPD Homicide." He fished around for the appropriate smile, pasted it on, and flashed his badge. "I'll take over now. You can get back to work. I'm sure the citizens of Bellaire would want you on the job, not standing out here in the cold." He purposely spoke to the youngest man, turning his back on the top dog.

"Now just one minute," the lead investigator sputtered

from behind him. "This crime is in Bellaire. We don't need any interference from Houston."

Noah reached in his pocket and pulled out a stick of gum. He took his time, twisting toward the other man. "Are you sure? According to my calculations, her car crossed into Houston at least twenty feet before she was killed." He slipped the gum into his mouth and waited. Would the Bellaire detective fold, or was his night about to get more complicated?

Noah held his breath as the man glanced to the car and back again several times before answering. "She was shot approximately in front of the dry cleaners. Her car rolled to the intersection and the bumper may have kissed the Houston city limits, but the crime, the car, and the body are all in Bellaire."

The Bellaire detective's face grew redder with every word. He pulled his puny shoulders as high as they'd go and puffed out his chest. Noah sighed and pushed the gum to one side of his cheek. *Great, a Napoleon complex.* He took a step forward, towering over the smaller man.

"I don't know what they teach you in Bellaire, but in Houston, we learn exactly where our city limits are. On the west side of the freeway, the city limits are at this intersection. But for some unknown reason, on the east side they start a block back. That means the whole crime scene, from the first shot to when the car stopped, all belong to me."

The detective chewed on his lip and scratched his bald head. "You want it, buddy, you take it. We've got plenty to keep us busy." He spun on his heel and had his cell phone to his ear before Noah could answer.

Noah sucked in a deep breath. The raw air burned his lungs but couldn't dampen the moment. *That's one for the win column.*

Seemed like confrontations with other officers was all the fun he had these days, and no matter how many cases he worked, he couldn't stay busy enough.

Footsteps on the icy roadway caused Noah to glance behind him as his partner approached, the frost on his breath almost obscuring his face.

"Started a fight and finished it before I could park the car. Thought you were going to wait for me." Conner Crawford was a hair under six feet and whip thin. Noah topped him by two inches and twenty-plus pounds, but Conner could hold his own in any situation and Noah never worried about his back with Conner around.

"No sense letting 'em get the drop on us. It was an argument that could have gone on for days. Now it's settled and we can get to work." Noah had never been good at politics. Lately, he just did what needed doing and let his partner clean up the mess.

Conner trailed behind Noah as they made a wide circle around the crime scene before approaching the vehicle. The stoplight overhead cycled to red, giving the area an eerie glow.

As they approached the car, Conner took a moment to mumble a private prayer. After six years of working together, Noah still didn't know if his partner prayed for the deceased or for his own abilities to offer justice. It seemed too personal to ask.

He just hoped the prayer covered him, too.

Noah leaned in the shattered window and studied the body. She'd once been a beautiful woman. Not anymore. "Looks like a single shot to the left temple. A through-and-through, judging by the amount of brain matter on the passenger seat." The coppery smell of blood filled the car and turned Noah's empty stomach. Or was it the sight of a woman whose life was snatched away much too early?

A thought pricked at his heart. Would anyone mourn for her?

He swallowed back the question. This wasn't the time to be sentimental. "We'll have to wait for the M.E. to give us official time of death, but this weather might skew the numbers. Looking at her, I say less than an hour. You checked with the responding officer on the way in. What'd he say?"

Conner pulled out his pocket spiral. "Fletcher over there," he pointed his chin at a motorcycle patrolman, "arrived at 8:17 and switched off the engine. Said he didn't want to take a chance the body would shift and she'd bump the accelerator. It's 9:00 now, so yeah, less than an hour. You want to question him about it?"

"Hell no. Much as I hate anyone messing with my crime scene, it takes a set of stainless steel *cojones* to ride a donor-cycle on a night like this. I'm not going to cross him."

"Wise choice. Personally, I planned to step back out of the way if you did. The DMV lists the car as belonging to Gary Hudson. Address a few blocks from here."

"Our vic doesn't look like a Gary." Noah ignored the honks and shouts as drivers objected to the cordoned-off street. Didn't anyone have respect for the dead anymore? These were probably the same people who blew past funeral processions, horns blaring.

"Big diamond, fancy car, trophy wife. Gary must be doing well for himself." Conner made more notes in his spiral.

"Yeah, but she's just wearing some kind of sweats."

"Yoga pants and top. See the emblem on her left shoulder? That means designer duds. I'll wager my left nut they cost more than your suit."

"I already own your left nut from our last case, and I sure as hell don't want the right one. Besides, this is a nice suit." Noah brushed dog hair off his jacket. He decided not to mention the pieces of crumbled liver treats in the pocket.

"It may be the best suit Men's Warehouse sells, but it's not a *nice* suit." Conner adjusted his perfectly fitting jacket. "*This* is a nice suit."

Noah eyed Conner's suit and groaned. *What a waste of money.* He owned one expensive suit and he'd worn it exactly twice: to one wedding and one funeral. He didn't plan to ever wear it again. Except maybe to his own funeral, but that was somcone else's problem.

For the moment, his only concern was a dead woman in a red car. "One bullet to the side of the head. That's a hell of a shot into a moving car. So was the shooter mobile or stationary?"

"No way the shooter stood beside the freeway. Anyone could have seen him. Must have been from a car."

Noah twisted to stare down the street. "You're right. The shooter would have been completely exposed. Not likely he was standing out there, waiting in ambush. We'll have to check anyway, but what are the odds?"

"About as good as the mayor inviting either of us to dinner." *That slim, huh?*

"Could be road rage. A bright-red BMW sometimes hints at an aggressive driver. Doesn't take much to set some people off. Might be a good idea to check her driving record."

"Already on my list." Conned tapped his spiral.

He could always count on Conner. Best paper-jockey, detective, friend he'd ever had. "So was the shooter angry and trying to scare her, the bullet connecting by accident, or cold and calculating, pulling off a one-in-a-million shot?" Noah tried to breathe warmth onto his frozen fingers.

Conner scanned the area, measuring, angles, distance, visibility. "I'd call it more of a one-in-a-hundred shot, but as soon as we finish here, let's go talk to the husband."

Sure, because talking to a grieving husband is so much fun.

Noah turned his back. He'd seen enough. "Wonder if he's missed her yet? Maybe he isn't actually expecting her to return."

Brightly lit store fronts illuminated the parking lot, but left the street dark. Noah and Conner cased the area, their flashlights poking temporary holes in the gloom. Fragments of broken glass littered the pavement, marking the spot where the BMW was hit. The raised side of the freeway dropped down to meet the street with no curb. The slush beside the road had iced over and showed no sign of footprints. Noah squatted and poked at the slush with one finger. The ice gave way, sending his finger two inches into semi-frozen muck.

He motioned for a forensics tech. "Step in this ice, then time how long it takes to freeze over again. Does it freeze smooth or leave a footprint?"

The tech frowned, but Noah ignored him. The tech was dressed for this weather—parka, rubber boots, gloves—let him run the tests.

Conner joined him in the street. "Nothing's open for a block either direction on this side of the freeway. An ExxonMobil station is the first business open to the north. An Auto Zone stays open till nine to the south. I've told them both that nobody leaves till we talk to them. I suggest we start with the Exxon. They have hot coffee."

Noah stuffed his hands back in his pockets, fingering the crumbled dog treats, and spun toward the gas station. "Sounds like a plan. I need to get out of this cold soon, or I'm going to develop frostbite on parts of my body that I'm very fond of." Not that he'd had any use for that part lately. "If this weather keeps up, I may actually have to invest in a heavy coat."

"Weatherman says another seventy-two hours and we'll be back to normal, sunny and clear, just in time for the groundhog to see his shadow."

"Fuck the groundhog. He's just a big rat with good PR. What does he know?" Noah studied Conner under hooded eyes. "Why aren't you colder? Do you have on long underwear or something? Don't answer that. I don't think I want to know."

Conner gave a how-did-you-guess grin. "Toasty warm all the way down. Only problem was fastening my pants. I took a cue from when Jeannie first got pregnant. I stuck one of her hair bands through the button hole and looped it around the button for an extra couple of inches, then put a belt on top of it." His lips clamped shut as if he could move fast enough to prevent the words from escaping or suck them back in before they reached Noah's ears.

Well, shit. Now what?

Talking about Jeannie's pregnancy in front of him made Conner uncomfortable, but they had to get past it if they were going to keep working together. Noah cast around for something to say that would put his partner at ease. "Women. Pregnancy brings out the mama bear in all of them. I'm surprised she didn't put you in one of those knit hats with flaps hanging down over the ears and a puff ball on top. If you pull one of those out of your back pocket and put it on, I'm walking out of here right now."

"Nah. If she'd tried that, I would've refused. I still have some backbone left." Conner's voice eased as if the moment had never happened.

And Noah wished it hadn't, but if that's what it took to get his partner back, he'd gladly endure two minutes of discomfort.

The ExxonMobil station smelled of scorched coffee and wet clothes, but the attendant spoke English with an accent that wasn't too heavy to understand. "My last customer left at least fifteen minutes before all the commotion down the street. He paid cash, and no, that's not unusual. He's been in before. I think he's a waiter. He always has small bills. I had several customers shortly before that and I've got their credit card receipts ready for you. I know you'll want the surveillance video. I took it out when I heard the sirens. I've been expecting you." He held out a paper bag with the video and receipts.

Noah glanced at Conner. Was this guy for real? Witnesses were never this helpful. No point asking what he saw, the windows had fogged over, and the guy insisted he hadn't left the building. Noah handed him two cards. "Thanks for your help. Call me if you remember anything else. And if the waiter comes in, get his name and ask him to call."

He grabbed his coffee and faced Conner. "You take this side of the freeway, and I'll cross over and take the other side. I'll meet you back at Auto Zone."

Noah hiked across the feeder-road and through the underpass, cradling the Styrofoam cup in both hands for warmth, occasionally sipping a brew so foul, most would have tossed it away in disgust. He'd be willing to swear in court they had fished used oil filters out of the trash to do double duty in the coffee pot.

The air was so cold, it hurt to breathe. How did people live in climates where this was normal winter weather? At least this norther would pass in a few days. If it froze again this year, it wouldn't last long. He'd spent two winters in New York when he was young. It was exciting, but not anything he'd ever want to do again.

Forty-five minutes later, every shop inspected for occupants or security cameras, he joined his partner at the auto parts store. If he'd been cold before, he was frozen now. His feet were wet and his nose running. That heavy coat was sounding better and better. No, it would feel like a straitjacket inside of an hour.

The employees sat in the break room, fidgeting. Their shift was over, and one glance said they wanted out. Taking one person at a time, he and Conner interviewed all four workers. Three were in the back at the time of the shooting, leaving one at the counter, facing the street. Like the gas station attendant, he claimed the windows were too fogged to see anything.

Unless the security tape showed something, this was another dead end.

The wind had died down and the sleet stopped a few hours earlier, but the temperature had dropped several degrees by the time they left Auto Zone. Conner pulled his coat tighter and headed for the car, but Noah stopped him. "Take a look up and down this street, then check the other side and tell me if you notice any difference."

The two men trudged through the underpass to the west side of the feeder road. Conner didn't speak, but studied the businesses carefully. He even stood in the street and scrutinized the freeway before crossing back to the east side and checking it again.

"West side's a lot darker. None of the businesses have bright lights, and the nearest streetlight on the freeway is out. The pavement's dry next to that dumpster. Something kept the sleet off that spot. A car sure could hide there and wait unnoticed. Then pull out when the right vehicle came around the corner. And that's the route she'd probably have taken, according to the address on her drivers license."

The wind whipped Noah's hair and he raised his voice to be heard over the horns and shouts and sirens. "Then why the job on the east side? Auto Zone and ExxonMobil both have security cameras, and the bank has one on the ATM. All three of those places are brightly lit, and the strip center hasn't taken down their Christmas lights."

"Something happened. Another car came by, he couldn't make his shot, he got nervous. I don't know. But he got up his nerve and tried again on the east side without all the planning."

"Why didn't he try to catch up? What else is different?" Noah waited while Conner chewed on the problem. He didn't have to wait long.

"The city limits. It's too early to know for sure, but maybe he wanted to do it in Bellaire and didn't realize the line didn't run straight. Can't say I blame him. Without a Homicide department, Bellaire's no match for us."

Noah started for the car, breath-frost trailing behind him. "Don't fault Bellaire. Working a little of everything makes a well-rounded detective. They may not have as much specialized experience as we do, but they're sharp and have a smaller case load. But you're on the right track. I'll bet *my* left nut the perp wanted to do the job in Bellaire, and when we figure out why, we'll be a long way toward knowing who."

The Hudsons' home was only a few blocks from the crime scene but a world away from the noise and traffic of the freeway. Extensive outdoor lighting showed off a manicured lawn rolling up to a two story stucco eyesore that was big enough to hold Noah's house, yard and car with room left over to host a gala for three hundred of his closest friends.

The click of Conner's seatbelt unfastening pulled Noah from his study of the house. He put his hand on his partner's sleeve. "I'll give you back your left nut if he asks how to contact the victims' fund about paying for the funeral."

Conner gave an I'll-take-that-bet chuckle. "Your loss."

Noah removed his gum, wrapped it in paper and tossed it into the car's litter bag. "Let's go see what Gary has to say and where he thinks his wife is," he paused to check his watch, "at quarter till eleven on the nastiest night of the year."

He opened the car door and stopped, one foot on the pavement. "Fuck, I hate this part of the job." Notifying loved ones sucked. If they were taken by surprise, their grief was a kick in the gut. If they were involved, watching them pretend was ten times worse.

Conner clicked the key fob and grunted in agreement.

The yard may have been well lit, but the house was dark. An upstairs window glowed and the frosted glass in the front entrance showed a thin line of light seeping from under a closed door near the back of the house. No welcoming light had been left on for a returning wife. He wouldn't have wanted anyone he loved coming home to such an unfriendly place.

Conner stomped his feet on the mat and smoothed his hair. "How do you want to play this, grieving widower or prime suspect?"

The darkened house sent a be-on-your-toes warning down Noah's spine. "I'd like to get a feel for him first. Let's give him some rope. See if he makes a noose before we do the official notification business."

He rang the bell and waited. By the time he'd counted to ten, the light increased and footsteps sounded on a wooden floor. Hard-soled shoes, not slippers or bare feet. He glanced at Conner and raised his eyebrows. "Think he's expecting someone?" he mouthed.

The door flew open and a middle-aged man stood on the other side. He carried twenty extra pounds, and his hairline had retreated several inches. Otherwise, he looked in good shape for his age. He'd removed his suit coat and tie and rolled his sleeves part way up with a knife-edged crease, but could have been ready to leave for the office with three minutes' notice.

He stood in the doorway and stared at the two men. He didn't move or speak, only blinked several times.

"Mr. Hudson?" Noah waited a beat, but the man didn't answer. "I'm Detective Daugherty from the Houston Police Department, and this is my partner, Detective Crawford. May we come in?" He held his badge in his left hand, keeping his right hand loose and near his weapon.

The man shook his head as if clearing it. Noah had seen better acting at his niece's grade school play.

Another moment passed before the man stepped back and

opened the door wider. "Of course, of course. I expected to see my wife, that's all. I thought she must have her hands full and couldn't open the door." His voice was too pleasant, too welcoming, too accepting.

Noah's bullshit antenna activated instantly.

He expected his wife to come in the front door? No one but trick-or-treaters and mourners had ever come to Noah's front door. If the bell rang, it wasn't someone he wanted to see.

The man led the way through the house, flipping on lights as he went, and stopping in an ornate room containing furniture Noah was afraid to sit on. "Make yourselves comfortable, gentlemen. I'll be right back."

Noah glanced at Conner and narrowed his eyes. He'd never knocked on anyone's door, day or night, who didn't ask why he was there before inviting him in.

There was no way Noah would ever be comfortable in that room, but he lowered himself into the sturdiest chair he could find. Conner shrugged and sat on a small sofa that had a curved back at one end and a seat extending another two feet with no back rest. He tried several different positions before giving up and taking the most uncomfortable looking chair Noah had ever seen.

At the far end of the room, a grand piano gleamed under multiple coats of furniture polish. A pang of guilt hit Noah as he thought of the old upright sitting in his living room, dusty and unused, with one temperamental key that he'd never gotten around to having repaired.

Was the victim the one who played? On tough days, did Hudson perch on that torturous sofa and let the notes of *Clair de Lune* wash away his cares? Did they sit on the piano bench, side by side, on Christmas Eve and sing carols while they waited until midnight to open their gifts?

Mr. Hudson returned, followed by a maid carrying an ornate silver tray containing china cups filled with coffee. Cream and sugar containers matched the flowered pattern of the cups. After the burnt sludge from the ExxonMobil station, it smelled like Heaven. The maid hovered as each man fixed his coffee, then she placed the tray on a piece of furniture Noah hadn't realized was a table and left the room.

Noah inhaled the rich brew and eyed the cup, worried he might crush the delicate porcelain if he gripped it too tightly. *Where am I supposed to put my fingers? Not through that tiny handle.*

"Now, what can I help you gentlemen with on such a cold night? I always like to assist the police whenever I can. Another donation? Buy some more vests? You could have just called. I would have had my secretary send a check." Mr. Hudson sat on the sofa Conner had vacated. He leaned back into the corner and stretched his legs down the cushion.

Smooth. He's already managed to tell us we're rubes while he's a wealthy sophisticate with connections in the department.

"We're here about your wife, Mr. Hudson." He glanced at his notes, as if he had to remind himself. "Crystal, isn't it?"

Hudson gave an exaggerated sigh. "What is it now? She didn't get another ticket, did she? I should have known better than to buy her a red car. It brings out the worst in her driving. She speeds, weaves in and out of traffic and thinks a yellow light means 'go faster.' Well, this time she'll have to attend one of those defensive driving classes. I'm not paying the ticket until she does."

Conner finished his coffee and set the cup on something that might have been a table. The room was warm, and Noah's feet were beginning to thaw. He unbuttoned his coat and glanced at Conner. Beads of sweat were breaking out on his forehead and he tugged at his shirt collar. Noah tried to hide a smile as he noticed the edge of Conner's long underwear peeking out from his pant leg.

"Where is your wife now, Mr. Hudson?" Noah kept his voice calm, casual. Just your normal everyday conversation with two detectives in the middle of the night, visiting.

"Lord only knows. She has different classes on different nights. I don't have any idea what tonight's is. Then she goes shopping or has drinks with whoever else is in that class. She gets bored at night because I'm so often working. Like tonight, I've been on a conference call to Japan. You have to be available when your customers are awake."

Good one, he slipped in his alibi before we even asked.

Enough of this pussyfooting around. "Mr. Hudson, I'm sorry to inform you a red BMW registered to you was damaged earlier this evening, and the woman driving was killed. We suspect it might have been your wife and we need someone to make a positive identification."

Hudson's eyes went wide, and his mouth formed an O shape. He set his coffee down with an exaggerated tremble, causing the cup to rattle and slosh coffee into the saucer. "You must be mistaken. Crystal liked to push the speed limit, sure, but the car has air bags and she always wore her seatbelt unless she was headed to a party and didn't want to wrinkle her dress."

Noah kept his eyes on Hudson. He hadn't even made an ID and he was already speaking of her in the past tense. "It wasn't a traffic accident, Mr. Hudson. Did your wife have any enemies that you know of?"

"Crystal? Heavens, no. She shopped, she lunched, she took classes. You think someone shot her because she played better tennis?"

Conner leaned forward in his chair. "Shot? Why do you say that? We never mentioned she was shot."

Hudson jerked toward Conner, knocking over his coffee cup. At least this time his surprise didn't look staged. "Well, you said enemies. It's hard to poison someone while they're driving. I naturally thought of a gun. Is that what happened? Did she cut someone off in traffic and they retaliated?"

Five minutes and the man had already accepted his wife's death, provided himself with an alibi and solved the crime.

"Why don't we try to get a positive ID before we speculate?" Noah stood and motioned

Hudson to follow. He'd witnessed enough phony concern. "If you'll come with us, we'll drive you downtown and you can view the body."

"The body," Hudson said, a hiccup hiding in his voice. "That sounds so cold." For a moment, he actually seemed shaken.

Conner drove and Hudson sat in the back, staring silently at the floor. Noah twisted in his seat to face him, but any questions he asked went unanswered.

At the morgue, Noah led Hudson to the family viewing area. The room, which was kept ten degrees too cold in the summer, was now too hot and someone's attempt to cover the chemical odor with flowery deodorizer had failed miserably. Conner left in search of an aide to bring the body around.

The aide arrived and placed the body with the damaged half

of her face away from the window. With all the blood washed away and her hair smoothed down, it was almost possible to believe she was sleeping.

If you didn't look too closely.

Hudson placed his hand on the window and leaned his forehead against the glass. Noah turned his head and let Conner do the observing. The scene was too familiar, the pain still too raw. Noah unconsciously twisted the gold band he now wore on his right hand.

"Is that your wife's body, Mr. Hudson?" Conner softened his voice, smoothing the sharp edges off the worst words in the world.

"Yes." Hudson swallowed deeply and spun toward the two detectives. "Do you have the son-of-a-bitch who did this?"

Noah put his arm around Hudson's shoulder and led him down the hall. "Not yet, sir. But we will."

On the surface, his words may have sounded reassuring, but there was no mistaking the underlying threat.

Noah mounted the steps silently, but as soon as he turned the lock, he was met with a cacophony of yipping and growling. A tiny Yorkshire terrier backed away from him while curling her lips and baring her teeth.

"Hi, honey, I'm home. Nice to see you, too." Noah said, tossing his keys on the kitchen table. He lowered himself onto the nearest chair. "You do realize I'm the one who feeds you, don't you? And the one who cleans up your mess and takes you for walks."

The dog fell silent but showed her teeth again when Noah

reached out his hand.

"I swear, if you bite me one more time, you'll never see another doggy treat."

Noah sighed and pushed up from the chair. The dog watched from across the room as he opened a can of dog food and filled her dish. "If you'd eat the dry stuff I leave out, you wouldn't be so hungry when I get home. It's good stuff. You used to eat it all the time."

The dog eyed her food bowl, but didn't move toward it until Noah backed away. While she ate, Noah cleaned up the gifts she'd left on the kitchen floor and put out new papers. He didn't even notice the smell anymore. "You get worse every day. You used to tolerate me. Hell, you used to *like* me."

Once the dog finished eating, Noah scooped her up and held her in his lap. She stiffened but didn't snap at him. "What am I going to do with you, Sweet Pea? If I knew someplace to take you where you'd be happy, believe me I would. But no one really wants an angry, barking, biting dog."

Or an angry, grouchy man.

Sweet Pea wiggled free. Noah felt something warm on his leg and looked down to see a wet spot spreading down his slacks. *What the fuck?*

The day he was going to have to make the decision to put her down was getting closer, but so far he didn't have the heart to do it. Noah let Sweet Pea out and waited while she made a quick circle of the yard, squatted and hurried back inside. At least the cold weather was good for something.

As she scooted past him, he glanced into his empty house and thought of Crystal Hudson slumped against her seat belt. It was going to be another long night.

CHAPTER TWO

THE DRIVER SHIVERED as he stood at the window, watching the morning sun reveal a frozen landscape. The few fools who ventured out slipped and slid like they were on an ice rink. Good thing he didn't need to leave the room for several hours.

Red numbers glowed on the clock beside his bed. Still time to catch the early news. Would the mark's death be the lead story? Grabbing the remote, he flipped on the TV. If the Bellaire cops had connected her death to the others, he was in trouble. No, he'd been too clever. They'd never see the strings.

A portly, bald guy was finishing the weather with a special report about driving on ice-covered roads. Five minutes for him to say "Don't do it." When the bleached blonde came back on, a picture of the red BMW flashed on the screen behind her. He leaned forward to catch every word.

When she finished, he released a relieved sigh. The media seemed to be blaming the attack on road rage caused by icy streets. According to their report, more of it was likely to happen if people didn't stay home till this front passed in a few days.

Stay home for a few days? He barked a short laugh. No one in Houston was going to admit they didn't know how to drive on ice. They wouldn't stay home a few hours, forget days. The ice, which had almost ruined everything, might turn out to be the perfect cover.

The cop they interviewed didn't have a clue. They never did. Stupid civil servants. You get what you pay for, his mother always said. But the guy did seem familiar, or did all cops look alike? He chuckled at his own joke, his spirits rising. Payday was right around the corner, but outsmarting the cops was even more fun.

His heart slammed against his rib cage. Did the reporter just identify the man as an HPD detective? What happened to Bellaire, where were they? Had the car rolled into Houston? Even so, the shot was fired in Bellaire.

This was a cluster fuck if ever there was one.

Heat boiled inside his gut and he threw the remote across the room. It hit the wall with a *smack* and the back flew off, spilling batteries on the floor. Watching the batteries disappear under the bed was like watching his money roll away.

A tap on the door startled him, and his heart jumped into his throat. His head swiveled, searching the tiny room. Nowhere to go except out the window. From the third floor, in boxers and a T-shirt? *Calm down.* This was the kind of panic he couldn't afford. The type exhibited by the dumb criminals he read about in the paper. He was above all that.

A blast of cold air swept in, and he swung around to see the shooter slide through the door and pull it closed behind him. "Hot damn. They're already calling the job road rage. With everything they'll have going on for the next few days, they'll box this one up and forget about it. Maybe we can get paid a few days early. I'm tapped out. I need the money." The shooter's voice edged up in excitement.

"Forget it. For some reason, HPD is investigating. They'll be all over this like ducks on a June bug. We'll either have to move up the next job, or convince this client to pay even if the cops are still sniffing around him."

Four hours of sleep did little to improve Noah's mood. He crept downtown over freshly sanded streets and waited while Conner signed for a pool car. Motor pool cars were a piece of shit, without decent AC in the summer and minimal heat in the winter, but no way was he driving his own car on icy roads in a city that experienced these conditions once a decade.

Conner brought the car around, a white Taurus with a dented rear fender and broken side view mirror. *Yep, another turdmobile.* But the service report listed the dash cam and siren as operable, so Noah climbed in. He turned the heat up and a trickle of tepid air oozed through the vents. It smelled like something filtered through old gym socks.

Without taking his eyes off the road, Conner brought up the question Noah had been wrestling with all night. "Do you want to start with canvassing the area or interviewing the neighbors?"

Noah flashed back to the racket Sweet Pea had made that morning when she heard a car door slam. "The neighbors. I'd like to talk to them before the victim's husband gets to 'em and plants any ideas in their heads. We'll let the sun do its best before we start the leg work."

Conner kept the speed low, but steady, and they made good time on almost deserted freeways. A few idiots zipped past them as if road conditions were normal, but Noah figured that was one way to keep the gene pool pure.

They reached the victim's home by nine thirty and it was even more enormous in the daylight. The Mediterranean monstrosity took up two lots at the end of a cul-de-sac. That left room for six houses on the block, each a mansion compared to anything Noah or Conner had ever owned. No one answered the bell at three of the houses, so Noah stuck his card in the door.

At the fourth house, a maid opened an ornate door. From the way her eyes widened when she saw Noah's badge, she had to be an illegal. He tried to question her in halting Spanish, but she shook her head. "*No hablo ingles,*" she insisted.

The card he handed her might as well have been hot lava.

"She'll be in the wind the moment we're out of sight," Conner sighed as they started down the sidewalk.

"Yeah, too bad, really. She might have been our best lead."

"How do you figure that? The Hudsons would never talk to her. They probably wouldn't notice if she stood in the middle of the street." Conner stepped carefully, avoiding patches of ice.

"They wouldn't talk to her, but their servants might. And they'd tell her things they wouldn't tell us." Noah shoved his hands in his pockets and continued down the deserted street. So far, the day had been a waste of time.

A blue plastic sledding disc the size of a garbage can lid leaned against the door frame of the next house. A Frisbee on steroids. Did they still make those things? Noah hadn't seen one since he cut classes and went to Vermont one winter weekend with a bunch of friends.

Nearly wrecked my football knee, but it was worth it, Noah thought, remembering a girl with long blond hair and fuzzy ski boots. They'd shared a sleeping bag and she'd ditched the boots and everything else. Not his first time, but close enough that it was the first time he could enjoy it with the confidence he was doing everything right.

What was her name? Allison. A smile quirked at the corner of his mouth. *Yeah, Allison.*

But that was long ago, when he was young and thought the world was a fair place. Six months later, he knew better.

He straightened his tie and reached up to ring the bell, but the door flew open before he had a chance to press the button. A teenage boy with multi-colored hair plowed into him.

"Whoa, dude." The kid jumped back. "Nobody's home, man. Come back some other time."

"You're home." Noah stared the boy in the eyes, but the kid didn't seem to comprehend the logic of the statement.

"Chill, dude. I gotta run." He pulled the door shut and tried to squeeze between Conner and Noah.

Noah held out an arm to block the boy's path without touching him. The look on the kid's face said no one had ever kept him from doing what he wanted. When he spotted Noah's badge, his eyes went wide and his jaw dropped.

"We need to speak to you about the people next door." He'd had enough of being brushed off. The kid was here and would stay here until they got some answers if he had to handcuff him. Maybe he could threaten to sit on him and dye his hair brown.

"You mean party central? The dude keeps the brights on round the clock. I had to get black-out curtains. They have parties where they hire valet parking and the music blasts all night. It would be one thing if it was *good* music, but man. . ."

"Do you know the family? Are your parents friends with them?" Now they were getting somewhere.

"They're not like *friends* or anything. They get invited to the parties, but just so they can't complain about the noise. At least that's what my dad says. My mom says who would want to be friends with them? She only goes to see what tacky thing they've done now."

A late model SUV barreled down the street, horn blaring, and skidded to a stop in front of the curb. The car vibrated in time to a bass drum Noah felt instead of heard. The passenger window lowered and from deep inside a male voice called, "Move it, dork breath. Once the sun hits that hill, all the ice will be gone in ten minutes."

"Later, dudes. The parental units'll be home tomorrow." The boy grabbed the sledding disc and slipped between Noah and Conner.

"This'll teach 'em to go to Aspen without us," he called as he dove into the back seat of the car and was gone.

Conner stared after the car. "Am I correct in assuming this is a school day?"

"I'm sure they're headed for a field trip."

"Yeah, that's what I always called it, too."

The partners picked their way cautiously across the street. Some of the ice had melted, but not in areas shaded from the sun. The final house was the smallest and had a For Sale sign listing slightly on the front lawn.

Noah rang the bell while Conner studied the house. "I don't think anyone's home."

After ringing the bell a second time and knocking on the

door, Noah shrugged and stepped back, but a sound stopped him.

The door opened to the width of the chain and one eye peered out. From the height of the eye, Noah decided the person on the other side was a woman. "I'm Detective Daugherty, ma'am, Houston Police Department, and this is my partner, Detective Crawford. We'd like to ask you a few questions about your neighbors, the Hudsons."

The door closed briefly while the chain was removed then opened completely. Backlight left the person obscured. Only a short, lumpy silhouette showed. "Crystal and Gary? What do you need to know?" She craned her neck toward the Hudson house. "Did someone try to break in? Is Crystal okay?"

"May we come in, ma'am?"

The lump swiveled her head from Noah to Conner and back. "Sorry. Could I see that badge again, please?"

Both men held out their badges and she studied them briefly. "Sorry. Living alone, you have to be careful."

Then she should have been careful before she opened the door. "You're absolutely right, ma'am. If it would make you feel more comfortable, you could call our boss and he'd describe us."

"No, that's not necessary. Come in, come in. It's cold out there." She spun around and shuffled toward the rear of the house. Noah and Conner followed.

"I'm having Chamomile tea. Would you gentlemen like a cup?"

"That would be lovely, ma'am. Nothing like a nice cup of tea on a cold day," Noah said, rubbing his hands.

Conner shot Noah a dirty look, but Noah ignored him. It was hard to throw someone out when they were sitting at your table, drinking tea.

The kitchen was over-warm and cluttered, but a draft said parts of the house were closed off, not heated. Noah unbuttoned his jacket and glanced at Conner. He looked thinner today. He must have left the long underwear at home.

When she set the cups in front of them, Noah relaxed. A nice, big mug with a handle he could grip, not some kind of kid's tea-party toy cup. Noah got his first real look at her as he turned and said, "Thank you." She was much younger than he had realized.

Her hair was honey-blond and had started out in a ponytail, but half of it had escaped, and was going in whatever direction it desired. Hard to guess when she'd last brushed it. She apparently had on several layers of clothes, the top one being an oversized Chenille robe belted loosely over flannel pajamas. No wonder he'd mistaken her for someone's grandmother.

On her feet were fuzzy striped socks and fluffy bunny slippers. Her nose and eyes were red, and she clutched a box of tissues. She turned her head as she sneezed and blew her nose like a honking goose.

"Sorry," she said, her voice raspy and raw. "I promise not to breathe on you."

Noah sat back in his chair, trying not to inhale any of her germs. He'd probably be in that condition or worse by tomorrow. His feet were wet again and would have to stay that way all day.

Conner whipped out his ever-present spiral. "Could I get your name, ma'am?"

"Oh, sorry. I'm Laurel Bledsoe."

Conner jotted, while Noah started the questioning. "What can you tell us about Mr. and Mrs. Hudson?"

"Are you trying to reach them? I have Crystal's cell number if you need it. I can't imagine where she is. She's usually kind enough to turn the lights down on this side of the house, so I don't think she came home last night."

"Do you know if she went out yesterday evening?"

"It was her yoga night. I used to go with her, but I can't afford it now. Class is over at eight, and a couple of times we stopped for a drink, but we were always home by nine thirty. I doubt she'd go to a bar by herself." She twisted from Noah to Conner and back. "Why do you ask? Is she missing? Did something happen to her? Where's Gary?" Her voice began to rise.

Noah generally asked the questions. He didn't answer them until he was ready. "What about her husband? Do you know him?"

"Of course I know him." She sneezed again, but the hint of distaste was evident in her voice. "He's more Peter's friend than mine, but I know him."

"And Peter would be . . . ?"

"My husband. My soon-to-be ex-husband." She pulled a tissue from the box and shredded it. "Those men were like two peas in a rotten, stinking, decaying pod of shit."

A smile twitched at the corners of Noah's mouth. He gave Conner a knowing glance. This was about to get good. Thank heavens for disgruntled wives. They led to more solved cases than the HPD, the Sheriff's Department and the Texas Rangers put together.

"In precisely what way is Gary Hudson a rotten, stinking, decaying pod of shit, Mrs. Bledsoe?"

"Call me Laurel. Mrs. Bledsoe's my mother-in-law. The best part of getting a divorce is that you get to divorce your mother-in-law as part of the deal. Oh, sorry. I probably shouldn't have said that."

Noah hadn't gotten that many apologies in the last six months, maybe a year. This woman must have the self-respect of a snail. Bad for her, good for him. Given time, he could find out her pin number and password. Scoop on neighbor guy was going to be a breeze.

She coughed into the crook of her arm, then pulled a wadded, damp tissue from the pocket of her robe and swiped at her nose. "Would you excuse me for a moment, please? I need to take some cough medicine and slip into some clothes. Help yourselves to more tea."

Well shit, there went his advantage. Anytime an interview was paused, he lost some degree of control. And with women, it was even worse. Once they combed their hair and put on underwear, he'd lost. It seemed like they kept their backbone hidden in their bra.

Laurel Bledsoe fled as fast as she could manage in bunny slippers, down the hall to her room.

What was she thinking, sitting at her kitchen table at ten in the morning with two good looking guys, while still in her robe and with a nose that must rival Rudolph's? More importantly, why in the world was she about to tell two strangers things she hadn't even told her mother, or her sister?

She needed to stall while she decided what to do.

In the corner was a deep purple warm-up suit that she'd worn . . . whenever the last time she'd had on real clothes. She slipped it on and then splashed some water on her face—great, there was crusted booger on the side of her nose—and put on a swipe of powder and a dash of lipstick. Getting the band out of her hair was no easy feat and running a brush through it was almost more than she could manage.

My God, when was the last time she'd brushed her teeth? Her breath would probably strip varnish. No wonder she hadn't wanted any food. Her mouth tasted like she'd licked a garbage can.

Five minutes after she reached her room, she felt more human than she had in days. If she used the phone in her room, the kitchen extension would light up. She dug through the debris and found her cell phone. The battery showed only one bar. Hopefully that was enough for a single call.

She punched Crystal's number in from memory and waited while it rang unanswered. Now what? As she thought about the conversation with Officer Grumpy and Officer Neatnick, she realized she hadn't gotten a single answer to her questions. Both detectives' eyes and hair could be considered brown, but Grumpy's edged closer to black. If eyes were the windows to the soul, Grumpy had pulled the curtains and didn't want anyone to see inside.

What was he hiding from her? Where was Crystal? And worst of all, was it her fault?

CHAPTER THREE

A S SOON AS the door closed, Noah was on his feet, prowling the kitchen. From the look of the dirty dishes, she'd been living on cereal and crackers. An inch of milk was left in a carton with an expiration date of yesterday. No real food was in the fridge, and only a few cans of vegetables sat in a pantry even emptier than his own. Could she not afford food or was she too sick to go out?

When Noah saw Conner step into the half-bath and close the door, he knew his partner was taking advantage of the privacy to make the phone calls necessary to check on Peter and Laurel Bledsoe without the lump hearing him. Noah stuck his head into the next room, but it was dark and musty. No wonder she kept sneezing.

Crystal's phone, sitting in an evidence bag in his pocket, vibrated. He'd been waiting to see who might call her, not realizing she was dead. Seeing Laurel's name appear was no surprise. He was pretending to refill his cup when the bedroom door opened.

Yep, she'd done more than take a dose of cough syrup. Her warm-up was loose fitting and rumpled, but still becoming. The pony tail was gone and her hair had been visited by a brush, but only briefly. She had on a hint of makeup and, thank the Lord, the crust on the side of her nose was gone. It was hard to look someone in the eyes when you knew that thing was sitting only a few inches down. It made him want to rub his own nose.

"Mrs. Bledsoe," Noah called out, louder than necessary. "I mean Laurel. Let me pour you another cup of tea." He pulled out her chair and placed the fresh cup in front of her as he glanced at the closed bathroom door. With several layers of clothing discarded and that God-awful pony tail gone, he couldn't think of her as the lump anymore. On a better day, or if he were a different man, she would even be considered appealing.

Of course, he never saw people on their better days. Too often, when he knocked on their door, it was about to become the worst day of their lives.

The toilet flushed in the half-bath and Conner stepped out, drying his hands. "Ah, Laurel, you look like you feel better." He nodded at Noah. "All nice and clean."

"You were going to tell us about Gary Hudson." Noah folded his hands and waited patiently. He was good at waiting patiently.

That hadn't always been the case. He'd lost his mojo for a while last year. His usual calm replaced with sighing and twitching and pacing, never giving the suspect time to trip himself up. At times, Conner had needed to take over the questioning. But he was better now. He could sit unmoving for half an hour, hardly blinking. Another couple of months and it would be an hour.

Laurel twisted her head from him to Conner and back again.

She took a deep breath and lifted her shoulders slightly. Not a good sign.

"I need to know what's happened to Crystal. I keep imagining terrible things." Her eyes, already bloodshot and puffy, brimmed with tears.

"Why do you think anything's happened to Crystal?" Noah's lips were the only thing that moved. The sound of a clock ticking in some distant room filled the air.

Laurel slammed her hand on the table hard enough to rattle the cups. "Answer me, damn it. No more questions until I know what happened to my friend."

Noah considered asking her why she hadn't asked about Gary, but one look told him she was on the edge. Best not to push too hard.

"Mrs. Hudson died last night, presumably on her way home from yoga."

Instead of dissolving into tears as he'd expected, Laurel's eyes cleared and she sat even straighter. So straight and stiff she looked as if one touch would shatter her into tiny pieces. "I don't guess you'd be here if it was an accident."

"No, she was shot. Most likely a case of road rage. I've been told she was a reckless driver." He watched her carefully, trying to gauge her reaction.

"Who told you that? Gary?" Again the note of distaste filled her voice. "Well, he's right, up to a point. When we'd go shopping or out to lunch, she'd drive faster than the speed limit. She liked to weave in and out of traffic. It gave her some kind of thrill. The red car Gary gave her for Christmas brought out the worst in her. She had a couple of tickets last year, but got two more already this year. She claimed cops picked on red cars."

"That's a fallacy, ma'am." Conner spoke softly. "Red cars don't get any more tickets than black ones or brown or white."

She had the grace to look embarrassed. "Maybe, but there's something Gary didn't know. She may have driven a few miles over the limit, but she was never reckless. Especially once the sun went down. After her Lasik surgery last year, she didn't see well at night. The lights bothered her. Gave her a starburst effect. She didn't want Gary to know, so she was always extra careful after dark. And a night like last night? With ice on the ground? She would have found her lane and stuck to it."

Noah's chest tightened. "So what do you think happened, ma'am?"

"Why don't I put on a pot of coffee? This is too important for candy-ass tea."

Laurel busied herself making coffee while she attempted to figure out where to start. She'd let Crystal down when she was alive. She couldn't let her down now. "You know Bledsoe is my married name. I was born a Newcomb."

The tall detective's face didn't change. If he knew, he didn't care. The slim detective glanced up from his notes and she knew he recognized what she was implying. She might as well have said her name was Houston. It amounted to the same thing.

"When Peter and I got married six years ago, we signed pre-nups. He said it was to protect me from him. I was the one with money, and it was old money. That's worth twice as much as new money any day. They say you can't take it with you, but when my dad died three years ago, that's just about what he did. It was all gone. I realize now that Peter already knew Daddy had lost, or was about to lose, everything and the pre-nup strongly favored him. But at the time, I was in love and believed everything he told me."

She set the cups in front of the detectives but paced the room while she talked. She was too skittish to stay still. "When Peter left me for a newer model six months ago, he took everything that wasn't nailed down. This house, that he claimed he bought for me as a wedding gift, is in his name only. And my car is leased through his office and the lease is up next month. The fidelity clause applies to me, not him. He can do it on the first green at River Oaks Country Club and he might be ejected from the club for indecency, but that's all that will happen to him."

The two men glanced at each other, then back at her, but didn't speak. She could feel her body start to tremble. If she didn't control herself, they'd think she was hysterical, and disregard anything she said. Then she would have failed Crystal again and she wouldn't let that happen. They'd just have to be patient a little longer

She clasped her hands tightly and took a cleansing breath, trying to remember everything the yoga instructor had taught her.

"If I don't get caught misbehaving, I'm due to receive one million dollars. But only when the divorce is final, and Peter's in no hurry for that. Why should he be? He's holed up in his love nest with his new bimbo. He can't possibly marry her until he gets rid of me. Meanwhile, he stuck an outrageously high price on the house and since I don't have any cash, I have to live here until it sells. Only I found out he's deducting exorbitant rent, taxes, and utilities from my million. If I ask for money to live on, he deducts that from my million also. He plans to hang on till the economy improves. If it's another year or two, what does he care? He can get what he wants for the house, trade in that bimbo for an even younger bimbo, and he won't owe me anything but pocket change."

She watched as Detective Neatnick closed his notebook and pushed it aside. "That's a very distressing story, ma'am. But I don't see how it helps us figure out what happened to Mrs. Hudson."

Detective Grumpy unfolded his hands and sat up straighter. "Because Crystal was in the same predicament as Laurel. Only she realized it ahead of time and tried to protect herself."

Yes! Finally. Someone who took the situation seriously. A wave of relief flooded over her. She plopped down in her empty chair, her legs weak as water.

The big detective had opened the curtains a sliver and she could see the intelligence shining through his eyes. She couldn't think of him as Detective Grumpy anymore.

"When did you tell Crystal exactly what Peter was doing?" He raked a hand across his chin and started at her intently.

"At first I was too upset about Peter leaving me to even think about the money. As soon as I started to get my feet on the ground, I learned he'd moved in with his secretary. That threw me back again. All I did was whine on Crystal's shoulder. 'Why me? Why me? What did I do to deserve this?'" Tears threatened as the truth hit home. She'd never see her friend again.

She ran her fingers through her hair and her ring caught in a tangle she'd missed. When she yanked her hand away, a clump of hair came with it. She flinched but kept talking. She owed it to Crystal.

"The week after Thanksgiving, my yoga teacher pulled me aside and told me my bill hadn't been paid. I was humiliated.

Everyone in the class heard. In the car on the way home, a little bell started going off in my head. I think Crystal caught on before I did. She placed her hand on my arm and asked, 'Laurel, how much is Peter giving you a month to live on?' She couldn't believe I didn't know."

"So she jumped in to help you figure it out, and in the process discovered how easy it would be for Gary to screw her in the same way."

"Yes, Detective Daugherty, I think that's what happened. Although it wasn't until Gary gave her that car for Christmas and she realized it was leased in his company's name that she confronted him."

Something close to a smile played across his face. "We're past the formalities at this point, Laurel. You need to call us Noah and Conner if we're going to sit here and drink all your coffee."

She hated admitting what a fool she'd been. Especially in front of two men who seemed so strong, so pulled together. They probably had no idea of the paralysis that followed having your entire world turned upside-down overnight.

But, like it or not, she'd live over her problems. Crystal hadn't.

CHAPTER FOUR

THE DAY WAS probably as warm as it was going to get. Half melted ice formed puddles on sidewalks and parking lots.

Noah's socks had dried out just in time to get wet again.

Almost noon, although you wouldn't know it from the gray sky.

"Learning which yoga studio our vic used was a big plus. Now we know how far to canvas. I'm happy not to walk around outside any longer than we have to."

Conner blew on his hands, creating a cloud of breath-frost. "It may be cold out here, but I'll take this any day to that nut-job yogi with his mood lighting, new-age music and incense. He would have *felt the negative energy* if Crystal was being harassed or followed."

"I like to be able to actually see a witness' face to judge their statements. The only thing bushier than his beard was that curlicue mustache."

"You're just jealous because he's in better shape than you are."

"Not jealous, disappointed. When we decided to interview the yoga instructor, I was expecting a lithe, sexy woman, not a seventy-year-old man with a ponytail. You have to admit, it's not natural for someone his age to be that limber. And his feet! Talk about ugly. I swear those toes where practically prehensile."

Conner took one last look at the yoga studio before turning to follow Noah down the street. "We did learn one useful thing. Crystal grabbed her things and left within five minutes."

"Which leaves us ten minutes unaccounted for because pulling a U-ie under the freeway and passing in front of the dry cleaners shouldn't take more than two or three minutes."

They checked every store in the strip center, but no one remembered seeing Crystal or any suspicious car. A Circle K near the corner explained the diet soda in her cup holder and the missing ten minutes. It had cameras both inside and outside.

Noah grabbed two coffees while Conner added those tapes to their ever growing pile.

By late afternoon, they had finished canvassing the other side of the freeway, collecting two more tapes, but no new information. They were almost back to headquarters when Noah's cell rang.

"Daugherty." He didn't recognize the number, but he'd given out at least twenty of his cards over the last two days.

"Noah?" The voice was soft and he couldn't place it.

"Yes." Why couldn't people identify themselves right away? Did they expect him to recognize their voice from one word?

"It's Laurel Bledsoe. Do you think you could come by my house? I have someone here you might want to talk to."

What now? Everyone thought they could be a detective, that

they'd found the one clue necessary to break a case wide open. A Hero complex.

He checked his watch. Already after four. This time of day it would take half an hour at least to get to Bellaire, and that was after Conner had checked in the Turdmobile and he'd pulled out of the garage. He'd be late getting home again, and Sweet Pea could add another item to the long list of grievances she held against him.

"Of course, Laurel. If you think it's important. I'm downtown right now, but I can head your way in about ten minutes."

Noah hung up and reached into his pocket, pulling out a quarter. "Want to flip me for it?"

Conner swung the Taurus into the parking garage. "No, you take her. I'll stay here and get the murder book up-to-date. Maybe I'll do a preliminary run through on these tapes before I log them into evidence."

"Don't forget the popcorn," Noah growled as he started up the ramp to his own car. If Laurel hadn't given him her cold this morning, she surely would now. His immune system must be on its last legs after a full day with wet feet, inside one overheated office for ten minutes before moving back out into the cold and on to another overheated store.

Ah, the glamour of police work.

Noah had to admit there was an upside to the shitty weather. Some businesses had closed, and rush hour traffic was lighter than normal. The sun had never made an appearance, leaving the sky a uniform gray. Exactly the way he pictured White Nights in northern latitudes.

He reached Laurel's by five fifteen. If she didn't talk too long, he could get home at a decent hour. There was one frozen dinner left in the fridge. He could put his feet up and eat in front of the TV. Even play with Sweet Pea, assuming she'd acknowledge him.

A quick phone call to his sister, assuring her he was all right, would keep her from popping over unannounced on the weekend.

This time, Laurel answered the door at his first knock. That wasn't the only thing different. She must have bathed and washed her hair because it hung in waves beside her face. She was wearing tight jeans and a red sweater. He would have said the sweater matched her nose, but she'd evidently put on make-up because while her nose still looked raw around the edges, it no longer glowed.

"Hi, Detective, uh, Noah. Come on in. I have someone who's willing to talk to you."

Noah wiped his shoes on the mat as he stepped inside. The curtains were open, allowing light inside and the house no longer smelled damp and musty. The hum of a vacuum came from another room.

She led him into the kitchen, which now sparkled. He sat in the same chair he'd used that morning, but the arm rests had lost their sticky feel.

Damn, she must be a little turbo if she's cleaned this much in only a few hours.

Maybe he should offer to hire her. Despite the half-hearted stab he made at house cleaning on Saturdays, he suspected his home was beginning to acquire a thin layer of grime. But who was to know except him and Sweet Pea?

Laurel leaned across the kitchen table and whispered. "I

need you to get her out of here."

Get who out? Did this have to do with his case or was she asking for help with a trespasser? Or worse, her ex-husband. "I thought you wanted me to talk to someone about Crystal's murder."

"I do, it's just that . . ." Laurel's eyes darted around the room. "After you left this morning, I kept thinking about Crystal, how I should have been a better friend. I needed to do something before I fell apart so I decided to go to the grocery store. I've had this cold lately and haven't felt like going out. Besides, I hate going to the store. Everyone's so happy and buying for their families."

He knew exactly how she felt. He usually did his shopping after ten at night. When all the families were home, tucked in safe and sound.

"But I really didn't have any food left and the ice had melted so I thought I'd better go before things froze again and that's when I saw her."

Noah nodded several times in hopes of encouraging her to get on with the story.

"Sorry, what I mean is. . . When I pulled out, I saw Rosaria walking down the street. She's housesitting for the Fords. They've gone to the islands to rest from all the holiday parties. Being rich is stressful you know. You have to pick just the right gift, and you can't wear the same thing to more than one party. And Heaven forbid you use last year's decorations." She rolled her eyes at Noah.

"Anyway, she used to work for the Fords three days a week and for me two days. Then I had to cut her back to one day and finally stop using her altogether. So, I'm sure she needed the extra money."

Noah was beginning to feel like a bobble-headed doll, but each time he stopped nodding, she stopped talking.

"So when I saw her carrying her suitcase, I knew something was wrong."

If he nodded one more time, his brain would turn to Jell-O. He tried to make an encouraging sound, but it came out more of a growl.

"I'm sorry. I know I'm babbling, but I think you frightened her this morning."

Yep, he should have put money on it. Rosaria was the maid from the fourth house, and she must have run as soon as he and Conner drove off.

"I brought her here to try to convince her to talk to you but she keeps cleaning instead and I don't have any money to pay her and you have to get her out of here before I spend all my food money on clean dishes and I still don't have anything to eat. I don't know what to do and you've got to help me." The words poured out faster and faster. When she finally stopped for a breath, her shoulders sagged.

So Rosaria was the cleaning whiz he ought to hire. "Does she know anything about this case?"

"I think so. She used to help out when Crystal and Gary had parties. She got very agitated at the last one and refused to work for them anymore. Crystal said Gary fussed at her for breaking a glass, but I think she saw something that upset her."

"Why don't you see if she'll come in here and talk to me?"

Laurel set a cup in front of him and headed for the sound of the vacuum.

He'd been demoted to tea again.

Rosaria followed Laurel into the room, almost hiding in her shadow. She sat only when Laurel pushed down on her shoulder, and tried to refuse the cup of tea placed on the table in front of her.

Noah knew instinctively she'd be a tough interview. Any interruption would be a deal breaker.

"Laurel, why don't you go on to the store and do your shopping. Rosaria and I will be fine by ourselves. We know how to find the tea if we need some more, don't we, Rosaria?"

Rosaria looked terrified at the thought of being alone with him, but he held Laurel's eyes until she picked up her purse and left.

"Now, Rosaria, you remember me from earlier this morning, don't you?" He took out another card and handed it to her. She had probably thrown the first one away. "I'm Detective Noah Daugherty. I'm with the Homicide Department. The only thing I'm interested in is the murder of Crystal Hudson. I don't care if you have traffic tickets or trouble with your green card. That's not my department and I won't talk about you to anyone in those departments. Do you understand?"

"*Sí.*" Rosaria agreed, but didn't relax.

"I'm giving you my personal word that anything you say to me is in strictest confidence. It's no different than talking to your priest." Bile rose in Noah's throat. It was a lot different than talking to her priest and the lie almost choked him. The fact that he would never have told that particular lie six months ago set like a stone in his chest.

But what had God done for him lately? Nothing good.

Rosaria still didn't look him in the eyes. This was going to be like pulling teeth. He decided to start with easy questions and give her time to warm up to him. Yeah, sure. Because everyone knew what a warm and fuzzy guy he was.

"How long have you worked for the Bledsoes?"

"Oh, I've worked for Miss Laurel for years. Long before she married that *hijo de puta* of a husband. She doesn't have any money now, but when she did, she was very generous. She used to give me a nice Christmas bonus and pay me when she went out of town. When my kids were young, she would buy them a new outfit to start school. But that's not why I like her. She always drove me to and from the bus stop. The other's—poo, they couldn't be bothered. Even if it was raining or cold. She remembers my kid's names. She once wrote a letter to a school to help my Emile get accepted. I think she asked her husband to write it, but he wouldn't."

Her English was accented, but easy to understand. He just needed to keep her talking and agreeing with her was the easiest way to do it. "In this business you learn to read people. I could tell Laurel was a nice person the first time I met her. I could tell a lot about Gary Hudson also, and I wasn't too impressed."

Noah waited while Rosaria fidgeted with her tea cup. Finally she raised her eyes and looked him in the face.

"I need to know everything you can tell me about the Hudsons. What was their relationship like? How did he treat her?"

"If Mr. Bledsoe was a *bastardo*, he learned it from Mr. Hudson. Mr. H was the king of all *bastardos*. He treated Miss Crystal worse than the servants. Always yelling at her. Saying how much smarter he was. Saying she was dumb like a child and should do what he said. I didn't like working there, but his money was good, and Miss Crystal was nice when he wasn't looking over her shoulder."

Now they were getting somewhere. Noah forced himself to take a sip of lukewarm tea and tried to look non-threatening. Not easy when they both knew he could ruin her life with one phone call. "I understand you had a falling out with Mr. Hudson recently. Can you tell me what happened?"

Her eyes dropped to the table, and she began twisting her napkin. "I broke a glass and he fired me."

"Rosaria," Noah reached out and took her hand. "We both know that's not why you're afraid of him. What did you see?"

"I saw him kissing the catering lady. He had his hand on her *culo*. I was so surprised I dropped a glass and it broke. He started yelling at me and threatened to call immigration if I said a word to anyone. Later that night, I was putting away dishes when I saw him in the back corner of the butler's pantry. He was on the phone. He never knew I was there."

This was why he loved police work. This moment. When all the pieces fell into place. "Who was he talking to?"

"I don't know his name, but Mr. H., he didn't like him, called him icky. Told the man he was the customer who had called last week about hiring a mechanic to take care of his wife. I remember, he said, no, he didn't mean his wife's car. He talked about checking out the website and something about a secret door. He mentioned finding the name on Craig's List. Then he said it should look like an accident, even if that cost more. I was so scared I backed out without making a sound. But I heard him say one more thing."

Noah's skin prickled. "What did you hear?"

"He said it would take him a month to get the money ready. That was on New Year's Eve."

He almost clapped his hands. This should be enough for a warrant. He'd have this case closed in no time. One more scumbag bites the dust. He glanced at Rosaria, nervously twirling her tea cup.

Fuck. How was he going to get a warrant for Hudson's phone and computer without using Rosaria's name?

CHAPTER
FIVE

THE DETECTIVE'S CAR still sat in front of her house when Laurel returned with the few groceries she could afford to buy and still have money left to pay Rosaria. That wasn't the car the two men came in that morning. This was a big, black pick-up. His personal transportation? Yeah, it looked like something he'd drive.

Peter would've turned his nose up at it, and Gary wouldn't want it parked on the same street as his Mercedes. But it was a nice truck. Late model, extended cab, probably clean before driving through all this slush. As soon as that thought crossed her mind, her foot sank into an icy puddle.

Laurel limped in the back door with two bags of groceries and one sodden foot. "Yoo-hoo, I'm home," she called as she hobbled through the laundry room. Her intent was to avoid surprising Noah and Rosaria, but when she realized this was how she'd always called out to Peter, it felt as if a knife plunged through her chest. She took a deep breath and willed her heart to behave.

Noah and Rosaria sat at the kitchen table, just as she'd left them. If possible, the detective looked even more haggard than he had when he first knocked on her door. Were they making any progress on Crystal's case?

He pushed back his chair and jumped to his feet as soon as he saw her. "Let me take those bags for you, ma'am." He towered over her, even bending slightly to take the bags from her arms.

Rosaria was on her feet also. "Oh, Miss Laurel, what happened to your foot? Sit down, sit down. Let me get you a towel."

Within seconds, her shoe was off, her foot warm, the muddy tracks through the kitchen cleaned up and the two visitors were putting away her groceries. She buried her face in her hands and pretended to sneeze while she wiped her eyes. She hadn't been this pampered in months. And by people she barely knew.

The ones she should have been able to count on—her mother and her sister—were too wrapped-up in their own lives to give her the time of day. Other than a few admonitions to pull herself together, they'd hardly spoken to her once they discovered she was no longer an easy touch for quick cash.

Crystal was the only person who had given her support and encouragement. And what had she done in return? Missed any sign that her friend was in trouble. How awful for Crystal. Did she know what was happening? Was she frightened or in pain?

The big detective hunkered down beside her chair, his face almost even with hers. When he reached into his back pocket and drew out his wallet, she was aghast. Surly he wasn't going to give her money? She'd die of embarrassment if he did. Instead, he pulled out a business card.

"I don't know if you have a lawyer yet, Laurel, but if you don't, you need one. And if you do, I suspect he may not be a good one or you wouldn't be in the mess you're in. This is a friend of mine. I've known him since high school. We played football together."

He gave a short laugh. "You know guys and football. Once you're on the same team, you're bonded for life. He may not be famous, but he specializes in Family Law—wills, probate, divorce. He knows how to counter every dirty trick your husband can pull on you. If you tell him I sent you, he'll fight to the ends of the earth for you."

Laurel tried to concentrate on the card, but her eyes wouldn't focus. She rubbed her thumb over the embossed lettering. All she could see was the scales of justice in the upper right corner. In the picture, they were tipped to one side. With someone on her side, would it be possible to right them?

Noah stood and pivoted toward the housekeeper. "I have to get to work on the information you gave me, Rosaria, but I'll be happy to drive you wherever you want to go. Remember, I gave you my promise that I was only interested in information about Mr. and Mrs. Hudson. No one's going to bother you if you go back to your housesitting job."

"He's right, Rosaria." Laurel straightened herself in the kitchen chair. "Go back to the Ford's. Don't risk your job by leaving. You can trust Detective Daugherty to see you're not disturbed."

Rosaria studied the big man, then glanced at Laurel and sighed. "If you think so, Miss Laurel."

Laurel watched Noah pick up Rosaria's suitcase as if it were a box of feathers and prayed her instincts were right. Unfortunately, past history wasn't on her side.

She'd trusted her father's promise to leave his family financially secure. And she'd trusted Peter when he promised to love her and she'd trusted his promise to be faithful when she married him. Three for three, not good odds. She hardly knew this detective, yet she'd just vouched for his word.

Maybe she should have advised Rosaria to run while she still could.

Noah escorted Rosaria to a small door on the side of the Ford's home. With no door frame, and painted the same color as the house, it was almost invisible.

Must be the servants' entrance.

Heaven forbid they let someone they trust with everything they own come and go through the front door. As soon as she slid the bolt into place, he pulled out his cell to dial Conner.

The phone rang twice before Conner answered. "Crawford."

"Where are you, partner? Still in the office or headed home?" Strains of classical music in the background answered the question for him. Damn, he'd wanted to get moving on this before another case came up. Now they'd have to waste half a day watching tapes.

"In my car, but still downtown. I've got the murder book in top shape in case the Lieutenant checks to see if we've been doing our job. The videos are logged in and will be ready to go in the morning, but I thought we might do better with fresh eyes. I can be back in the office in ten minutes if you need me to."

"No, go home. Check on Jeannie, eat a good supper, but don't watch too much TV. We'll need to be on our toes tomorrow. We have to invent an excuse for a warrant with no evidence to back it up and I'm hoping those tapes will help."

"Looking for a miracle?"

"I'll fill you in with the particulars in the morning, but remember the maid who didn't speak English? She does and she spilled a good story."

"Now that does sound like fun. See you in the morning."

Noah debated returning to the office and watching the tapes by himself. No point in that. He'd have to watch them again tomorrow with Conner. Might as well head home. He could use his laptop to prepare information for the warrant.

A quick stop at the golden arches—he substituted a fried pie for his usual milkshake due to the cold weather—and he was home for the night. The warm scent of hamburger and fries filled his nose as he held the to-go bag in his teeth while digging for the house key.

Sweet Pea met him at the door with her usual good humor. When she smelled dinner, she stopped barking and actually wagged her tail.

"Don't worry. I got you a hamburger all your own. You don't even have to share it with me." Noah set the bags on the counter and reached for the dog dish. Before he saw her move, the dog clamped her tiny teeth on his hand. He yelped in surprise and yanked his arm back, sending the dog spinning to the far side of the room.

"Son of a fucking bitch," he whispered in amazement. "Now I can't even feed you?"

He scooped up the dog dish and crumbled the burger into it before he changed his mind. Sweet Pea stayed in the corner, eyeing him while he set the dish on the feeding mat, not venturing out until he turned his back.

Noah turned on the cold water and held his hand under the stream. A semi-circle of red dots marked each side of the web between his thumb and forefinger. His heart felt as if it weighed a ton. Each breath ached.

When the dog finished eating, he opened the back door and watched as she darted out for a quick pee, a poop and a circuit of the backyard. Apparently satisfied that no cat had dared enter her territory during the day, she scooted back inside.

Under the counter in the half bath, Noah found a bottle of alcohol and poured a generous splash over his hand. The sting went straight through to his soul. Tomorrow was Thursday. On Saturday, he'd have to . . . Well, he'd think about that later.

Sweet Pea stayed in the kitchen as Noah made his way to the spare bedroom. Working on the computer would help postpone making any decision about the dog.

He dashed off a summary of his interview with Rosaria and forwarded it to Conner. The meaning of "icky" stumped him. Was it a name or was Hudson disgusted by the man? Had Rosaria misunderstood or could it be a Hispanic word he didn't know? His Spanish was good enough to get by, but far from fluent. He made a note to ask one of the Hispanic members of his squad and started work on the warrant for Hudson's home.

Two hours later, he'd worked up a satisfying list of reasons for issuing a warrant to search Gary Hudson's home, office, car, all phones and all computers. He emailed the list to his office computer. He could hit the ground running in the morning.

Exhaustion filled every corner of his body as he made his way to the bedroom. He left the door open in case Sweet Pea wanted to sleep in the dog bed that rested in the corner instead of the one in the kitchen. He lay in bed with his eyes open, staring at the ceiling until he heard the dog tiptoe into the room and curl up in her bed.

The driver lay in his single bed and stared out the window. A sliver of crescent-shaped moon hung framed by the sill. No stars were visible in the partly cloudy sky. His mind churned as he tried to figure out exactly why the police weren't writing off this latest job as a case of road rage. There'd been a small hiccup in his plan, but overall, it had worked.

What hadn't worked was the client's attitude. He was refusing to pay the second installment until he was sure the cops weren't looking at him. They hadn't said anything to him yet, but he claimed he could feel it in their attitude.

The one thing the driver hated most in the world was stupidity. And this guy was demonstrating it in spades. In their first conversation, he'd warned the client that cops always looked at the family before anyone else. That if he played it cool and followed all instructions, there'd be no trail for the police to follow and they'd move on. But what did the guy do? Called in a panic after the big cop frowned at him.

If the client couldn't hold up to a stern facial expression, he was going to shit himself if they ever truly interrogated him. And that made him a liability. No question the jerk had to go before he said too much, but could he afford to wait until after the last installment was paid?

Afford was the key word. While he'd carefully saved every penny, his partner had driven to Louisiana and tried his luck at one of the casinos; sure that he could double his money counting cards at the blackjack table. He might have managed to, if he had practiced first. Reading about a skill in a book and pulling it off were two different things. Especially after those sexy waitresses started plying him with free drinks.

Proof that his choice of partners was less than ideal. But shooting was a skill also. He didn't have it and his partner did, so he was stuck with the dick-wad for a partner, and the dick-wad hadn't saved enough to cover his expenses. Decision made; they waited for the client to pay up before cutting out that link of the chain.

On to the next problem—how to keep the client cool until after he paid the final installment. The driver got up and paced the room. He always thought better when moving. When he passed the window, he yanked the blinds shut. Cold air was seeping through the glass and it distracted him.

The old building wasn't insulated for this type of weather but the rules prohibited space heaters. He had nothing going on tomorrow afternoon. He'd go home and snag the electric blanket off his old bed. There was no rule against that. If he called in the morning to give his mom enough warning, she'd go by the store and buy something for supper. Maybe a steak.

The driver smiled. Just the thought of a home cooked meal and a warm bed calmed his mind and made planning easier. He slipped on his jacket and made another circuit of the room.

The next step was finding out how much the cops actually knew. Now here was a problem he didn't mind tackling. Understanding how to handle people was his weak spot, and he knew it. Uncovering information, making a plan on how best to use that information, there was where he excelled. One sure sign of intelligence was recognizing your weak points as well as your strong points, then learning how to maximize each.

That was what he didn't understand about cops. Why would a person with any sense take a low paying job handling other people's problems while putting themselves in danger? Take that tall cop. He had to have some basic intelligence to achieve the rank of detective. It must be what he'd heard called 'street smarts.' But essentially he was like the rest—a big, dumb, flatfoot.

He gave a soft chuckle as he hugged his jacket tighter. There was a use for stupid people after all. They certainly made his life easier.

CHAPTER SIX

NOAH'S HAND WAS tender and slightly swollen the next morning. The teeth marks stood out like a semi-circle of dots from a crimson marker and the surrounding skin was pink, but not angry looking. He decided to ignore it. Otherwise he'd have to think about what that bite meant for Sweet Pea's future.

The dog was on her best behavior, as if nothing had happened. She made a quick lap of the backyard, her usual check for overnight intruders, and hurried back inside to warm up. No new ice had formed, but patches remained in protected spots. She waited patiently while Noah scooped dog food into her dish and put out fresh piddle pads. She even played with the squeaky toy he tossed her.

Maybe it was his fault. He'd moved too quickly when he reached for her dish. He'd startled her. Yeah, that was all.

He'd slipped back to the bedroom to grab his keys when he noticed the smell. She didn't usually make a mess in the house.

Only outside or on the paper. The hamburger had probably given her gas. Much as she loved it, her stomach didn't handle people food well.

As he swung around for the door, something caught his eye. A small, steaming turd sat on his pillow. Guess that told him how she felt.

Morning traffic was back to normal. Businesses that had closed for the ice storm had reopened, and drivers were trying to make up for lost time. Noah needed a distraction to keep him from thinking about Sweet Pea, so he switched the radio from country/western to heavy metal. It didn't help.

By the time he reached downtown, he was in a sour mood. Maybe he should try classical music. Conner claimed it soothed his mind. No, it was likely to have the opposite effect on him.

Parking was tight at the Travis Street Headquarters, but he found a spot when a night shift worker pulled out. He took the elevator to the sixth floor without speaking to anyone.

Conner rounded the corner with an armload of tapes. "Perfect timing. I've got us set up in the viewing room. Let's see if we can catch the scumbag who fired the shot."

"I need coffee. Let me grab a cup and I'll join you."

"Already taken care of. Jeannie knew we'd be sitting here for hours. She fixed us a thermos of decent stuff."

Did Conner suspect he'd been pissed about his early departure last night? He had no right to expect his partner to work the hours he did. With nothing to go home to, he worked late to help pass the time. Conner had a life and someone warm waiting for him. Soon he'd have even more reason to hurry home.

Noah forced a deep breath. It was jealousy, plain and simple. And he'd better get over it or risk losing the best partner he'd ever had. "I always told you she was a keeper. Just don't know what she sees in you. It can't be looks or money."

Conner glanced over his shoulder and grinned. "I'm good in bed."

"I doubt that. You must be able to cook."

Perfectly brewed coffee in hand, the partners settled in to watch the videos. They moved the tapes forward and back, paused them and used slow motion. They adjusted the brightness and took notes of any car that looked suspicious.

After three hours, the thermos was empty and they had printed photos of four cars. They called the license numbers into Records and decided to look at some older tapes while they waited.

"Back up a little. I want to get a better look at this car." Noah sat with his nose inches from the screen. A tiny spark of interest took root deep inside his brain.

"That doesn't match any of the cars we're looking at." Conner dialed the video back thirty seconds.

"No, but there's something about it that rings a bell."

Conner paused the tape and printed a photo of the car that caught Noah's eye. "I don't get it. This isn't one of the cars we've been watching. It does go by a couple of times, but not on the night of the murder."

"If you were casing a job, would you use the same car?"

Conner stretched his neck, rolling his head from side to side. "Probably, that's why I'd get caught. What do you see besides the fact that it passes more than once?"

Noah tapped one thick finger on the lower left corner of

the back window. "Look at this smudge. It's probably a parking sticker. Now look at this car. It has a similar emblem in the same spot."

"That's not much to go on. Lots of cars have some type of parking sticker."

"Run through the tapes again. See if you find any other similar decals." Noah picked up his coffee cup and tossed it in the trash. He eyed the empty thermos and sighed. He'd have to make do with vending machine slop for the rest of the day.

Half an hour later, Conner had checked all the tapes twice. "Here's one sticker in the same spot, but it's long and narrow. I'll send both these photos to the lab and let them work their magic. Maybe they can enhance them, but even if they do, I have a sinking feeling all we're gonna learn is who this bozo voted for in the last election."

Maybe, but no matter how much work it took, if it brought them even one step closer to solving this case, Noah would stay and chase it down. When all you lived for was to close cases, one step was worth the effort.

Whoever pulled that trigger was in a car, and he planned to find it.

Noah sat in the break room, eating a cardboard sandwich from the vending machine. The tuna was so dry it stuck to the roof of his mouth. Several slugs of Diet Coke were required to wash down each bite.

The more he chewed, the more he thought. Which direction should he go first? He wanted to follow the car. That might lead him to the actual shooter, and the shooter trumped the client in his book. Yet the shooter was just doing a job.

As much as it disgusted Noah, he recognized that it was nothing personal. The client, on the other hand, knew the victim. If it was the husband, he'd slept with her, promised to love her, eaten breakfast with her.

That was betrayal.

If Hudson ever suspected they were looking at him, he'd have time to destroy any evidence. But Hudson would be easier to turn than a professional.

What a joke. Was he seriously considering a professional hit man? They might be the darling of B movies, but in real life, he'd never come across one. Sure, the mob and certain governments had people they used to dispose of problems, but they were employees, not some stranger who advertised over the internet.

Husbands and wives, even business partners, turned to relatives or lovers, maybe even a shady friend, with the promise of a cash payoff. But honest-to-God hit men, out there for hire by anyone with money, ranked with the Loch Ness Monster. Never let the truth stand in the way of a good story.

He threw the rest of his sandwich in the trash, glad for an excuse to avoid eating it, and started down the hall, looking for Conner. Chasing the car was a long shot. The shooter would be someone Hudson knew personally. There'd be some connection to him in that house. If they got there fast enough.

Where was that warrant?

Conner was on the phone with Jeannie when Noah's footsteps echoed down the hall. He hung up quickly and grabbed the license plate information faxed over from Records. Things had been smoother with his partner the last few days, and he wanted to keep it that way.

Noah had earned the right to his sour moods. In fact, Conner doubted if he would have handled things as well. Still, this tiptoeing around, pretending he didn't notice, was getting old.

The idea of taking time off with Jeannie and the baby was all that kept him together. Handling a colicky infant had to be easier than a grumpy partner.

When Noah glanced at the phone, Conner felt the back of his neck heat up. He'd never managed to put anything over on his partner yet, no point in starting now. "I told Jeannie how much we appreciated the thermos of coffee. It's tough for her to make when she's not allowed to drink any."

"I can't imagine going nine months with no coffee. Beer and wine I could give up with no problem, if I had a good enough reason, but I have to have my caffeine. Is she feeling better these days?"

A weight lifted off Conner's shoulders. Avoiding any discussion of the most important thing in his life with his best friend had been tough. One glance said it still wasn't easy for Noah, but the man was obviously trying. "At the moment, she's doing great, and I'm enjoying the calm. The first three months she puked every time I looked at her. Her hormones were raging enough to make PMS look like a walk in the park. I understand the last trimester she'll be tired, uncomfortable and grouchy, but I've worked with you so I figure I can handle it."

"I don't complain," Noah shot back.

"No, you don't. Sometimes I wish you would." *Damn.* Had

he really let that slip out?

"I'm not going to get all touchy-feely at this point, if that's what you mean."

"God, no. I'd probably have to shoot you if you did."

Noah's eyes turned hard. "So, what is it? What do you want from me?"

I want my old partner back. But that wasn't going to happen. He had died in a fiery crash on the Sam Houston Tollway the last week in August, as surely as his wife had. He'd never be the same man who'd played practical jokes on him while acting as best man at his wedding. Or drove him to the airport when his mother got sick, then showed up in South Carolina in time for her funeral. That man was gone forever.

Noah had been better the last month or so, but even that worried Conner. It felt like he had made a decision of some kind. Conner didn't know what it was and that frightened him. Homicide was the top of the heap for a detective, but it meant looking evil in the face every day. Noah might not have the heart for it any longer.

Conner squared his shoulders. The truth might hurt, but what they had now was death by a thousand cuts. "I want you to say whatever's on your mind. If I screw up, tell me about it. If you think I'm slacking off, chew my ass out. Don't shoot me dirty looks and act like you're disappointed."

"A call home to check on your wife isn't slacking off, and if I act like it is, that's my problem. But if you screw up, your ass is grass." Noah actually smiled. "Now, where'd you put that warrant? We need to go catch us a bad guy. That's why they pay us the big bucks."

CHAPTER SEVEN

GARY HUDSON'S FACE turned seven shades of purple when he opened his door to Noah and saw the warrant in his hand. He stuttered and sputtered and sprayed spit on Noah's suit as he threw out an arm to block the door. "You can't come in here now. I'm trying to plan my wife's funeral. This is a disgrace. It's harassment. I'm going to call my attorney. You'll have to wait outside."

As if hiring a hit man to murder your wife is no disgrace at all.

The sight of Hudson squirming brought a smile to Noah's face. This was going to be fun.

"Call your attorney if you wish, sir, but this warrant gives us immediate access. We won't be waiting for anyone." He folded the warrant and stuck it in Hudson's shirt pocket.

Hudson gaped at him. "What's that on your hand? It looks like a bite. You could have AIDS. Or rabies. I don't want you touching any of my things."

Noah stepped closer and lowered his voice. "You don't have

to worry. It's from my own dog and she's perfectly healthy. But since I don't know what germs you carry, I'll be using these." Noah took a pair of latex gloves from his pocket and pulled them on with a loud snap as he pushed his way inside.

Conner, two uniformed officers, and a string of forensic techs streamed in after him.

"I wouldn't have a dog that bit." Hudson looked like his head might explode at any moment. "I'd shoot it myself."

Noah eyed him with a look that had brought stronger men to their knees. "Is that a fact, sir? And do you keep a gun on the premises?"

Hudson must have realized his error because he clamped his mouth shut and didn't answer.

Conner started up the stairs, chuckling. Before he had climbed halfway, a young blonde scurried down, brushing past him.

"This is Madeline Davies, my secretary. She's helping me plan Crystal's funeral." A muscle on the side of Hudson's face twitched.

Conner looked down to the first floor. "From your bedroom?"

Hudson pulled himself up and tried to look indignant. "The funeral home called and asked me to bring over a dress for Crystal. I needed a woman's opinion."

The secretary pulled out a tissue and blotted her eyes. "Crystal always took such care with her appearance. I know she'd want to look her best."

Noah stepped back and appraised the secretary. A few hairs had come loose and curled around her face and most of her lipstick was gone, but it was late in the day. Maybe that was to be expected. It wasn't until she turned around that he noticed the back of her blouse was untucked.

If she was helping pick out clothes, she must have been doing it by trying them on, modeling them for Hudson.

"Miss Davies, please give my partner your contact information, then you and Mr. Hudson can wait in the kitchen with one of these officers." The secretary sniffed loudly and stalked toward Conner, her stilettos clacking on the marble floor and perfume trailing in her wake.

Noah spun on his heels and marched to Hudson's home office. The information would be in there. He knew it.

Hudson's office outshone anything Noah had ever seen, and he'd been in a multitude of homes and offices in his years on the force. The mahogany desk was polished to a high gleam and the flat screen computer monitor rivaled most people's TV. To the side sat printers, copiers, faxes, and machines Noah didn't recognize. On the wall, a bank of screens monitored the perimeter of the house. Several of the screens were blank and Noah pushed buttons and turned switches until they came to life. Now many of the rooms inside the house were displayed. In the kitchen, Hudson and his secretary sat inflexible as a church spire, staring straight ahead.

Too guilty to even talk?

Noah watched as Conner searched the drawers of a nightstand in a small, side bedroom. He pulled out several sex toys and laid them across the bed.

Noah flipped a switch and Conner's voice floated out of a speaker hidden behind a set of books. "Take these and we'll check them later to see whose DNA is on them. If it isn't Mrs. Hudson's, we'll have proof he was having an affair."

A techie dropped the item in an evidence bag and chuckled. "You know what they say… A man only buys toys if his own toy isn't up to the job."

So Hudson had his entire house bugged. Any time Crystal used the phone, he could hear every word. Had she talked to Laurel about her suspicions? If he was that paranoid, he must have made tapes to cover the times he wasn't home.

A side room contained file cabinets and Noah began rifling through them. Finally he gave up and started filling cardboard boxes with the papers. This was more than a one day job. If he rushed, he'd miss something. Better to take them back to the office and comb through them slowly.

He was almost finished when he stumbled on an accordion file tied with a bow. Inside were four mini-cassette tapes. As excited as Noah was to discover the tapes, the ten stacks of hundred dollar bills was a bigger find.

Unfortunately, it wasn't against the law to keep ten thousand dollars hidden in a file cabinet. But it was damn suspicious.

Hudson shot out of the kitchen as Noah passed carrying boxes of papers. "You can't take those. They're work papers. How am I going to conduct business without my files?"

Noah shifted the boxes to his hip. "Your papers will be returned to you as soon as copies have been made. Until then, you're in mourning, Mr. Hudson. You shouldn't try to work. You need to plan your wife's funeral and take time to grieve. I'm sure your clients will understand."

Hudson stood at the door with his mouth open and his arms out, but Noah kept walking.

An hour later, Noah was carrying a computer to the forensics van when Laurel Bledsoe's car pulled into her driveway. Even across the lawn he could see her eyes widen in surprise. He had made two more trips to the van when he saw her approaching him, her high heels sinking in the soggy grass.

She had a coat wrapped around her shoulders and the frost on her breath framed her face. Her hair was up and back in some type of simple style, exposing ears tinged with red from the cold. "Is it true? Are you arresting him? I know I thought he had something to do with it, but somehow I can't believe a person I've had in my home would do such an evil thing."

"No, he's not under arrest. We've got a warrant to search his house, cars and office. Experts will be going over his computers and I'll need another warrant for his service providers to dump the logs on all the phones. I'm glad you came over. I need you to identify something. Have you ever seen this? I found it hidden in a bowl, inside something called a Butler's Pantry, whatever it is." Noah waggled a cheap, throw-away phone.

Laurel eyed the phone and shook her head. "It's not Crystal's. And I've never seen Gary with anything like that. He fancies himself a techno-wizard. He only has the latest, most expensive gadgets. Whenever a newer model came out, he had to have it. He would never own something like that. Crystal gave him a new iwhatever for Christmas, but it wasn't fancy enough and he exchanged it the next day. He acted like she had insulted him."

Well, he can't claim this is an old one he forgot to dispose of. He downloaded new minutes for it two weeks ago and half of them are gone. Noah sealed the plastic bag holding the phone and signed his name to it.

She shivered and hugged her coat tighter. "Will you be much longer? I'd really like to talk to you about something. Do you think you could come over for a few minutes when you finish? I could give you a hot drink. You must be cold."

Noah stalled. "Tea?"

"Oh, I think this deserves coffee. Or something stronger if you're off duty."

"I'll probably be another hour."

She smiled and when he smiled back, it hit him how much he was looking forward to that coffee. That didn't mean shit, he told himself. He was only curious about what she had to tell him, nothing more, damn it.

The sun was sinking fast and it coated the few remaining clouds with an orange tinge. With the sky so clear, the temperature would likely flirt around the freezing mark before the night was over, at least on the north side of town. Noah didn't care. He'd wrapped his pipes months ago, and any plants that couldn't take the cold were dead already. He hadn't bothered to cover them this year.

As he trudged across the Hudson's manicured lawn to Laurel's somewhat shabby yard, he rubbed his hands together and blew on them for warmth.

Laurel opened the door and stood silhouetted in the light. Wow. How could he ever have thought of her as The Lump?

She grinned. "I thought we were good enough friends by now for you to come to the back door."

His mother had divided people into front door friends and back door friends. He hadn't thought of that in years. "Next time I'll try the back door, I promise."

But why would there be a next time? She wasn't a suspect and he had no reason to interview her again. He felt his shoulders sag slightly at the thought that this might be his last cup of coffee with her.

Shoot, he'd even have taken tea.

He followed her through the house to the kitchen and pulled out what he'd begun to think of as his chair. The smell of coffee hit him in the gut. His half a tuna sandwich had worn off hours ago.

She filled his cup, passing him sugar and flavored creamer, as he studied her. For the first time since he'd met her, some portion of her face wasn't red and raw, and he realized how attractive she was. Well, why not? If he could appreciate the sunset, he could appreciate an attractive woman. There wasn't anything wrong with that. He wasn't dead yet.

She nodded toward a folder of papers on the table. "Thank you for giving me your friend's name. I called him this morning and when I mentioned you, he worked me right in."

"Wonderful. Will he be able to help you?"

"Only time will tell, but he says he can. He's going to get on it right away. He says Peter can't pull half the underhanded tricks he's trying to do."

At least things were looking up for somebody. He spent most of his time dealing with the chaos caused by selfish, greedy people. He had to take good news wherever he found it. She obviously felt better about life. She'd dressed in nice clothes, fixed her hair and makeup, and was sitting up straight, looking him in the eye. She hadn't even said "Sorry" one time. "I'm glad it's working out for you. Roy's one of the best. He'll take good care of you."

"Well, the thing is, I need to apologize."

The contrast was almost immediate. She slumped in her

chair and hung her head, avoiding looking at him.

"When I said you sent me, he must have thought we were close friends. He asked how you were doing and said he hadn't seen you since he handled your wife's probate last November. Said he'd been worried about you at the time and meant to call you over Christmas."

She shifted in her chair and glanced up and back down quickly. "I should have stopped him, but it was like a train wreck. You know you should look away, but you can't. Anyway, I apologize for nosing into your business. I didn't want you to think I asked."

Fuck. Damn lawyers, he knew he couldn't trust them. Now what was he supposed to say? He could handle the loneliness, he could handle the dark thoughts, but he couldn't handle it when people tried to make him talk.

Now it was his turn to avoid eye contact. "Don't worry about it," he mumbled.

She pushed back her chair and stood. "Let me heat up that coffee for you. Or I could warm it with something stronger."

Noah cradled the cup, drawing strength from its warmth. "Just coffee for me. I'm still on duty. I have to go back to the office in a few minutes."

"This late?" she asked, refilling his cup.

"There's something I need to ask you about. Did you and Crystal ever talk on the phone?"

"You're kidding, right? Almost every day."

"Did she talk about her situation? What she might be planning to do?"

Laurel played with her coffee cup, pushing it around on the table. "Mostly we talked about me, and now I feel like such a shit.

All the times I cried and whined on her shoulder. If I'd been a better friend and asked how she was doing . . ." She twisted in her chair and wiped tears from her eyes.

At least someone's crying for her. Her husband acts like her death is an inconvenience. "Did she ask any questions or give any suggestions that would lead you to think she might be making plans of her own?"

"I can't remember. But when she took that car in a couple of days after Christmas to pick up the floor mats, and found out it was leased in his company's name, she was livid. There was no doubt she was in the exact same position I was in, and she knew it. Did we talk about it on the phone or in person, I'm not sure."

I'll know as soon as I hear those tapes. And if I know, then Hudson knew.

He placed his hands on the table, ready to push himself up. "I better get moving. Have to make sure all the evidence is logged in correctly. I'd love to start going through it tonight, but I better wait and look at it fresh in the morning. Don't want to take a chance on missing something."

She reached out and touched him. "What in the world happened to your hand? It doesn't look good."

He was so surprised, he almost jerked his hand away. How long had it been since someone touched him? His sister, sure, she was always hugging him and his nieces kissed him, but that didn't mean anything. He'd tried to hug his mother-in-law after the funeral, but hugging Betsy's mom was like hugging a marble column.

He cleared his throat. "My dog. It's just a little nip. I don't think she knew what she was doing."

She ran her fingers over the teeth marks and Noah couldn't

decide if the tingling came from her or from the bite.

"Let me put something on it. It isn't hot to the touch, so I don't think it's infected, but no reason to take a chance." She rummaged in a cabinet until she found peroxide and gauze and cleaned both sides of his hand.

He wasn't used to being taken care of, and the contrast between the sting of the peroxide and the softness of her hands was disconcerting, but he left his hand in hers for several seconds longer than necessary.

"You do know that dogs can grieve just like people. If she's acting out too much, you might want to talk to your vet."

"I'm not putting her down," Noah snapped. He could understand Hudson suggesting it, but it was like a punch in the gut to think Laurel would say the same thing.

"Heavens, no." Laurel looked shocked. "I meant doggie Prozac or something. Of course you don't want to put her down. It's just that the vet might have some suggestions on how you can help her. Behavior modification, training, stuff like that."

Noah flushed. He hadn't shown that much emotion since, well, he couldn't remember. He pushed his cup away and stood. "Thanks for the coffee and the advice. I'd best be getting back to the office. Don't want to leave Conner with all the work."

He would never have thought of Prozac for a dog. And he certainly hadn't realized that Sweet Pea might be grieving as much as he was. Maybe talking wasn't the worst thing in the world.

Tonight he'd go home early, leave the log-in to Conner. He'd feed Sweet Pea on time. Take her for a walk. Show her a little more attention. That would be a start.

CHAPTER
EIGHT

THE DRIVER'S CAR was slow to start, producing a loud grinding sound before finally turning over. It hadn't been driven in more than a week and the weather was unusually cold, but it reminded him that the car was now five years old. It irked him to drive a car that could no longer be called a late model. Intellectually, he realized he didn't *need* a nicer car at this point, nor could he afford the attention a new car would bring, especially with his parents. Still, he was used to better, he deserved better.

He took his time driving home. If he arrived too soon, he'd have to listen to his father gripe about everything from the economy to the programming on TV. Any respect he'd had for his father had vanished when he lost his job and made no attempt to find another one.

He'd had to step in before his parents headed for welfare.

If he timed his arrival correctly, he could do a load of laundry, eat, grab his electric blanket, and be gone with as little conversation as possible.

He smelled food when he walked in the door, but it wasn't steak. Chicken. His mother had stopped for take-out fried chicken. He hadn't been home since New Year's Day and greasy fast food was the best she could do?

She set the table in the dining room, as if that would make up for the lousy meal.

He was finishing a piece of dry, store-bought cake when he noticed a large man with a tiny dog stroll past the dining room window. The cake caught in his throat as he recognized the man. It was dark outside, maybe he was mistaken.

"Who's that?" he asked his mother. "I think I've seen him before."

"The policeman who moved into the Yates' old house. I can't think of his name. You met him at the Fourth of July picnic. His wife brought that delicious cobbler. Then a month later, she was gone. Killed by a speeding driver on her way to work. I think she was a teacher."

His mother slid another piece of cake onto his plate. "Are you sure you can't spend the night? We never get to see you anymore. I bought those sweet rolls you like."

Now he knew exactly where the cop lived. And how to get in there. Fortune did sometimes smile on the worthy. If he could put up with his parents for another couple of hours, he'd have all the information he needed to throw the cops off his trail. How deliciously ironic that it was the same cop who spoiled his plans in the first place. "I suppose I could stay. But I'll have to get moving first thing in the morning."

"Of course he can stay. There's free food involved and his mother to wait on him," his father grumbled.

The driver sat with his parents and watched an inane reality cooking show. Why did they watch such drivel? Neither one of them cooked.

His mother went to bed before the news started. She had to get up early for work in the morning. But his father showed no signs of retiring. When the driver turned the TV to an in-depth program on global warming, his father headed for the bedroom.

After fifteen minutes, his father's snores shook the house like a semi with a bad muffler and the driver picked up his laptop and slipped out the back door. Keeping to the shadows, he made his way down the street to the Yates' old home. He knew the house well.

As a kid, his mother had forced him to play with the Yates' son, Kenny. She thought it would be good for him to socialize with kids his own age. What a joke. Kenny was dumber than a bag of dirt, but tormenting him was always good for a laugh.

A light was on in the back bedroom. The cop must still be up. With any luck, he'd be on his computer. Using his sweatshirt as protection against fingerprints, he jiggled the side garage door until the lock let loose.

The door gave a *screech* when it opened and his heart skipped rope in his chest. What was he thinking, breaking into a cop's house? Sure, he'd done this dozens of times in the past, but then the worst that could happen if he got caught was that his mother would ground him. This guy had a gun. He might get shot.

Still, he needed the information and this was the best way. The fact that this nosy cop had spoiled his perfect crime had nothing to do with his decision.

The cement floor looked cold and hard. The driver found an old lawn chair cushion and pulled it off a shelf. Last summer's pollen flew into his nose and eyes as he set it on a stack of brand new, tightly rolled garden hoses. Turning on the overhead light was too risky, but he'd planned ahead and brought a headlamp. He pulled it over his forehead and switched it on low.

In less than ten minutes, he'd hijacked the cop's computer and was reading everything the cop did. He had expected porn. Didn't macho men like cops troll those sites all the time? But this guy was studying dog behavior. No matter. He'd found the password and would come back tomorrow to discover how much the police knew about the Hudson case. That cop's computer belonged to him now.

When the cop turned off his computer, the driver powered his down and stood to leave. The back door slammed and he recognized the cop's voice from TV.

"Get a move on, Sweet Pea. It's too cold to dawdle."

Bad enough the guy looked ridiculous walking such a tiny dog, but he named it Sweet Pea? This was going to be a piece of cake. The guy obviously had as much brain power as the dog.

Before he could slip out the side door, the dog began barking ferociously. Tiny claws scraped against the brick, but the only door on that side opened into the house.

The cop called softly, probably worried about the neighbors. "Sweet Pea, Sweet Pea, stop that. Come back inside. Nothing's out there. I'll set traps tomorrow, just in case."

The driver eased the door shut and hurried home through darkened streets. He needed to get into that house tomorrow to look for any papers that might tell him how the investigation was going. Getting inside would be easy. A passage from the garage up through the attic led into the laundry room. He'd slipped inside to play practical jokes on Kenny several times when they were kids, moving things and hiding his homework, and no one had ever figured it out. Of course, it might be a tighter fit now that he was grown. And the stakes were much higher.

The dog was the problem. If it carried on like it did tonight, the neighbors might hear. But all problems could be solved with a little ingenuity.

His father's snores still filled the house and he tiptoed into the master bathroom. On the counter were his mother's sleeping pills. He helped himself to four: two for his father and two for the dog.

That dog was toast.

The alarm woke Noah at five-thirty with an annoying *beep, beep, beep* that set his teeth on edge. The first thing he saw when his feet hit the cold floor was Sweet Pea, glaring at him.

"Sorry to wake you so early, Pea, but that's the price you pay for having me come home in time to walk you last night." The dog turned her back on him and sat down.

By the time he had showered, shaved and dressed, the aroma of coffee filled the house and he poured himself a cup, savoring the first sip. He placed some bread in the toaster and heated a sausage patty in the microwave before carrying his cup to the back stoop where he waited for Sweet Pea to do her morning business.

The sky was still dark and the air cold, but several degrees above freezing. "No barking this early, girl. We don't want to wake the neighbors. They've already complained about you."

The Yorkie made her circuit of the yard, stopping to sniff at the garage before moving on. "Nothing there, girl. It was all your imagination," Noah called softly. She refused to look at him as she scampered in the house. Noah set out food, water and fresh pads for her before buttering his toast.

The dog ignored the food so Noah picked up a toy and held it out to her. "Want to play? Here's Mr. Squeaky Man. Come get him. Here you go." He tossed the toy beside the dog but nothing happened.

Sweet Pea and Noah glared at each other while he drank a second cup of coffee and ate his breakfast. "I'm trying, Pea. Really I am. But you have to meet me halfway."

Finally, he held out a piece of sausage patty. "You know you're not supposed to eat people food. It doesn't agree with you."

The dog grabbed the meat and darted away again as Noah wiped grease from his fingers.

At least she didn't bite me. That's some improvement.

By nine o'clock, enough light seeped into the room to wake the driver. He rolled onto his back and stretched. The room was warm, the bed was soft, and the pillow smelled like home. He sighed and settled deeper into the bed until he remembered why he was there.

He padded barefoot into the living room, yawning and scratching his head. "Morning, Pops. Any coffee left?"

His father glanced up from his favorite spot in front of the TV and frowned at him. "Thought you were in some kind of hurry to get out of here this morning."

"I have to be back by eleven-thirty, but I don't need to rush.

" He poured lukewarm coffee into an old Santa mug and heated a sweet roll in the microwave. On a shelf next to the spice rack, he spotted a pill bottle with his father's cholesterol medication. He smiled. *A solution always presents itself, if you stay prepared.*

"Hey, Pops, did you take your pills yet?" He held his breath and waited.

"Don't Mother-Hen me. I'll get to them during the next commercial."

"Give me a second. I'll bring them to you." The driver fished in his pocket and pulled out two sleeping pills. He ground them into powder and reached for a glass. No, the pills might make the water cloudy. He poured the powder into a coffee mug, added water, and stirred until it dissolved.

"Here you go, Pops. No need for you to get up."

The older man held out his hand without taking his eyes off the TV. He popped the pill in his mouth and grabbed the cup, downing the medication with one quick swallow before handing the cup back to his son.

"Uh-uh, the directions say to take with a full glass of water. Drink it all."

"Don't pull that tone with me, kid. You aren't any kind of doctor, not yet anyway." Pops up-ended the cup and drank the rest of the liquid. "Are there any sweet rolls left? Those pills left a nasty taste in my mouth."

Would the sugar in the sweet rolls offset the sleeping pills? "Mom said you were on a diet. I'm not getting into the middle of that one. What's on TV?"

"These guys buy abandoned storage lockers and sell the stuff inside. Some of the stuff is really valuable. I've been thinking I might try that. It looks like good money and no boss to give you a hard time."

Shit. Those guys were professionals. They knew what things were worth and where to sell them. They'd see Pops coming a mile away. Like playing poker with card sharks. If you looked around the table and didn't know who the mark was, you were it.

If his folks weren't bankrupt yet, they would be when Pops started gambling what little was left of their nest egg. That wasn't his problem. He didn't plan to support them. He'd already done his good deed.

When Pops first lost his job, his mom had applied for a promotion. She complained bitterly that while she had seniority, another woman seemed to have an inside track. "She must be sleeping with the boss. It's the only explanation."

Yeah, right. Like his mother's sloppy work habits hadn't entered into it. The driver expected Pops to find a new job soon—he was an engineer for God's sake—but if they got behind in their bills and tightened the purse strings, they could refuse to pay his room and board. He might have to move home.

Taking out Mom's rival was easy. A carjacking gone wrong. A garrote around the neck meant no blood on his clothes. The three hundred dollars in her purse was a welcome extra. Now his folks should be able to hold on until Pops got a new job.

Only Pops didn't get a new job. He took to the sofa instead, complaining how life did him wrong. Without his parents to count on, *he* was the one who discovered a new sideline. One that took skill and planning. One that suited him to a T.

When Pops began to snore, the driver put on his shoes and headed for the back door. The kitchen reeked of grease and fast food. He reached into the garbage for a few chicken bones and started down the street.

At the cop's house, he acted as if he were ringing the bell but then slipped around and entered through the side door to the garage. Two rat traps were set that hadn't been there the night before. Lifting a ruler from the unused workbench, he touched the spring on first one and then the other, smiling as they snapped closed on nothing but air. If the cop suspected anything, he'd think it was rats.

A cord hung from the ceiling. One pull opened a panel and a ladder unfolded, allowing dust and insulation to drift down into his face. He stifled a sneeze. No one to hear him but the dog.

The stairs creaked and groaned as he climbed into the attic. How many years had it been since he'd last oiled them? He pulled the ladder up behind him, closing the door completely. The morning sun seeped through a louvered vent, but did little except accentuate the darkness. Holding a penlight in his mouth, he crawled toward a small square of light. The panel lifted out as easily as if he'd used it yesterday.

The dog growled and the hairs on the back of her neck stood up, but she didn't bark out loud. He coated a chicken bone with the powdered sleeping pill and dropped it into the laundry room from the hidden opening to the attic. The dog grabbed the bone and carried it to her bed in the kitchen.

Within minutes, the dog began to stagger in circles. The driver lowered himself out of the attic, stepping on the dryer and then the floor, just as he had when that little numb-nuts Kenny lived here. He watched the dog's shallow breathing for a moment, then scooped the remnants of the chicken bone into his pocket and looked for the computer.

The floor plan of the house was familiar from when Kenny lived there, and after watching the lone light the night before, he felt confident which bedroom the cop used as an office.

Still, he couldn't resist a quick look through the house, just to see how the man lived. *Know your enemy*, he told himself, refusing to admit the charge he always got from snooping in other people's lives.

A king size bed took up most of the space in the small master bedroom. A flowered spread was folded back over half of the bed. The other half had the blanket pulled up, but not smoothed out. The pillow looked lumpy. Women's clothes and shoes filled more than half the closet space and spilled out onto the floor. A silk robe hung off a knob on the open closet door. Perfume and jewelry boxes sat on the dresser.

An ornate perfume bottle caught his eye and he lifted it to his nose. Light and airy. *Probably something cheap.*

Damn, the wife's been gone since August and he still lives this way? I thought a big tough guy like him would already have some blond he was doing. Maybe he's not so butch after all.

The lid on the largest case sat open and he poked through a jumble of costume jewelry. His mother's birthday was coming up. He picked up a silver bracelet with colored stones and slipped it in his pocket. *This should do nicely.*

A pink, glittery key chain fell to the floor and he scooped it up. If he had to come back, he could use the door. Avoid that stuffy attic.

In the living room, the upright piano was a surprise. Sheet music for some classical piece he didn't recognize was another jolt. No way that cop played delicate music with those big, thick fingers. A step closer said he was right. He ran his finger over the bench seat. Dust covered every surface.

The smallest bedroom held an elliptical machine and loose

weights on one side of the room and a computer on the other. This was more like what he'd expected. A muscle bound jock using brawn instead of brains to get through life. The shelves were overflowing with books, but that didn't mean he read them any more than having a piano meant he played. A violin in the closet only confirmed that the wife had been musical.

He already had the password for the computer, so searching the files was a snap. What he found wasn't good. They were definitely looking at the client. That was to be expected. But who was the unnamed witness the search warrant mentioned, and what had she overheard? Still, it was mainly a fishing expedition with no solid link to him or his partner unless the client had been foolish enough to put something in writing.

If the client kept his mouth shut, they would all walk away with what they wanted.

He grabbed a beer from the cop's fridge and slipped out the back door. No need to go through the attic again. He paused behind a tree and looked both ways before stepping out. If the cop came home now, he'd be in deep shit.

As he strolled casually down the street, he thought about how jumpy the client had become. Could he trust him to keep silent or should he cut his losses and remove that link from the chain now?

No, they needed the money. The client could wait until after he paid up. So, get rid of the witness or the cop, but he didn't know who the witness was. The cop. With that link removed, the investigation would stall and he'd have time to find the witness.

First the cop, then the witness, then the client. Once they were eliminated, he'd be safe. The two brand new garden hoses he'd seen sitting in the cop's garage gave him an idea. Considering the way the cop lived, no one would even ask questions. Hell, no one would even miss him.

He took a sip from the beer can and grimaced. He'd only drunk a couple of beers in his life, and this one didn't do anything for him. Domestic. He should have guessed. The cop was low-class through and through. He tossed the half-full can in the bushes and kept walking. He wasn't worried about prints. The guy would be dead before he ever realized someone had been in his house.

Lifting the keys was a stroke of genius. Another example of superior intelligence overcoming unexpected problems.

CHAPTER NINE

NOAH'S BACK ACHED and his eyes burned, but he finally had Hudson's papers organized into piles in descending order of importance.

He turned off his desk lamp and briefly considered having his eyes checked. Nope. No point in that. He'd stop by the dollar store and buy some cheaters. That would last him as long as he needed.

Conner had spent the morning sitting in the audio/video room working on the phone logs. The office had a constant hum of activity which could be ignored when dealing with paperwork, but interfered with sound recordings.

When Conner stuck his head around the corner and motioned to him, he stood, downed the last dregs of cold coffee, and tossed his cup in the trash. *Jeez, that was nasty*. He pulled a stick of gum from his pocket to cover the bitter taste.

"What ya' got, partner? I hope it's something we can use, because the guy doesn't have anything labeled 'Contract for

Killing My Wife," at least not that I've found yet." Noah stepped into the audio room and pulled the door closed behind him.

"I've got something, but it's not what we expected." Conner spread out his worksheet and pointed to a phone number. "Someone at this number started calling Crystal at regular intervals about seven months ago. She called him occasionally, but not often."

Noah interrupted. "How do you know it's a he?"

Conner reached over and pulled a stack of papers closer. "Phone is registered to this guy." He handed Noah a driver's license copy of a man with dirty, scraggly hair, tattoos crawling up the side of his neck, and the brown, rotten teeth of a meth user. Just picking up the photo made Noah want to wash his hands.

"Guy's name is Harlan Prince. And he's a prince of a guy," Conner continued. "His rap sheet starts when he turned sixteen, but I'm willing to bet there's a juvie record somewhere. Now he's nearing forty and still making his living stealing other people's hard earned money. He does mostly penny-ante stuff. Crimes of opportunity. And he was definitely angry with Crystal at the time of her death."

"Wait a minute. Crystal wouldn't have had anything to do with him. Her bathroom had more face, hair, and skin products that a mid-sized drug store. I can smell this guy's stink just looking at his picture. No way they were having an affair. And how do you know he was angry?"

Conner pulled the phone log back. "When he first started phoning, the calls lasted ten to twenty minutes. If he missed her and left a message, the one minute calls, she phoned back within a couple of hours at most."

He moved his finger down the list. "A week ago, he phones and waits all day for her to call back. He calls again and waits a couple of hours. Then one call an hour. Finally, he's calling every ten minutes for twelve hours straight. He skipped an hour here, maybe he fell asleep or had to take a dump, I don't know, but he started right back up."

Noah leaned over the paper, studying it closely, his back and eyes forgotten. "Yeah, then he goes to three or four times a day until the day she dies. Then no more calls."

"You haven't heard the best part." Conner held his finger over the play button of a recording device. "I've got his last message. She never deleted it."

He pushed the button and a scratchy voice filled the room. "You can't treat me like this, you bitch. Don't think you'll ever be safe in your fancy house with your fancy car. I'll make you pay, one way or another."

Noah raked a hand through his hair. He stared at the photo and rap sheet then shook his head. "I can't see Prince being organized enough to pull this off. He might walk up to her front door and blow her away. But this job took skill and planning. I know in my bones Hudson was behind it and he would never hire this guy. The proof is somewhere in the stuff we took from his house and we need to keep looking for it. Hudson radiates evil. I can it feel down to the soles of my feet."

"We can't overlook this, partner. It's a lead and we have to follow it. If we ever got Hudson to trial and his attorney found out we didn't chase this down, he'd walk."

Fuck. He didn't mind Conner being right, he just hated being wrong. He'd wanted to solve more cases, get a few douche-bags off the street before it was time for him to go. But if he couldn't do that properly, he was spinning his wheels, wasting time. Worse, he was allowing bad guys to slip away and ruin more lives.

Noah turned on his heels. "Let's go find this Prince character. It'll be interesting to see how he explains his last message."

Conner spent a frustrating hour tracking down Prince's last known address before heading for the motor pool to check out another rolling pile of dung. Noah had grabbed a couple of sandwiches and sodas from a deli down the street and was waiting for him by the curb. He pulled over and unlocked the door, then held the take-out bag while his partner buckled up. As soon as the click sounded, he pulled out into traffic.

He drove with one hand while they chowed down. He hated eating in the car—no matter how careful he was, crumbs fell on his suit—but if they arrested Prince, it would be hours before they had another chance for a meal. It wasn't as if their lunch could make the car smell any worse.

After several wrong turns onto streets with no markings, Conner found the address he had copied from the last arrest report. Prince lived in a run-down four-plex. Conner eyed the house and decided the whole building was leaning dangerously toward the east. Was it even safe to enter? The added weight of two more people might bring it all down.

If this was the correct address, Prince should be in the upper, right hand apartment. An outside staircase rose unsteadily to a side door. Piles of trash bags littered the ground. Someone apparently considered tossing the bags out the door as taking out the trash. From the size of the piles and the stench that carried down the block, this method had been going on for quite a while.

Conner hurried up the stairs before Prince could notice them.

He watched Noah grip the banister as he climbed, testing each step before placing his full weigh on it. "What a shit-hole," Noah whispered as he reached the landing. "This place should be condemned before somebody gets killed."

He and Noah stood on either side of the door. Noah nodded and he reached over to knock.

A muffled, "Who's there?" drifted from behind the door.

Conner slurred his words. "Hey, Prince, come on. Open up, man."

Footsteps shook the landing and the door flew open. "I told you to beat it . . ." A giant of a man in his late-thirties stood in the doorway. He wore a stained and torn undershirt. His sweatpants looked and smelled as if he hadn't bothered to remove them the last time he relieved himself. Conner had seen people in many stages of withdrawal, and this guy had it bad.

His eyes flew open when he saw Conner and Noah. He tried to slam the door, but Noah's foot was in the way.

"Good afternoon, Mr. Prince. I'm Detective Noah Daugherty, this is my partner, Detective Conner Crawford, May we come in and speak to you for a moment?" Noah's arm was hanging loose, close to his weapon. Conner twisted slightly so his hand wasn't visible and placed it on his Glock.

"Do you have a warrant?"

Conner spoke up. "Why no, we don't, Mr. Prince. We just want to chat. To see if you can answer a few questions for us." This guy might be a slob, but he was no dummy.

"Then no, you can't come in. Stand out there and ask your questions. If I feel like it, I'll answer. But hurry, I don't want to miss my show." The theme from *Who Wants to be a Millionaire* played in the background.

If Prince could answer anything past the $500 question, Conner would mail his BA back to Texas A&M.

Noah managed to move closer without taking his foot out of the door. "Do you know a woman named Crystal Hudson?"

"That bitch," Prince almost screamed. "Did she send you? That's just like her. She doesn't want to deal with me so she hires someone to do her dirty work for her. Tell her one time, that's all. Pay for me to go to that fancy rehab where all the stars go and she'll never hear from me again."

Conner blinked. That wasn't exactly what he expected to hear. "How well do you know Mrs. Hudson?"

"Oh, I know her alright. I know all about her, and believe me, she's not the fancy-schmancy high society bitch she likes to pretend. I could tell some tales. Tell her to do right by me or I won't be the only one who knows about her."

Most suspects didn't make threats in front of police officers, but Conner doubted Prince had any idea what he was saying. "Why don't you come downtown with us where we can talk in comfort and I'll see if we can get you a hamburger, maybe some fries?"

"Fuck this. I'm not getting in a car with you. I'd never be seen again." Prince tried several times to slam the door, but Noah held his foot steady.

Prince growled and rushed at Noah, placing his hands around his neck. Conner reached for his gun, but Noah was between him and Prince. The staircase wobbled and swayed as

Conner tried to reach around his partner, but the small landing left no room to maneuver.

Noah swung a meaty fist into Prince's midsection but the man didn't loosen his grip. Conner grabbed a section of Prince's undershirt and pulled. The fabric was so rotten it crumbled in his hands. He turned his Glock around and tried to club Prince in the head just as Noah took a step sideways. The blow fell on Prince's shoulder. Noah's face was turning red so Conner straightened his gun. *I'll have to shoot the SOB no matter how close Noah is. I'm not sure even that will stop him.*

The staircase shuddered as Noah threw himself against Prince. The banister snapped with a loud crack and both men flew off the landing. Conner raced down the stairs. His heart climbed up his throat. His foot crashed through the last step and he fell forward.

The men landed on the pile of trash bags, Noah on top and Prince still struggling. Noah swung his fist again, this time connecting with Prince's jaw. Prince lay still and Noah rolled to the side, gasping for breath. The trash bags had ruptured, covering both men in three-week-old garbage. The beer cans were bad enough, but maggots had started in on the pizza crusts.

Conner's pants were torn and his shin bleeding as he limped to the two men. He hoped to God neither one noticed how much his hands shook as he slapped the cuffs on Prince.

"I told you this place was a death trap," Noah wheezed.

Noah and Conner sat on one side of a battered table that was bolted to the floor. Prince sat opposite them, his legs and arms chained securely. Noah eyed him suspiciously. The man was huge and coming down from some powerful narcotic. Was there any chance he could pull the bolts loose and vault over the table after them?

He scooted his chair back slightly, ready in case the man made a move toward him. Conner took notes, although the interrogation was recorded.

Prince glared across the table. "I thought you promised me a hamburger and Coke. I'm hungry."

Noah snorted. "I'm not in the habit of spending my own money to reward a person who tried to kill me."

"I didn't want to kill you. I just wanted to get past you. I was worried you were trying to kill me. I wouldn't put nothing past that bitch. She has the money to hire something done, no questions asked."

Noah took a sip of ice cold soda. His throat burned with each swallow. "What'd you do to piss her off? Did you threaten to tell her husband about your affair?"

"Are you crazy? Yeah, I only met her last year, but still, she's my sister. That's just sick."

Nothing about this interview was going the way Noah expected. At least he'd been right to insist they weren't sleeping together. "She's your sister and you only met her last year?"

"Okay, half-sister. I've known about her for years, but never set eyes on her. When Mom found out Dad had a second family on the other side of town, the shit really hit the fan. I was about five when Mom saw the birth announcement in the paper. We moved to Houston and Dad didn't come with us."

"Where were you living at the time?"

"Tyler."

Conner shuffled some papers. He pulled out Crystal's birth certificate and handed it to Noah. Yep, she was born in Tyler.

"So how did you finally meet?"

"I saw her photo in the paper, some society deal. They were listed in the telephone book, so I went to her house. I waited outside till I saw her husband leave. Then I rang the doorbell."

"I'll bet she was just thrilled to see *you* on her doorstep."

"Actually, she was real nice. She invited me in. Gave me tea." Prince rolled his eyes.

What was with these rich people and their tea? Remembering how much trouble he'd had with those tiny teacups, Noah almost felt sorry for Prince. Until he thought about those gigantic hands around his neck.

"Something must have gone wrong. You weren't too friendly when we came to your door."

"I shouldn't a called her those names, but she bailed on me. Just like everyone else I've ever known. She promised to get me some help. Put me in one of those rehab places. A good one. Not like in jail where they just let you sweat it out. But I had a little relapse and she stopped returning my calls. When I saw you guys, I figured she was gonna wash her hands of me so I couldn't bother her no more."

Noah leaned forward in his chair, looking Prince in the eyes. "So you decided to get rid of her first, before she hurt you?"

Prince shook his head, as if to clear it. "No. What? I don't understand. Did something happen to Crystal?"

Conner softened his voice. "Crystal was killed a couple of days ago on her way home from yoga."

"Noooo," Prince moaned, as if some part of him had ripped in half. "Not Crystal. Are you sure? She was all I had in the world.

She was going to help me get clean, then she promised to make her husband give me a job." He tried to put his head in his hands, but with his wrists chained, they wouldn't reach.

Sobs racked his huge body until Noah could feel the waves of grief. He glanced at Conner. They both knew that in his condition, it was possible to have done something in a fit of rage and not remember it later.

"She was so sweet. She never got mad at me, no matter how bad I screwed up. She didn't blame me for all the shit our dad pulled. Why did it happen to her? Was she in a wreck? I know I don't deserve it, but I want to go to her funeral and tell her husband how much she meant to me."

"It wasn't a wreck, Harlan. Someone shot her." Noah waited.

Prince's head shot up. "No one would hurt Crystal. Were they trying to hit her husband? She never said nothin', but I got the feeling some of his business was crooked."

"No, she was driving home alone. Where were you on Tuesday night?" Here it came. The moment they had been waiting for. Would he break down and confess or deny everything, try to blame someone else?

Prince's eyes were red and his nose covered in snot, but he looked Noah in the eyes. "Are you trying to put this on me? I don't even have a car. Or a gun. Besides, on Tuesday night, I was in the county lockup. I just got out last night."

Noah booked Prince while Conner finished the paperwork. When Noah returned to the office, Conner looked up and wrinkled his nose. "You need to go home and take a bath. You smell like shit, and I mean that literally."

"You aren't exactly a bed of roses yourself." Noah eased himself gently into his chair which let out a groan that matched the way he felt.

"I can't. When Jeannie sees what I did to this suit, she's going to have a fit."

Exactly why I have the sense not to wear expensive clothes. "It's your leg you should be worried about. If it gets infected, I might have to take it off at the knee with my pocketknife."

"Fuck that, I poured alcohol over it in the bathroom. Didn't you hear me scream?"

"Yeah, I could hear it over at the jail. I though a hooker had grabbed the Chief by the balls and twisted." Just a few minutes talking with Conner and Noah could feel his nerves settle down. "Did you find any record of Prince's bust on Tuesday night?"

"Yeah. He was arrested in a vice sting at a bar on the east side at 7:12. That gave him an hour to get across town. Could be done, but how'd he get there? He doesn't have a car. Bar's walking distance from his place. He was supposed to have been there all night, but who knows if the undercover kept track of what time everybody came in or out."

Noah raked a hand across his face. "So we'll put him on the back burner for now and keep looking."

Conner swung his chair toward Noah. "What'd you decide to book him on?"

"For the moment, it's just assaulting an officer and resisting arrest. If these red marks around my neck are still here tomorrow, I might up it to attempted murder." He wouldn't do that no matter how red his neck was. That would mean photos, depositions, and everyone in the building knowing how close he'd come to buying the farm.

"I hate to bring this up, partner, but there's something that concerns me a lot more than the red marks on your neck. Your hand is still swollen and more colors that a six pack of Crayons."

Noah flexed his hand and pain shot up his arm. "It's not infected and the swelling is going down. At least it was until I bashed it against that piece of concrete Prince uses for a jaw."

"I'm not talking about that. I'm talking about Sweet Pea. I'd hate to admit that Hudson was right about anything, but you need to think about doing something with that dog."

Noah's jaw clamped and his hands balled into fists. "I'm not putting her down just because she's too much trouble." Conner might be his partner, but he was overstepping on this.

"Not because she's trouble. Because she's miserably unhappy. You're not doing her any favors by making her keep going when she hates everything about her life."

If only Conner knew how close he'd come to echoing Noah's own feelings.

"Is there anyone who'd take her? What about your sister, or Betsy's mother? Didn't she keep her while you were on your honeymoon or the time you two went to Austin for a few days?"

"Rachelle can't take her. She might bite one of the kids. And Betsy's mother took her for a few days, but Sweet Pea bit her too. And she's diabetic. The bite didn't heal well."

Besides, she barely remembers who I am. Another link to Betsy broken.

"I'm going to give Sweet Pea a few more months. If things aren't better for us by then, well, I know what I need to do." He knew. He knew exactly what he was going to do and he didn't plan to discuss it with Conner, or Rachelle, or Betsy's mom.

Noah crammed papers into his desk drawer and slammed

it shut. He was going home and stand in a hot shower until the tank emptied. It was early, but he'd stayed late too many times for his boss to say anything. He stood and shoved his chair back. The mood he was in, he'd have liked to kick it, but his foot hurt where Prince had slammed the door on it. Almost as much as the rest of his body did. Falling off a second story landing had taken its toll, even if he did land on garbage bags.

"We should have the information on the cars by Monday. We can start there. Hudson's behind this. Prince didn't kill his sister."

"The man tried to kill you. We can't discount him entirely."

"No, he was just trying to get away. I'm a lot harder to kill than that." *At least until I decide I'm ready to go.*

CHAPTER TEN

THREE STEPS UP to the back door were all Noah could handle. Every inch of his body protested. He sighed with relief when Sweet Pea failed to bark as he unlocked the door. *Shower first or eat first?* Either way, he planned to be in bed within the hour. He was too young to feel this old. Or maybe he was too old to pretend he was young enough to wrestle a giant off a two-story landing.

One step inside the kitchen, and the stench slapped him in the face. The room smelled worse than Prince's three-week-old garbage bags. Fuck. Pea had barfed and had diarrhea all over the linoleum. The thought of cleaning up the mess was almost more that he could handle. Especially since it was his own fault. He should never have given her that sausage. He knew people food upset her stomach, but it usually just gave her gas.

Sweet Pea lay curled in her bed, her back to him.

"Okay, Pea. Stop playing possum. I'm not mad at you. Let's get your bottom rinsed off and I'll give you the tummy medicine the vet sent home for you. Thank goodness I came home early. Another two hours and you'd look like one of those baboons with the multi-colored keister. Not to mention that the gifts you left me would have set up harder than concrete on this floor."

Noah stared at the dog, but Sweet Pea didn't move. Heat rose up the back of his neck and he swallowed several times. Half of him wanted to kick the dog and the other half wanted to cry. He'd done all he could, yet she still growled at him, bit him, and ignored him. What was he supposed to do? He'd given himself eight more months to make things work, but on nights like this he seriously considered moving up the timetable.

Groaning audibly, he squatted beside the dog. "Come on, Pea. Let's get up." He ran one finger across Sweet Pea's head. When the dog didn't move, he slipped his hand under her body and lifted her.

"Pea? Are you alright?" He put his ear to her chest. For one long moment, he didn't hear anything. Finally, a faint sound greeted him.

Rushing to the laundry room, he pulled a towel from the cabinet. A small pile of dirt covered the washer and he brushed it away as he wrapped the Yorkie in the cloth. "Don't worry, Pea. I'll take care of you."

His feet flew across the kitchen and he was out the back door without stopping to lock it. Carrying the tiny dog through the cold night, he jumped into his truck and cranked the heater to high. To the vet's or straight to the animal emergency clinic? He glanced at the clock on the dashboard. Five-fifteen. Could he make it to the vet's before they closed? Rush hour traffic was starting up and the streets were still a mess. Too risky.

He hadn't been able to save Betsy, but he'd be damned if he'd let anything happen to her dog.

He pulled into the emergency clinic on two wheels and leaned on the horn. He had Sweet Pea inside before the sound died from the air. An aide ushered him to a back room and the vet on duty, a doughy looking man with thick glasses and thin hair, took the dog from his arms. "Do you know what happened to her?" he asked.

"She was like this when I came home from work. She'd vomited and had more diarrhea than you'd think possible for an animal this size. I gave her some sausage this morning. I shouldn't have, she can't really handle people food, but it's never been this bad before."

The vet frowned at Noah and disappeared into the next room. When he returned, he held a syringe, tubes, and a bag of fluid. He took a blood sample and started an IV. "No point in waiting. It'll be several hours before we know if she's going to make it. Stop in front and leave your contact information. I'll call you as soon as I know anything."

Noah scratched the dog behind her ear and she opened one eye. The look of pleading stabbed his heart. "Good dog," he said in his softest voice. "You're going to be just fine. The doc here is going to take care of you." He turned away before his voice cracked completely.

How could he have allowed himself to feel such anger just because she didn't respond when he called? Was he willing to give up that easily? He could see she was sick, and from something he'd given her.

In the lobby, he reached for a clipboard and filled in the required information. A wave of dizziness swept over him. The sound of his pen scratching on the paper and the universal hospital smell of antiseptic, cleaner, and general misery, was too familiar. Five and a half months. Too soon to go through this again.

He sat the clipboard down and hurried out the door. The cold air hit him in the face and he leaned over the fancy landscaping and threw up behind a bush before rushing to his truck. He drove slower and slower as he neared his house, afraid of the phone call he might receive.

The foul smell of Sweet Pea's accidents hit Noah the moment he stepped inside. He left the back door open despite the temperature and started toward the laundry room for cleaning supplies. The house was silent except for his footfalls. A crunching sound caused him to look down. White powder coated the bottom of his shoe. Most likely spilled laundry detergent. The dirt he had swept off the washer glared up at him. He lifted the lid of the washer and the odor of wet clothes assaulted him. He hadn't put the last load in the dryer yesterday. So when had the dirt fallen on the washer? And where had it come from?

Was he that poor a housekeeper? Probably.

He spent the next twenty minutes dealing with the mess Sweet Pea had left and trying not to think about how empty the house would be if she didn't pull through. When the floor was clean, he moved the wet clothes to the dryer, put the towels in the washer and added bleach.

Sighing, he closed the back door. The room still wasn't a rose garden, but it was livable.

No point in taking that shower now. There wouldn't be any hot water till the washer finished. He pulled off his suit and dropped it in the dry cleaning pile. No point in trying to sleep, either. Not until he got some kind of phone call, one way or the other.

Five minutes later, in jeans and a sweatshirt, he grabbed the vacuum and started attacking his office, then his bedroom and then the den. Cheetos, peanut shells, and old shoes littered the floor around his spot on the sofa. Just because his life was a mess didn't mean he had to live like a slob.

He didn't need to hire Rosaria, he just needed to get off his butt and get the job done. He and Betsy always split the cleaning. On Saturday morning, he would vacuum and mop, while she dusted and cleaned the bathroom. She did the laundry, but he took care of the dry cleaning. He had honestly believed that he shouldered half the housework. Now he realized how little he did to help.

Finally, he couldn't put it off any longer and he ventured into the one room he tried to avoid. It had been so long since he entered the living room, it even smelled musty. He opened the curtains and dust motes flew into the air. He vacuumed quickly and pulled out the dust rag that dangled from his back pocket. But there was only one piece of furniture that needed attention. The piano. How long had it been since he'd been able to look at it?

Memories of Hudson's gleaming baby grand swept over him. He'd vowed that night to repair the stuck key on his own unused upright. He stared at the piano for the first time in months and the broken key stared back, like a one eyed Cyclops blaming him for every promise he'd ever broken.

Spray polish in one hand and dust rag in the other, he leaned over the bench seat. The movement allowed the overhead light to shine directly on the seat and a line cutting through the dust caught his eye. He stood up again and the line disappeared. He moved to the side and it reappeared. Had Sweet Pea jumped on the bench? No, the dog couldn't jump that high anymore and she would have left paw prints, not a line.

The line looked exactly like someone had run a finger across, checking for dust. Who would have done that? Betsy's mother would, but she hadn't been over since the day of the funeral.

Conner had picked him up once about two weeks ago, but had he come into the house? Yes, but only the kitchen.

His sister. Was Rachelle checking up on him? She'd brought over a casserole, but that had to be a month ago, maybe longer. He squatted beside the mark. No fresh dust. The mark was recent.

The phone rang, startling him, and he spun on one heel and rushed into the kitchen. Only one person would call this late on a Friday night. Well, two, but he and Conner weren't on call this weekend.

"Mr. Daugherty," the vet started immediately. "Sweet Pea is improving. The shot I gave her has settled her stomach and the IV is replacing the fluids she lost. She's sleeping now, and I'll check her again in the morning, but unless something happens, I think she's turned the corner."

"Thanks, Doc." Noah's heart hammered in relief. "When can I pick her up?"

"Let's wait till mid-morning at least. Noon would be better. I want to keep an eye on her until I'm sure she won't relapse."

Fatigue consumed Noah as he stumbled to the bedroom, dropped his clothes on the floor and fell into bed without a shower or food.

Daylight woke Noah and he groaned as he rolled out of bed. Every inch of his body ached, but nothing compared to his hand. Fresh bruises from connecting with Prince's jaw overlaid the fading yellow areas from Sweet Pea's bite. The swelling between his thumb and index finger had diminished, only to be replaced by more across his knuckles. He flexed his fingers twice, but wasn't willing to make that mistake a third time.

He stepped into a scalding shower and let the water pour over his head and down his body. That seemed to ease everything except his hand, which throbbed worse than before. Too late, he remembered Betsy telling him, "Ice first. Then heat."

Two cups of coffee and a bowl of cereal later, he almost felt human. The empty house echoed every sound. Placing his cup and bowl in the sink might as well have been fingernails on a blackboard. He switched on the TV but couldn't sit still long enough to watch it. The digital clock on the stove read 10:37.

To hell with this. It might not be noon, but it certainly qualifies as late morning. He grabbed his keys and, slamming the door behind him, strode to his truck. It would be eleven by the time he reached the clinic.

He drove one-handed and it slowed him down some, but pain shot up his arm when he tried to grip the steering wheel with his sore hand. At the emergency clinic, he paced in the small room as he waited for the lab tech to bring Sweat Pea. What was taking them so long? His gut clinched with worry. Maybe she was sicker than he thought.

The same vet from the night before appeared holding an open manila folder filled with papers. He kept his eyes on the papers, not looking at Noah. "Mr. Daugherty, what type of medications do you take?"

Noah blinked in surprise. How was that any of this guy's business? "I don't take any medication, Doc. I have a bottle of fish oil and some vitamins in a drawer somewhere, but I seldom remember to take them. What does that have to do with Sweet Pea?"

The vet looked at him for the first time. "According to these reports, Sweet Pea didn't eat something that disagreed with her. Our lab here isn't sophisticated enough to say exactly what, but it looks like she ingested some type of drug. We try to caution all pet owners about the danger of using drugs that might spill onto the floor or be left out where an animal could reach them."

What the hell was this guy talking about? There weren't any medications at his house. His sister had brought him three sleeping pills the day of Betsy's accident. He had taken one and felt worse the next day than if he'd stayed up all night. The other two were safely stored in his dresser drawer for a future occasion. Probably laundry detergent. He could have spilled some of that.

The lab tech, a skinny kid with the faintest wisp of a goatee and arms like twigs beneath scrubs decorated with kittens and bunnies, stepped into the small room. The interruption saved Noah from answering. Sweet Pea never liked strangers on the best of days, and now she was visibly trembling.

"How you doing, girl?" Noah lifted the dog gently from the young man's arms. Had she been this thin before? He could feel every rib. He searched her face, and she gazed back with mournful eyes.

"She'll need to be on a special diet for a few days. Feed her small amounts, several times instead of a large meal once or twice a day. Kevin here will have the cans waiting at the front desk." The vet glanced over his glasses toward the lab tech, who scurried out of the room like he was afraid to be caught eavesdropping.

"Watch her carefully and bring her back at the first sign of a relapse. And don't let her get hold of any sausage–or anything else." The vet turned his back to Noah and closed the door behind him with a solid thump.

Noah stared at the closed door for several seconds before taking Sweet Pea to the front desk, collecting several cans of special diet dog food, and paying the exorbitant bill. He climbed into his truck and settled Sweet Pea on the seat beside him. His sore hand rested lightly on the little dog during the drive home, and he was careful not to make any sudden stops.

Noah tried to coax Sweet Pea to eat a few bites of the new dog food, but her expression clearly said she wasn't interested. Smelling it, he didn't blame her. He lifted her dog bed onto the sofa and she dozed next to him for most of the afternoon. He kept one hand on the dog and the other in a bowl of ice. Whenever he got up, she lifted her head and followed him with her eyes.

By evening, she still hadn't eaten and Noah sat on the floor and held her in his lap. "Come on girl, try a little. You might like it. If you won't eat, I'll have to take you back to the vet's." He scooped a tiny amount on his finger and put it against her lips. A small, pink tongue took a hesitant lick, and then cleaned his finger. Two more scoops and she started to eat on her own.

He carried her to the backyard where she made a half-hearted circle, checking for intruders, then stood by his leg, waiting to be carried inside.

Although the rule had been 'no dogs in the bed,' he always suspected Sweet Pea slept with Betsy when he had to work all night. He'd come home once to find his pillow warm and the dog glaring at him. He'd been secretly glad that Betsy had a warm body to keep her company when he was gone.

What an ass he'd been. Was he jealous of a little dog because she'd known Betsy longer than he had? It wasn't like the dog took up that much room. No wonder Pea resented him. He'd kicked her out of her own bed.

In those first months after Betsy died, if he'd taken Pea into bed with him, they could have comforted each other. Maybe they'd both be stronger for it now. Instead, they shared the house in silent resentment—each sure the other had stolen some of the love that belonged to them alone.

His bones ached, and he headed for the bedroom before the news was over. He bunched the spread into a nest and settled Sweet Pea into it before dropping his clothes and stretching out on top of the sheet. One hand encircled the little dog, as it had most of the day, and he felt her lick his arm before he fell asleep.

CHAPTER ELEVEN

THE DRIVER CIRCLED the block several times before parking one street past the cop's house. Not a light was on anywhere in the neighborhood. Of course not, they rolled up the sidewalk by ten on weeknights and by eleven on weekends. At—he checked his watch—half past two, it might as well be a graveyard. The thought made him chuckle.

Don't get cocky. That's how fools are caught. He stayed in the shadows as he approached the cop's house, too excited to care about the cold air. The side garage door opened easily and he switched on his headlamp as he tugged it closed behind him.

There was the cop's truck, waiting for him. He pulled out the pink key ring and slid the key marked 'Ford' into the ignition. A perfect fit. He turned it to accessory and watched the gas needle move to a fraction below the full mark. He patted the steering wheel. *Good cop. I knew I could count on you to keep your tank full in case you got called out on an emergency.*

No time for self-congratulations. Best to get in and get out before someone woke up, even if it did mean leaving without a memento. In this neighborhood, some old fart would need to pee, or a baby would want his mother's tit.

Although he could come back after and clean out the cop's wallet. No, the risk/ratio wasn't worth it. The cop was unlikely to have much cash. He hated to do a job for free, but working alone again after so long was enough of a thrill.

The gemstone bracelet he'd picked up on his first visit would have to satisfy him. Even if he did have to give it to his mother.

The two hoses were still in the same spot and he began unrolling them. He fastened the ends together and pulled the larger one to the rear of the truck. He jammed the end as far into the tailpipe as he could manage and held it in place with a rag he found on the workbench, plugging the extra material around the opening.

The folding stairs lowered without a sound. He'd oiled them on his last visit. The wind outside was kicking up and he tied a bandana over his nose and mouth in case dust was stirring in the attic. He didn't want to cough or sneeze at the wrong time. Another example of a superior intellect planning ahead, considering all possibilities.

Now for the hard part. Dragging the hose up was difficult, but he carried the roll over his shoulder, unwinding as he went. He already knew the way.

A poorly connected vent had allowed him to watch Kenny's parents, rutting vigorously in the same bedroom. Seeing Mr. Yates' fat ass bouncing and Mrs. Yates with her legs spread and her boobs jiggling had been both disgusting and intriguing, but he didn't look away. After several minutes, Mr. Yates had rolled to the side, hissed angry sounding words to his wife, and she finished the job with her mouth.

The driver had stared in disbelief. At thirteen, he hadn't realized such an act existed. Pressure built in his jeans and he experienced his first erection. Over the next year, he checked in on the Yates from time to time. Saturday night seemed to be their preferred time, and he was often waiting.

While there was never any outright violence, the act was always rough and demeaning, without the expressions of love he'd read about in magazines. Mr. Yates tugged and twisted and pinched his wife until she cried out. He bent her over the bed and entered her from behind, entangling his hand in her hair and pulling her head back.

The driver would hurry home, his pants bulging, and relieve himself in private, remembering every detail.

Now the act of killing had the same effect. Planning, he considered foreplay. The instant he was sure the mark was dead, he rushed back to his room, locked the door, and unzipped his pants. Each job gave him hours of pleasure. And this one would be the best. He would savor every moment, over and over again.

The streetlight on the corner bathed the room in a soft glow. He could see the cop asleep on his half of the bed. He knew the man was big, but hadn't considered what that actually meant. His arms, shoulders, and chest were perfectly sculptured. But it was his legs that caught the driver's attention. Strong and muscular, disappearing into his boxers just as things got interesting.

He wasn't gay, certainly not. But he didn't have time for the distraction of women at this point in his life. Maybe in five or six years. Besides, the women he was around now seldom flaunted their assets, concentrating on intellectual abilities. When he was ready, he'd find a wife with both *Playboy* looks and a Mensa mind. He deserved nothing less.

The temperature in the attic was only slightly above the outside air, and his hands were beginning to go numb. Time to get moving. He positioned the hose carefully and used the rest of the rag he'd found in the garage to ensure that the fumes went into the bedroom instead of the attic.

The cop sighed and shifted slightly. No, he was wrong, that chest was riveting, and the thin line of dark hair that disappeared under the waistband of his boxers drew his eyes. It wasn't the man that aroused him. Anyone could admire the beauty of a painting without wanting to buy it and take it home. It was only the thought of all that power brought down by someone as small and weak as himself, using only his superior intellect.

His erection was so strong, it was painful. *Do I dare stay here and let myself go while I watch him die?* He stifled a chuckle. *Coming while he's going, that's rich.*

A strange sound caught his ear and he peered down into the shadowy room. A small head popped up from under the covers and looked around.

That fucking dog.

How had she managed to live after eating all those sleeping pills? He watched as the dog pulled its head back under the covers. As he sat back, a small shadow on the cop's chest caught his eye. Something was there, on his left peck. A small line, too faint to distinguish in the dim light. Was it a scar? Had he been shot, or maybe knifed?

The thought was titillating. He ached to know what it was. He adjusted his glasses, but the line remained a faint blur.

He eased out of the attic. *Stick to the plan. Don't dilly-dally around just for the extra kick.* He could hack into the autopsy report to find out. Until then, there was enough pleasure from bringing down that nosy cop all on his own. What a waste. All those muscles, that beautiful body, and what good had it done him? A few minutes of breathing exhaust fumes would shut him down the same way it would a man half his size and condition.

The driver started the big truck and waited to be certain most of the gas was traveling up the hose.

Outside, the sleet had started again and it stung his face as he hugged the shadows on the way back to his car. As his puny compact sputtered to life, he could still feel the power of the cop's big truck, and imagine all the exhaust that super-sized engine would produce. His heater struggled against the cold, but he felt warm, envisioning the gas, making its way from that truck, curving through the attic until, slowly but surely, it reached the air vent.

He could picture it drifting silently into that room, blanketing both the man and the dog in poisonous vapors.

Two for one. Even better than he'd planned.

Sweet Pea whined and Noah rolled over and wrapped his arm around her. He buried his face in the extra pillow, but it had lost its scent. Time to dab a few drops of perfume on it again. Sleet peppered the window and an ice coated limb cracked like a rifle shot and fell to the ground, causing Sweat Pea to tremble.

"That's okay, old girl," Noah's voice cracked and he tried again. "It's just Old Man Winter singing his song. I'm here. I'll take care of you."

His throat hurt so that the words were almost unrecognizable. His head pounded like a jackhammer. *Fuck, I knew I'd end up sick. Going from an overheated room, outside into the cold, and back again. My feet wet for two days. Witnesses sneezing on me. Wallowing in garbage.*

"We'll spend the day resting tomorrow. How's that sound, Pea?"

The words burned and he started coughing. His nose and eyes felt gritty. He sat on the edge of the bed, but the room started spinning.

Trailing his hand on the dresser for support, he made his way to the bathroom, opened the door, and closed it behind him. That habit had stayed with him from Before. He'd always left the light on in the bathroom but kept the door closed so that he wouldn't disturb Betsy if he came in late or got called out early.

Inside, he fumbled in the cabinet for the bottle of aspirin, shook out three and washed them down with cold water from the faucet. The water felt so soothing sliding down his throat that he took several more gulps. When he straightened up, his head still hurt and the room still spun, but not as much as before.

One step inside the bedroom and he was coughing again. His nose burned and his eyes watered. He tried to make sense of it, but his head wouldn't work. Something was wrong, he knew that.

He took a step, then two, before he stumbled. He fell to his knees beside the bed. His legs wouldn't obey his instructions and he hung onto the sheet while the room whirled about him. His eyes were level with the edge of the mattress, where was Sweet Pea? He'd thrown the sheet back when he got out of bed. He pulled it toward him and saw her, buried under the blanket. She didn't move and her head lay in a small pool of vomit.

Anger swept over him. He didn't mind going, but it should

be his choice of when and where. Even if it was his time, it wasn't Sweet Pea's. She deserved better.

A giant roar filled his body and he opened his mouth, but only a squeak came out. He heaved himself to his feet and swept the Yorkie into his arms. He ran through waist-deep molasses toward the kitchen and threw open the back door.

At the first step, his bare foot hit a sheet of ice and he landed on his butt, sleet pelting him from all directions. He sat on the icy stoop, wearing only his boxers, and tried to blow into the little dog's mouth, but air wouldn't come. After several painful gasps filled his tortured lungs, he tried again and was able to blow a steady stream of air into Sweat Pea's snout. He rubbed her chest and did it again.

"Come on, come on, Pea. You can do it. Breathe for me." He blew again and she gagged, a thin trail of vomit trickling from the corner of her mouth.

"That's my girl. I knew you wouldn't leave me." Did the blanket he accidently threw over her head save her?

Each breath of the freezing air helped brush the cobwebs from his mind. His head still pounded, but the spinning had stopped. Sweet Pea shivered and he knew he had to get her someplace warm. But where? They couldn't go in the house. It was full of gas.

Gas? What the fuck? His kitchen was electric. Maybe the hot water heater. Or the central heat. He'd turned it up before bed to keep Sweet Pea warm.

Melting ice had soaked through the seat of his boxers and sleet continued to assault him, hitting bare skin like icy buckshot. The garage. But if the house blew up, so would the garage. *Okay, make a plan.*

Through the house and into the garage as fast as possible. Leave the doors open for fresh air. Once in the garage, put Sweet Pea in the truck, go back inside and open windows. Figure out what's leaking gas and turn it off.

He felt better as soon as he had a plan, a course of action. He stood, but his legs hadn't gotten the message. They trembled so that he grabbed the door for support. One step into the kitchen and he started coughing. His lungs burned and tears poured from his eyes.

Too fucking bad.

He clutched Sweet Pea to his chest like a football and ran through the kitchen. This time, the molasses was only up to his ankles.

In the garage, he hit the button to raise the door, opened the truck and climbed in. The towel he'd wrapped Sweet Pea in was still there and he settled the dog carefully. Wonderful, blessed warmth. His body was still shaking. Why was the truck so warm, was it still running? Had he forgotten to turn it off when he came home from the vet?

No, the gas gauge said almost full. It hadn't been running long. He reached for the ignition to turn the truck off and his hand closed on something that was familiar and foreign at the same time. His heart stopped and he opened his hand to reveal a pink, glittery key fob.

He shook his head to clear it and something caught his eye. The attic stairs were pulled down. *How did that happen?* His eyes followed the hose as it snaked its way up the folding stairs. Had he been dreaming, sleepwalking? Had he done this himself?

It was exactly his plan, what he'd been thinking of doing. But the timing was wrong.

A few weeks after the funeral, his sister, Rachelle, had taken him aside. "Did you read the book on grieving I gave you?"

He'd never been a good liar and didn't have the strength to try. "No. I can't sit still long enough to read."

"That's okay, read it when you're up to it. But until then, there's one important piece of advice to remember. Don't make any major decisions for at least a year."

And he'd agreed. Promised, even. Of course, she'd been talking about quitting his job or moving away.

The one year anniversary would be tough. So he'd decided on fourteen months. He had the date, October 25th, marked on his calendar. And he'd need every one of those days to atone for the sins of his past if he had any hope of joining Betsy in Heaven.

A Sunday School teacher had once cautioned him that for every sin you committed, you must redeem yourself not seven times, but seven times seven. He'd wasted the first few months moping, but now he was in full swing, and he needed to make his city safer for his sister and her two girls by taking forty-nine miscreants off the streets of Houston. And he still had thirty-four left to put away.

But this was February. He had eight months to go. And somebody was fucking with him.

CHAPTER TWELVE

CONNER WAS DREAMING of a warm beach. He could even smell the salt air. Jeannie was wearing a bikini. That pink one. The one that always drove him wild. She looked at him and smiled. He was about to get lucky. And with Jeannie, that meant very lucky.

At first, the buzzing of his cell phone was a breeze through the palm trees, then it turned into an angry swarm of bees. He answered without bothering to glance at the number. "This better be good. We're not on call this weekend."

"I need you here. Now." Noah's voice sounded rough, raw.

"Lights and siren?"

"Only on the freeway, not in my neighborhood."

Even on his weekend off, Conner had his clothes laid out and ready to go. In two minutes, he was dressed. Before leaving, he leaned over to kiss Jeannie on the cheek and whispered, "Emergency. I have to go."

She nodded without opening her eyes. As he stood, she

grabbed his hand. "I love you. Be careful."

"Always," he said. "And me too." He allowed one hand to linger on the swell that would soon be his daughter. A small kick told him she was awake. "And good night to you too, kiddo. Be still and let your mother sleep."

Even with icy streets, he pulled in front of Noah's house in fifteen minutes. All the lights were on and the garage door was up.

Noah stood in the driveway, waiting. Conner parked the car and stepped onto frozen grass that crunched under his feet.

"I need to use your car." Noah met him halfway across the yard. "I have to take Sweet Pea to the vet."

Conner noticed the bundle in his arms for the first time. He leaned to the side to look into Noah's garage. "For this you called me at four in the morning?" Something was up. Something more than a sick dog. He stalled while he tried to figure it out. "Your truck not working?"

"The truck's running fine. Too good in fact. I thought it best not to disturb anything. You giving me your keys or what?"

"They're in the ignition. Want me to drive? You don't look too good." Noah's hair was disheveled, his eyes red, and his voice sounded like old sandpaper. He was wearing jeans, no belt, a stained sweatshirt, and . . . flip flops? Noah gave him grief for noticing things like that, but it was surprising what you could learn about the person you were dealing with by being observant.

"No, stay here. Protect the scene. Don't touch anything and don't call anyone." Noah sprinted for the car and peeled rubber for half a block.

Conner stood in the ice-crusted grass for a full minute, watching the taillights disappear. He pivoted and nearly fell when his foot slipped. The garage would be warmer than standing outside in this weather.

He was still on the driveway when he noticed a bright orange hose snaking its way from the exhaust pipe of Noah's truck, across the garage, and up a set of wooden folding stairs. Halfway up the stairs, the orange hose screwed into a yellow hose, then disappeared into the open attic.

Fumes stung Conner's eyes as he stepped into the garage. He coughed and moved closer, squatting beside the truck exhaust. A rag held the hose in place and would have blocked vapor from escaping. He immediately recognized the remnants of Noah's hideous traffic-cone orange and white striped golf shirt that he'd squirted mustard on one weekend last summer.

Betsy had laughed and clapped him on the back as he rubbed the stain into the fabric, ensuring that it could never be worn again. "Thanks, Conner. I was trying to figure out how to get rid of that shirt." Noah had sputtered, but went inside to change.

Now here was a torn strip of Noah's shirt, tied to a hose funneling exhaust fumes into his attic. Conner closed his eyes. Had it come to this?

He'd been so worried for so long, but lately Noah had seemed better. He smiled, made an occasional joke, even laughed once in a while. He still only nibbled at his food, and the dark circles under his eyes said he didn't sleep well, but he gave every indication he was stronger, that he'd rounded a corner.

I dropped the ball. He was trying to convince me he was better. All the while the devious son-of-a-bitch was making plans.

Conner dropped to his butt and lowered his head into his hands. As he stared at the rag, the message light at the back of his brain began blinking.

Noah had joked about being an Eagle Scout. In this very backyard, he'd taught Conner how to tie different knots and what each was used for. The knot used to tie the rag on the tailpipe was sloppy, loose. Fumes still lingered in the air and a gap showed where gas had escaped.

If Noah had done this, he'd have done it right. And he wouldn't have asked Conner to protect the scene.

What other things had some fucker screwed up and left behind?

If Noah had pulled into the emergency clinic on two wheels last time, this time he executed a power slide inches in front of the main entrance. When he hit the clinic door with the heel of his hand, pain shot all the way up his arm. He was inside before the sound of Conner's engine had died away.

The skinny lab tech dropped his clipboard and gaped at Noah.

"I need the doc right away. She's got carbon monoxide poisoning. She stopped breathing for a while, but I got her going again." Noah's words tumbled out.

The kid didn't say a word, but disappeared into a back area, then reappeared down the hall, motioning Noah to follow him.

He led Noah to an exam room then disappeared again. Before Noah had time to object, the same pudgy vet appeared.

"She's breathing better now, doc. But she was in bad shape for a while and it's all my fault. She got a lot more gas than I did, and she's so much smaller. Can you save her?" He raked a swollen hand through matted hair, his voice a hoarse whisper.

The vet glanced at Noah before taking Sweet Pea. "Wait out

front, I'll get her on some oxygen, then I'll come talk to you."

Noah paced the tile floor of the waiting room, his footsteps the only sound. He ignored the orange plastic sofa and the year-old magazines, even the hospital smell, but he couldn't ignore the hammering of his heart or the burning sensation behind his eyes.

Minutes passed, or maybe it was hours. He couldn't tell the difference. When the vet appeared, Noah sank onto the sofa, unable to control his trembling legs.

"Did I get her out in time, doc? Is she going to make it?"

"Sweet Pea is recovering, but she's had a rough couple of days. She doesn't have any reserves left. Not only is she not strong enough to go through this again, she shouldn't have to. Just like a doctor or teacher has a legal responsibility to protect a child they suspect of being abused, I have a responsibility to protect Sweet Pea."

The vet studied Noah and continued. "It's up to me to see that she's safe and well taken care of. Do you understand what I'm saying, Mr. Daugherty?"

Noah pulled himself up to his full six-foot-two and glared down at the smaller man. The vet didn't back off and Noah had to give him props for that. "That's Detective Daugherty to you, and I am trying to see that she's safe. That's why I brought her to you. Now, I'm not sure what you think you know, but you're way off base."

"Mr. . . . Detective Daugherty, look in the mirror. In one glance, I can see a bruised jaw, abrasions around your throat, red, raw eyes, and possibly a broken hand. You've been fighting, drinking and doing drugs. I suspect you passed out in your car with the motor running. In the last two days alone, you've fed

Sweet Pea spicy food, allowed her to ingest a powerful narcotic, and exposed her to lethal gas. You're not capable of taking care of this dog."

"Giving Sweet Pea that sausage patty was poor judgment on my part, and won't happen again. But we both know throwing it up is what saved her life. As for the other, I had one beer yesterday evening." At least he thought it was only one beer. Two were missing. "I've never done drugs in my life and my father taught me as a teenager to avoid fights whenever possible. But some fights you can't avoid, and this is the way you look when a three-hundred-pound coke-head who doesn't want to spend the night in jail decides to throw you off a second story landing."

Noah took a deep breath, but it burned all the way down his lungs. "Now some low-life that's too much of a coward to come at me straight on, tried to get rid of Sweet Pea so she couldn't bark and warn me, then poisoned us both with carbon monoxide. I might need her to stay here for a couple of days until I know it's safe for her to come home. But make no mistake, she *will* be coming home with me."

The vet actually apologized, and, after subtle pressure from Noah, agreed to x-ray his swollen and discolored hand. If the hand was broken, Noah needed to have it taken care of, but if it wasn't, he didn't have the time to waste sitting in a hospital emergency room.

"I don't see any break," the vet had admitted, "but this is outside of my field of expertise. And with the number of bones in the hand, I can't guarantee anything."

"That's good enough for me. Thanks, Doc." Noah was out the door and in Conner's SUV before the vet could answer.

On the drive home, Noah felt empty, deflated. If he'd just rolled over and shut his eyes. Five more minutes and he'd have been with Betsy.

CHAPTER
THIRTEEN

NOAH PARKED IN the same spot Conner had an hour earlier. He felt incomplete without Sweet Pea. When he thought how close some scumbag had come to finishing her off, his hands clenched into fists. What would he do if she had brain damage?

The crescent moon was low in the night sky and the stars had started to fade. For the first time, he understood the phrase, "It's always darkest before the dawn."

His partner was nowhere to be seen as he trudged across the frozen grass, through the still open garage door, and into his house. The windows and doors had been closed, and Noah sniffed loudly, checking for fumes. The inside air was only a few degrees warmer than the outside, but it didn't burn his nose or throat, and he couldn't detect the presence of lingering gas.

Conner was sitting at his kitchen table, drinking coffee. He hated that his partner had been through his house, seen how he lived. But anger at the man who'd done this quickly replaced any embarrassment.

"There are things we need to talk about when this is over." Conner pushed a cup of coffee his direction. "But that can wait until after we catch this son-of-a-bitch. Do you think this was personal, or tied to a case?"

"I've been thinking about that. No question I've pissed off plenty of people, but I can't come up with one that would risk the shit that would rain down from killing a cop."

Conner tapped his spiral. "I've made a list of our most volatile perps. I'll check them out, but I believe they're all locked away. And none have family that care enough to take revenge. Most would be more likely to send you a thank you note."

"So that leaves the Hudson case. We aren't working on anything else where taking me out could make any difference, and this happened right after I appeared on TV talking about Crystal Hudson's death." *That son-of-a-bitch reporter. I should have ignored him when he pushed that microphone in my face.*

"I agree. Nothing else makes sense. This is an amateur. Someone who believes without you, the investigation would stall. Do you think Hudson ordered it?"

"That's possible. I wouldn't put it past him. The other side of that coin is the shooter. Hudson could be holding up payment till things cool down. With me gone, he might think Hudson would pay up faster." Noah took a sip of his coffee. The hot liquid scorched his raw throat, but soothed his jumpy nerves.

Conner's fingerprint kit sat on the table between them and he admitted he'd already tested the truck door handle, the key fob, the tailpipe, the two hoses, and the attic door pull. But Noah had touched most of those things, and the others didn't have a surface conducive for fingerprints.

Noah took another sip of his coffee. It burned going down, but not as much as before. "Check the side garage door, both knobs, then I have some interesting places I want to try."

When Conner returned, shaking his head, Noah showed him the ceiling panel over the dryer. Conner's eyes went wide with surprise. "That is an interesting place. I would never have thought of it."

"Yep, and while you're at it, try the dryer too. Anyplace someone might put their hands if they were climbing down." No point in getting Conner to test the handle on the fridge. He'd used it too many times since Friday.

"One more spot." Noah led his partner into the living room. "I'm not sure you can get anything from it, but do you see that line in the dust?" He flipped on all the lights and pointed to the piano bench.

Conner knelt beside the bench and studied the mark, before digging in his case for a small brush.

Noah stood, replaying in his mind every move he'd made when he came home Friday and found Sweet Pea sick. If only he hadn't cleaned the floor. He'd even put bleach in the washing machine with the rags.

He spun on one heel and rushed into his bedroom. Which shoes had he been wearing? He dug through the closet and pulled out his black loafers, still slightly damp from a day spent trudging through icy streets. One shoe was clean, but the other had tiny grains of a white substance stuck to the bottom.

Before taking the shoe to Conner, he checked the back of his sock drawer. Both his sleeping pills were nestled safely in a small plastic container.

Conner held the shoe in one hand and a small plastic

evidence bag in the other. "Are you sure you want me to do this? I didn't let you touch anything, but any decent defense attorney would use my involvement to cast doubt on everything I've collected tonight."

"I don't care about that. I don't want the SOB for attempted murder. I want him for the actual murder of Crystal Hudson. And anyone else he's hit. This wasn't his first time at the rodeo. He's done this before and I'm going to stop him before he does it again. These prints may point us in the right direction."

Noah finished his coffee while Conner packed up the evidence he'd collected. "I'm headed home after I drop these off for forensics. I'll call you as soon as I hear anything. Try to get some rest. We have to hit the ground running as soon as we know anything. Do you want me to help get the hose down?"

"No, I can do it. You get moving so you can spend at least part of the day with Jeannie."

He stood in front of the garage and watched Conner drive off. The sun was up and the sky had cleared, but his yard was littered with limbs that had broken during the ice storm. His neighbors, their faces slack with shock, began to venture out and survey the damage to their own yards. He'd seen hurricanes leave less debris behind.

Three hours later, he was sweating and freezing at the same time, but his yard was clear and neatly bundled piles of tree limbs waited at the curb for the city to pick them up. He stumbled inside and tried to convince himself to eat something. A piece of toast and some coffee were all he could force down.

He sped through his house, a whirlwind of cleaning, until

no trace of fingerprint powder remained. He even opened the windows to air out any hint of gas fumes. While cleaning the yard, he'd gone in and out the front door, unable to face the garage. Now he wanted that hose out of his house.

In the garage, he disconnected the two hoses and untied the rag holding them to his tailpipe, but not before he noticed the sloppy workmanship. His own shirt and his own hose. He kicked the jumble of tangled hose, and pain shot up from his sore foot.

The attic stairs were still down and he climbed them carefully. Crawling through the small space, he had a moment of claustrophobia. He shook it off. If some stranger could do it, so could he. The space narrowed even more, but he could see a glimmer of light ahead.

The hose, which had snaked its way across the attic, ended at the small square of light. Noah tried to sit up on his knees, but banged his head on a rafter. Two hundred pounds resting on hands and knees on a two-by-four, with his head crouched down. The pain in his knees would have been excruciating if he hadn't been so busy concentrating on not getting stuck.

How did the guy know where to go? He almost had to have been here before.

Light drifted in through the latticework at the far end of the attic. Dust motes floated in the air and Noah rubbed his nose. The streetlight would have given minimal lighting at night, still, one wrong move and the guy would have fallen through the ceiling.

He crawled forward a few more inches and peered into the opening. *Fuck.* Directly over his bed. Had the guy stayed here and watched him sleep? This was beyond weird. He sat back on his haunches and banged his head again.

Noah tried to turn around, but there simply wasn't room. He had to back out. As he reached the stairs, he remembered that he hadn't untied the hose from the air vent. A groan escaped when he realized he'd have to go back. That could wait until he had a hammer and nails, something to fix that vent properly. Before climbing down, he glanced toward the kitchen. Marks in the dust showed someone had traveled that way recently.

If necessary, he could have forensics test the area for prints and fibers. For now, he shoved the last section of hose into the attic and closed the door.

Sitting at the kitchen table, he replayed everything he knew. The killer had obviously been stalking him, but for how long? Had that been the noise Sweet Pea heard on Thursday night? The killer had definitely come in sometime on Friday and tried to poison Sweet Pea, probably to keep her from barking, but was that the first time he'd been in the house?

Noah thought of the air duct pushed to the side, and the clear view of his bed. Chills ran down his spine. Had the killer started spying when Noah appeared on TV discussing Crystal Hudson's shooting, or had he started sooner, while Betsy was still alive?

He had a flash of memory of Betsy, running from the shower to the closet wearing only a towel. His hand had darted out and grabbed a corner of the towel and yanked. They had fallen onto the bed, Betsy's rich, throaty laughter filling him. Had that pervert been watching?

His chest tightened until not a sip of air could pass. The thought of some low-life sitting safe in a jail cell, remembering his Betsy . . . He couldn't let that happen.

He would have to kill the guy.

An hour later, Noah hadn't moved from the kitchen table. The phone rang several times before he answered. Even then, he only grunted.

"Hey partner, you there? I heard from forensics."

"What's the word?" Noah's voice was rough, just above a whisper, but in the last two days, he'd been strangled and gassed, so Conner didn't seem suspicious.

"Nothing. Most of the prints were useless. A couple were good, but they didn't lead anywhere. Still, we'll have a comparison if we catch the SOB."

"When we catch him." Noah fought to keep his breathing steady. "What about the white powder?"

"Not yet. Maybe tomorrow. I stopped by to check with the video tech guys, and they promised to have a list of possible license plates first thing in the morning. How about I come over and we start canvassing the neighborhood? Maybe a nosy Nellie was watching out the window and saw a strange car or somebody hanging around."

"I've already asked the neighbors for two houses on either side and across the street. You know how it is, nobody saw nothing. I figure he came around two or three in the morning. Only moms with bawling babies are up at that time and there's none of those on this street." Noah's heart skipped a beat. *No use crying over that now.*

Noah squirmed. Omitting information wasn't the same as lying, but hiding something from his partner didn't sit well with him. And neglecting to mention what he found in the attic was only half of what he left out.

An almost full beer can was caught in a hedge two doors down. And the brand was the same as the can missing from Noah's fridge. Too bad the neighbor had crushed it and tossed it in the trash.

So the creep had headed east after his first visit, which was more likely the direction he felt comfortable with. If he was going to find the guy on his own, that was the direction to start.

Conner's voice brought him back to the present. "He wouldn't have parked in front of your house. We should check for a couple of blocks around."

"True, but we'll wait till Monday. I don't want to warn him we're coming."

After he hung up with Conner, Noah heated a can of tomato soup and drank it from a cup while standing at the back door. The setting sun gave the sky and any remaining patches of ice a rosy pink glow, which contrasted uncomfortably with his black thoughts.

Keeping his partner out of the way while he tracked down this killer would be tricky, but he'd made his decision. It couldn't be handled any other way. He refused to risk having any dirt blow-back on Conner. Not with Jeannie and a baby to take care of. At the very least, he had to know he was safe in his own home.

His bedroom was a mess, so he went into the guest room and stretched out on top of the covers. He set the alarm for eleven-thirty. That would give him almost five hours. Sleep came immediately.

When the alarm rang, he was ready. He set his bedroom just as it had been: with the bathroom light on, but the door closed. He pulled the curtain on the back wall tight, leaving the room slightly darker. In the garage, he opened the attic and reconnected the hose.

Crawling into the attic was more difficult this time because he already knew how tight the space was. He pushed the box of unused Christmas decorations ahead of him as he crawled to a far corner and stretched out. The box wouldn't stop a gun shot, but it might hide him.

He was perfectly positioned over the garage. He would hear if anyone came in. He could see both the attic opening and the vent into his room. If the light was switched on or the bathroom door opened, he would know immediately. His Glock dug into his hip and he pulled it out and sighted it where a head might pop up at the top of the attic stairs.

The slats in the air vent were narrow, so he reached over and pried them apart. He tested the opening with his gun barrel. A perfect fit. The shot would be tricky, but doable.

No need to waste time identifying myself or to shout a warning. Anyone creeping around my house this time of night is up to no good. Just line up and shoot, then worry about the consequences later.

The driver had fantasized about that unrecognizable scar on the cop's chest all afternoon. He'd managed to jerk-off a couple times that night, but it wasn't as satisfying as it should have been. He needed to *know*. Had someone else tried to kill the cop? Had he succeeded where a lesser man failed? And where was that person now; in jail or dead?

Ooh, that was a thought. Had the cop actually killed anyone? Did they have that in common? He lay in bed, wondering, while he tried to coax some life back into his tired dick. Watching the cop die should have been good for three pops at least.

Nope, wasn't happening again tonight, not even with the heated K-Y jelly. Neither was sleep. He stood and paced the room, visions of a thin line just out of reach.

Fuck this. He threw on a jacket and some shoes and headed toward the parking lot. His car started on the first try. *Must be a good omen.*

No point in waiting for the heat to kick in, he'd be halfway there by the time it started working. His glasses fogged over and he cleaned them before he buckled his seatbelt. He drove with care, as he always did. Tickets left a paper trail.

Twenty-five minutes later, he was circling his old neighborhood. His house was dark and he'd swear he could hear his father snoring inside. He had a key. He should slip in the back door and help himself to half the contents on his mother's wallet. She'd think his father did it, and never say a word. Not this time, but it might be fun sometime in the future.

Maybe he should snag one of his father's beers. That would drive the old man crazy. He chuckled as he circled again.

Nothing stirred at the cop's house. No lights, no sign of any activity. There had been no mention of his death on the news, but that was to be expected. He lived alone. It was possible no one had missed him yet.

He came to the spot where he'd parked before and pulled to the curb. It would be easy to slip inside, see what the mark on his shoulder was. Maybe take another memento.

Noah did a series of push-ups every half hour to keep limber. The night was much warmer than the previous one, but after two hours in the attic, the cold began to seep into his bones. *Why didn't I take the time to put on socks?*

He had thought to bring a water bottle, and he took an occasional sip. But mostly he remained still and remembered. He thought back over every hour, every minute, of his three years with Betsy. He'd always known it wouldn't last. That's why he'd rushed into the marriage.

Sooner or later, she would have seen through him. Seen the blackness in his soul. But while he'd been with her, she'd washed him clean. If angels walked the earth, she was his.

When he stepped in the door at night, she kissed him and all the ugliness of the day flew away. He became like any other husband; laughing, eating dinner, watching TV. Making love.

Without her, he was afraid the blackness would take over again. So far, memories of her had kept it at bay, but his decision to take out this guy–no trial, no jury–showed he was slipping.

Finally, his mind took him where he had refused to allow it to go even once over the past months. The place he thought he'd sealed off permanently. To that last morning, the last minutes of the Before in his life.

Betsy had read that the first pee of the day was the most accurate. She sat in the bathroom, giggling, while he paced nervously in front of the door.

"Would you stop that? You're giving me a case of bashful bladder. I can't always do this on demand you know." She turned on the faucet, either to help get things flowing, or to camouflage the sound. He never knew which.

Then they sat together, on the edge of the bed, watching the white plastic stick, as the pale blue plus sign appeared in the little window. His breath caught in his throat. God *had* forgiven him for the sins of his past. He had allowed Noah to give Betsy the one thing she wanted most in the world.

Betsy squealed, "We did it, we did it, we did it," and threw her arms around him. Noah fell back on the bed, pulling her with him. Soon, he was lost in her softness, her warmth.

She laughed again and tugged on his hand that had somehow managed to slide under her gown. "Not now, honey. I have to be at work in thirty minutes."

He had teased her nipple slightly. Just the way she liked it. "You don't have an exact time today. It's an in-service day. The kids don't even start until next week. You can slip in the side door and old Mrs. Clemmons will never know what time you got there."

He felt a shiver run down Betsy's spine and knew he had her. He pulled the gown over her head and began trailing kisses down her neck and across her throat until he reached that spot where he could feel her pulse racing, the spot that seemed made to fit his lips. Soon neither one of them could have stopped if Mrs. Clemmons had been standing in the room, watching.

And that was it. The last time he saw her, the last time he kissed her, the last time he would make love. Ever. The last moments of the Before. And it was his own fault. He'd caused her to be late. If she'd left on time, she would have been safely parked at school when that sleepy son-of-a-bitch speeding down the freeway had lost control of his car. But no, he'd been selfish and horny and she'd paid the price.

Now he lived in the After. At least he didn't have to worry about being horny. That part of him was as dead as his soul. No little tingles at the sight of a sexy woman, no early morning wake-up calls from dreams he couldn't remember. As if it didn't exist. And that was fine with him.

Until the day Laurel Bledsoe took his hand and held it while she checked his bites for signs of infection. *Whoa, where did that come from?* He tried to push the thought aside, but he could still feel the softness of her hand on his and the tingle it sent straight up his arm and then on down south.

He didn't have time to wonder what that meant before a sound snapped him back to reality. He closed his eyes and strained to hear.

A car drove slowly past and he checked his watch. Two-fifteen. He filed the sound away. Older car, loose muffler, needs a tune up. Ten minutes later, the same car drove past again.

He did three quick push-ups, flexed his fingers, and held his Glock steady.

The driver's foot had just hit the pavement when a light flicked on across the street. He jerked back and slammed the car door. Probably an old fart taking a piss, but using the same spot was foolish. Best to move to another street.

The ignition dragged and groaned and didn't turn over on the first try. His second try was more successful but by then his heart hammered and his hands shook.

How could he have been so reckless? He'd let his emotions override his intellect. The one thing he had sworn never to do. He needed to remember this moment, how frightened he was. Nothing like a near miss to teach an unforgettable lesson.

The cop was gone. The dog was gone. That thought made him smile. Soon the witness and the client would be gone. A few more jobs and he'd get rid of the shooter. No links, no chain. Start over with a more dependable partner or work alone.

He followed all traffic laws back to his room.

CHAPTER FOURTEEN

NOAH SQUINTED AT the luminescent dial of his watch. Four-forty. The killer wouldn't come this late. The neighborhood would be waking up soon. He untied the hose and nailed the air vent in place.

Crawling slowly out of the attic, his knee caps became a circle of pain with each move. The cold air and hard, cramped position had left his body so stiff he had trouble navigating the stairs.

One good yank brought the orange hose tumbling down. He didn't bother disconnecting it from the yellow one, but dragged them over the damp grass to the trash pile. *I might still need hoses, but not these two.* In fact, he didn't want them sitting there staring at him, reminding him of the decision he'd be making next October. If he prepared now, it meant he'd already decided.

Twenty minutes in a shower so hot his skin pickled and the room fogged over, loosened his muscles and warmed his bones. He gathered the soiled bedspread and dropped it by the dry cleaner's before stopping at Denny's.

The moment he pushed the restaurant door open, the smell of bacon and coffee enveloped him. His stomach immediately sent him a message. "Feed me, feed me," it cried.

A short stack of pancakes, two eggs over easy, bacon *and* sausage with wheat toast revived him. He wiped the plate with the last corner of toast and sat back. How long had it been since he'd enjoyed a meal? Even tasted what he ate?

Driving through rush-hour traffic into downtown, Noah realized that the swelling had gone down in his hand. Gripping the steering wheel caused only a slight twinge of discomfort. Good, he might need that hand soon. Depending on what he learned today, some SOB might be enjoying his last few breaths. He smiled and took the stairs six floors to his office.

He'd settled in his chair by seven and had already finished off his first cup of vending machine coffee when Conner arrived at seven-twenty, carrying two Starbucks cups and a manila folder.

"I stopped by and picked up the reports from the techno geeks. They gave us five possibles on the dark car from the night of the murder, and three on the white car from the week before." He plopped the folder and one coffee in front of Noah, then snagged his chair and rolled it next to him.

Noah drummed a pen on his desk. "Eight cars in eight different parts of town that aren't going to be at that address when we get there." He pulled the Starbucks closer in hopes the aroma would help erase the vile taste of the vending machine brew.

"This guy is seventy-six years old." Conner tapped a finger next to one name. "Although he might have a son or grandson driving around shooting people, let's put him at the end of the list. Same with this lady. She's sixty-eight. Possible, but not likely. These three live close together. We can knock them off in no time. Other than that, well, we might as well just get to it."

Noah dropped the pen into his drawer and pushed his chair back. Time to find that housebreaking scum. Twelve years experience. All he needed to do was look the suspects in the eyes and the hairs on the back of his neck would tell him when he'd found the right guy. If Conner pinged on the same one, fine. If not, Conner was on his own. This was personal.

Checking out a pool car and driving across town ate up an hour of the morning. No one responded for several minutes at the first house. Noah rang the bell again and knocked harder until a voice answered from somewhere in the back. When the owner opened the door, Noah could smell the booze before he introduced himself.

The woman was obviously still drunk from the night before. Her hands shook so violently, he had to help her light her cigarette. She was tall, but cadaverously thin. *Did she drink her meals?* Matted hair hung to her shoulders and her clothes had probably been slept in—more than once.

She led them unsteadily through her house. Noah had seen pigsties that looked and smelled better.

She claimed not to have left the house in several days. One look at her car and he believed her. A thin layer of grime coated every surface, and leaves obscured the windshield. No sticker decorated her back window and no residue indicated one had been removed.

Conner shook his head. "Her hands haven't been steady

enough to fire a gun since the Bush administration. And I don't mean Junior."

"There's a liquor store half a block from her house. I hope like hell she walks there. I wouldn't want her on the road under any conditions."

The second house contained a frazzled mother with two toddlers and an infant. The older kid stuck his tongue out at Noah and poured juice in his sister's hair. The infant wailed until Noah's ears rang, then she threw up on her mother's shoulder, traces of the vomit splashing on his shoe.

How could such a little kid smell that sour? His nieces had always smelled sweet, like powder or something.

The woman's husband worked on an oil rig in the Gulf and hadn't been home in two weeks. The car sat in the driveway. A row of baby seats filled the back. An aged, pealing bumper sticker, located on the wrong side of the back window, proclaimed a firm belief in The Rapture.

Noah tripped on a toy, hidden in deep weeds, on the way back to the car.

"Hell, I'd cruise the freeways shooting people too, if I was cooped up in that house with those little hellions." Noah pinched the bridge of his nose.

"I don't know about shooting people, but I'd pray for The Rapture to take me first." Conner stopped abruptly and hung his head. "Oh Lord, is that what I have to look forward to?"

Noah grinned at him from across the top of the car. "If so, I'll have pity on you and take you out for a beer occasionally. Now get moving. We have five more upstanding citizens to check out and one low-life murdering scum.

The third house was empty. A neighbor said that the family

had moved back to Tulsa six weeks ago.

Conner drove to the end of the street and stopped. "What's the verdict? Lunch, or on to house number four?"

"Let's take one more before lunch. I couldn't eat a thing after smelling that little kid. Her diaper must have been on overload."

Another day wasted while the guy who killed Crystal Hudson, and probably tried to kill him and Sweet Pea, got further away.

Monday was the driver's least favorite day. He had an early lab, then nothing till after lunch. Surely the Powers That Be could have arranged a better schedule. One with less wasted time.

The TV hadn't mentioned anything about the cop's death when he turned it on at seven, but he hadn't really expected anything that early. Now, with nothing to do for almost three hours, he decided to go back to his room and Google the cop's background. Maybe he could find out how he got that scar. Had he been shot or knifed? Would news of that be in the paper? If he'd killed anyone, there would definitely be a record. He felt the edges of his lips curl up. That information should supply hours of pleasure tonight. His eyes flitted under the bed. Yep, plenty of K-Y at the ready.

He settled himself in his desk chair and glanced at the clock. He could work for two hours and still have time for lunch.

Most of the information he found was mundane, but one item held a surprise. At seventeen, while still in high school, Daugherty had spent two weeks in China with a city-wide choir. Then he'd gone to Juilliard. But wait a minute, he'd graduated from the University of Houston.

He probably discovered the competition at Juilliard was a lot stiffer than he'd expected. That made him a quitter. A helpful piece of information.

A short bio showed that both his parents were gone, but he had a little sister. *Someone to keep in mind if things got too dicey.* He should have found out these things first. He was slipping, not doing the research he usually did. He'd let his emotions override his good judgment. A lesson to remember in the future.

The driver glanced up. Only thirty minutes had passed. Good. He still had plenty of time.

Going back several years, an article on violence in the downtown area reported that the cop's father, a concert violinist with the Houston Symphony, had been killed in a mugging outside Jones Hall. A valuable violin had been stolen and never recovered. His mother apparently died a year later. The paper listed her as having 'been with' the Houston Grand Opera. What did that mean, a ticket taker, seamstress? Her obituary didn't say how she died, but requested donations to the American Cancer Society.

So that was why he left New York and came home to Houston. Was he so soft he sacrificed his own dreams to take care of his mother and sister? A definite weakling, but was he not willing to do what was necessary to achieve his full potential, or had he used that as an easy out when he discovered he wasn't up to New York standards?

The desk chair felt hard, and his back was tight from sitting in one position for too long. His stomach growled and he knew time was getting short.

He moved to the next Google listing, and that's when he saw it. Just what he'd been searching for. An Officer Involved

Shooting. The cop had shot a teenager. Boy, the shit had hit the fan over that one. Eventually Internal Affairs cleared him of all wrong-doing, but it had gotten dirty for a while.

Looked like the cop had been on a gang task force when a seventeen-year-old pulled a gun and aimed it at a civilian. The kid's age caused the driver to pause. Apparently youth alone wasn't enough to make the cop hesitate. The kid had lived, so maybe the cop wasn't that good a shot.

Still, he'd been willing to take a life. They did have that in common. The driver felt himself come awake. This was enough to stir his juices. Maybe he could make it to threesies tonight after all.

His door flew open without any warning. He jumped and clicked off his computer. It wouldn't do to have anyone see what he was researching.

The shooter grinned at him. "Hey, the sun's out and I've been suffering from cabin fever. Let's see if we can gather up a crowd and walk over to Burger Barn."

"I thought you were short of cash."

"I figured I could count on you to spot me a burger. If that old man doesn't pay us soon, I might drop by his house some night and remind him we have a contract."

Ah, fuck. The jobs were easy. It was dealing with people that always tripped him up. He didn't trust his partner enough to tell him what had happened to the cop, and he couldn't risk having him decide to visit the client on his own. "Don't do a thing. I have it under control. Come on, I'll carry you till we get paid."

Half an hour's drive from the last house they visited, Rice

University was an oasis of calm in a city of four million people. The campus itself was shielded from view by thick hedges of wax leaf ligustrums. Towering oaks clasped hands above winding paths, and red brick buildings housed a student body comprised of only the brightest minds the country had to offer. It might have been harder to gain admission to Harvard or Yale, but not by much.

All that serenity and elitism set Noah's teeth on edge.

As a courtesy, Noah and Conner checked in with the campus police when they arrived. The officer on duty was about three weeks short of ninety. His white hair and beard made him look more like a skinny, ill-tempered Santa Claus than a cop. Even a rent-a-cop.

He had a meatball sandwich spread out on his desk. A soft drink, chips and a pickle were arranged at ten, two, and four, with a container of Parmesan cheese marking twelve o'clock. The smell of garlic hit Noah like a slap across the face and drove any remnants of dirty-diaper from his nose.

Conner left the office door open while they talked.

"You guys sure you're not going to arrest anyone? I'd have to go with you if you do. I've got one guy out—that ice storm dropped a tree on his house—and two guys checking into a disturbance over at the athletic compound. Then there's Marvin. He's supposed to be patrolling the science building, but I know damn well he's hiding somewhere. I just haven't been able to find his spot." The guard sucked meat sauce through yellow teeth.

"Nope. It's just a fishing expedition. We have to eliminate several dozen dark cars before we can convince a hard-nosed judge to issue a warrant for the guy we like." Noah didn't want the old guy walking around campus with them. That could turn a one-hour job into three hours spent with someone whose breath made his toenails curl. Besides, the faster they checked this kid off their list, the sooner he could move on to a real suspect.

"Well, you go on then. But be sure to let me know if you decide to arrest one of the little Einsteins. It's the fourth building on the left. I'd say the old, red-brick one but that wouldn't be much help." The guard either laughed at his own joke or had some type of seizure.

Noah glanced back as he pulled the door closed. The guard already had his face buried in his sandwich.

Rice operated on an old English model—students lived in colleges, not dorms. The walk to the college took less than ten minutes and Noah relished the chance to stretch his legs after a morning spent in the car.

Conner lifted his head and studied the sky. "I told you this would happen."

Noah glanced around. The day was ideal—cool, but not cold, sunny, with only a few white puffy clouds. "What are you talking about?"

"Groundhog Day. That old fella is gonna see his shadow for sure. Six more weeks of winter." Conner stepped in a puddle of melted ice and cursed under his breath.

"And I told you. Fuck the furry rodent. I'm done with winter. I'll give it two more weeks, tops." This winter had lasted way too long already. He felt like his insides had frozen over.

He needed to take Sweet Pea for a long walk, or to the dog park. Maybe invite Rachelle and her family over for hot dogs in the backyard. A couple of hours playing with his nieces and listening to Rachelle laugh was exactly what he needed. He'd even put up with his brother-in-law for that long.

But could he keep them in the yard and out of his house?

Noah pushed open the heavy wooden door and stamped his feet on a worn mat before entering the lobby. After the fresh air outside, the lobby smelled musty. Like a wet dog.

Conner glanced at the paper in his hand. "Second floor. Number 217."

Noah looked left and right. "Elevator?"

"In a building this old? What do you think?"

The stairway echoed as they tromped up to the fire door. Conner nodded toward the left. "I think it's this way."

"I'm not worried about finding the room. I'm more worried there won't be anyone in it when we get there. Shouldn't the little geniuses be in class or at lunch this time of day?"

"If he's not in, we can cruise the parking lot. It's a long shot, but maybe we can find his car. If not, we can check the room again. He might be back from lunch by then. Besides, you're the one who wanted to keep moving, not stop to eat."

Noah kept his mouth shut. Conner was right and if he disagreed, it would only be for the sake of starting an argument. And he was tired of doing that. Acting like an ass simply because his life sucked, pulled him down as surely as if he had a weight tied around his neck.

CHAPTER FIFTEEN

BOARDS CREAKED IN old hallways that took off in no logical direction as Noah and Conner searched for room 217. The numbers ran in a pattern understood only by some long dead architect. Noah realized his mother, with her love of antiques, would probably have appreciated the old lighting fixtures, but in truth, they cast only a shadowy glow that failed to illuminate the patina-covered number plates on aging doors.

"I guess the first test in determining if you're smart enough to come here is if you can find your room." Noah was ready to locate this kid and move on. The dark, narrow hallway was stirring hints of claustrophobia. The cop in him rebelled at tight places with only one exit.

"That must be why I went to A&M. The corps likes everything in straight lines. Numbered consecutively. Like an orderly mind."

"I could be wrong, but I don't think this university values an orderly mind. I think they encourage students to let their minds run free. To see what discoveries they can make. All the things that make the world go round." Noah debated pulling his penlight from his coat pocket to see if he could read the room numbers any better.

"Well, I'm not going round one more time. If this isn't the room we're looking for, I'm going to pull the fire alarm and interview students on their way out."

Wow. Conner must feel the same about dead ends to make a statement like that.

Two-seventeen was the last room on a short hallway with a window overlooking what Noah supposed was called The Quad. The kid that opened the door had caramel skin and black hair. He was tall, but on the chubby side, with wire-rimmed glasses and a bad case of adolescent acne scarring. His blue and silver Rice Owls sweatshirt exposed a sliver of doughy stomach.

The room was small, simply but adequately furnished, and had a large window with an excellent view. If not for the overwhelming aroma of Cheetos, Noah would have said the room was nice.

The fact that he could recognize Cheetos from one whiff worried him. *I need to change my eating habits or I'll end up looking just like this guy.*

The kid's computer was running, and a stack of textbooks lay open beside it. And yes, there sat an open bag of Cheetos.

"Ignacio Ramos?" he asked.

"Yes." The kid looked irritated at the interruption, but not frightened.

Noah introduced himself and Conner but didn't specify what department they represented. No point in putting the kid on edge if he didn't have to. He'd learn more that way. "May we come in for a moment?"

The kid shrugged and stepped aside. "Sure, come on."

Either the kid didn't know to ask questions before he let them in or he didn't have anything to hide. Unless he had a lot to hide and didn't want them to know it. Anyway, the room was university property, and a case could be made that they had the right to enter if they wanted.

"Could you make this quick? I only have an hour till my next class and I haven't eaten lunch yet."

Noah tossed out the same lie he'd already used twice that day and held his breath. Would the kid cooperate or try to stall them? "We're trying to track down a dark sedan that was in a hit-and-run accident last night. Do you mind if we look at your car?"

"My car hasn't been out of the parking lot since I got back from Christmas break. You can see it from here." He peered out the window and pointed to a parking area beside the building. "It's the," he counted, "one, two, third row from the front and the fourth car in."

Noah leaned to the side and spotted the car. "Where do you keep your keys?"

The kid pointed to a small basket on a table near the door. "You're welcome to look it over, but it wasn't me. I was in study group last night."

"You have study group on Sunday night?" Conner's brow narrowed and Noah smiled. He knew that look all too well.

Ignacio wiped his hands on his pants and Noah realized it was the first hint of nervousness he'd seen from the kid. "I've got a full-ride scholarship. If I don't keep my grades up, I'll lose it. So yeah, I have a different study group every night except Friday and Saturday. My dad's an auto mechanic. No way I could afford to come here without help. I can print you off a list of all the groups if you want to check."

Conner smiled. Back to being the good cop. "That would be very helpful. Thank you."

Ignacio sat at his computer and with a few keystrokes, a list of his study group partners, complete with contact numbers, rolled off his printer.

The door was still open, and Noah stood behind it, checking the contents of the basket holding the kid's keys and spare change so Ignacio handed the list to Conner.

The door swung in several more inches, almost hitting Noah. "Hey, Icky, my buddy. Want to head over to Burger Barn for lunch?"

The hairs on the back of Noah's neck stood at attention. He couldn't see the owner of the voice, but he could see Ignacio flinch.

"Not today, Ryan. I have company." Ignacio gritted his teeth as he spoke.

"We won't be more than a few minutes, if you want to join your friends." Noah stepped around the door and got a good look at the two intruders. Now his whole body was on alert. "In fact, we can all walk down together."

The kid in the back seemed surprised that Ignacio had company, but the kid in the front, the one with the high-pitched, squeaky voice, dropped his books and a can of Coke. The brown liquid spread across the floor and onto the kid's shoe, but he didn't seem to notice. He tried to speak several times, his mouth opening and closing like a trout dropped on the deck of a boat, but no words came out. His eyes doubled in size behind thick glasses and his face turned the same shade of red as his hair. He reached down and grabbed his books, but left the soda can.

"Well," he finally stammered. "We're in a hurry. You can join us when you're finished here." The kid spun on one foot and slammed into the boy behind him as he hurried down the hall.

Conner's gaze followed the boys as they disappeared, but Noah kept his eyes on Ignacio, watching for his reaction to the two visitors. "Sorry to keep you from your friends. . . Icky. Is that what you like to go by?"

Ignacio slumped in his chair. "They're not my friends and no, that's not what I like to go by."

Conner pulled his pocket spiral out and flipped through his notes. He tapped a page near the front and held it out for Noah to read. Under the notes about Noah's conversation with Rosaria was the word 'icky.' Underlined three times and followed by a question mark. Noah gave a barely perceptible nod, but he didn't need reminding.

Noah pulled the extra chair around and sat, facing Ignacio. This day might not be a waste after all.

"If he's not your friend, and your name's not Icky, why don't you start at the beginning and tell us what's going on." *Because something sure as hell is going on, and I intend to find out what.*

There wasn't a number large enough in the universe for two people named Icky in one case to be simple coincidence.

Noah didn't move. He'd sit here all day if that's what it took. But he wasn't leaving until he knew what this kid had to do with Crystal Hudson's death and the attempt on his own life.

"So who are those two guys, and why did they call you Icky

if that's not your name?"

"Ryan Howell and Derrick McAllister. Ryan's supposed to be my tutor, but he hates me, and the feeling is mutual. He resents having to work for part of his expenses, he resents that I have a scholarship and he doesn't, although his IQ is probably the highest on campus. And that includes the professors, some of whom have Nobel Prizes. He *really* resents that I got into this university at all. I went to a second-rate high school in the Valley that didn't prepare me for a school of this caliber. But I did finish first in my class, and I did pass the admission standards. I'm working like the devil with his tail on fire with no real help from my assigned tutor and so far, my GPA is 3.9, thank you very much."

Noah nodded. For some reason, that always seemed to keep a story going. But inside, he longed to grab the kid and shake him until the information he wanted spilled out. "If he hates you, why'd he invite you to lunch?"

"He doesn't want my company. He gets paid by how many hours he spends with me. At lunch, he'll ask me how I'm doing. I'll say fine because if I actually admitted how hard this is, he'd say something derogatory to make me feel worse. Then he'll turn in that he worked with me for two hours."

Conner paused in his note-taking. "So what's the deal with the name?"

Ignacio pinched the bridge of his nose. "The first day, when I introduced myself, he said, 'Just how dumb are you, Iggy, and how much of my time are you going to waste?' When I said I preferred Ignacio, he laughed and has called me 'Icky' ever since."

His chair scraped against the hardwood floor as Noah pushed it back and stood. "Do Ryan or Derrick ever borrow your car?"

"No, Ryan has his own car." Ignacio stopped. "Well, he borrowed mine once, when his wouldn't start. Didn't even put gas in it. Derrick doesn't have a car. He just tags along wherever Ryan goes. I don't know why Ryan likes him, but he's the only one who pays any attention to him. Derrick has plenty of book sense, but somehow still manages to be a misfit in a school full of nerds."

"Can you see Ryan's car from here?" Noah jammed his hand in his pocket and fingered the worry stone he kept there as he peered out the window. Something wasn't adding up here, but if he planned to settle this case himself he couldn't let on to Conner.

Ignacio craned his neck. "Same row as mine, two down. The pale blue Volvo. Now you have me worried. I'll walk down with you and check my car for damage."

Noah let Ignacio lead the way out. He hadn't left a trail of bread crumbs and wasn't sure he could find the stairs on the first try. The outside air was a relief after the wet, musty smell of the lobby.

Ignacio hurried to his car and circled it several times. "I don't see any damage. Where would it have been?"

"Right front fender." Noah squatted in front of the car and studied the fender with fake enthusiasm. "Looks good. I guess we can write you off. The impact would have left a dent for sure." He ought to feel guilty about lying with such ease, but like it or not, that was part of the job.

"Jeez, I was so worried about my own stuff, I forgot about the guy who got hit." Ignacio twisted his head from Noah to Conner. "Is he okay? Was he hurt bad?"

Noah waited for Ignacio to glance away then ran his hand over the license plate.

Conner put his arm on the boy's shoulder. "He's banged up, but it's not serious. We don't like to let someone get away with something so dangerous. Next time it might be worse. It was nice of you to ask though."

Noah glanced at Conner and winked. Time to ditch this kid so they could study the car closer. Then he needed to ditch Conner so he could study Ryan's car.

"Come on, partner," Noah said. "We better move on to the next name on our list. Good luck in school, son. Don't let a couple of assholes get you down. Sounds like you're gonna do just fine."

Conner flipped his notebook closed and fell into step beside Noah. Halfway to their car, they paused and glanced back. Ignacio was nowhere to be seen. They pivoted and started back to the parking lot, double time. "The sticker was the same size and shape and in the right spot. What could you tell about the license plate?"

"I felt a sticky spot, but I'd like to get a better look at it. For a car that hadn't been driven in two weeks, the dirt in the tires and sprayed up the side was still damp, and there was a puddle of water sitting underneath it." Noah tried to keep the excitement from his voice, but he could feel his heart picking up speed.

Conner made no attempt to hide his excitement. He rubbed his hands together as they approached Ignacio's car. He studied the back license plate from several directions. "I can definitely see where he's used some type of tape to change the three to an eight and the seven to a nine. And look at this. The P has marks indicating it's been changed to a B. I think we've got him. The right car, the name Icky, he needs money. Now that we know who, we'll find a connection to Hudson. You can bank on it."

He tapped the fender with his knuckles and laughed. "Can you believe our luck? Who would have thought someone would wander in and call him Icky? I almost didn't put that in my notebook when you told me the maid's story about the phone conversation."

Noah scratched his head. "Why don't you run back and bring our car around. I'll stay here and keep watch. I want to see if we can get a sample of the tape or pull off some fingerprints."

Conner hesitated a beat longer than necessary, but Noah didn't blink.

"Will do," he finally said. "I've got my kit in the trunk. Although I don't think we can prove anything if his fingerprints are on his own car."

"No, but we can see if he was in my house."

Noah leaned against the next car and waited as Conner rushed back to their motor-pool car. Those fingerprints would undoubtedly match the ones in his house, but he'd eat a live bug if they belonged to Ignacio. That fat little ball of dough never climbed into his attic and crawled around. And he'd have broken a leg and the dryer both if he'd tried to drop down into the laundry room.

As soon as Conner was out of sight, Noah strolled over two spaces to the pale blue Volvo. It wasn't on their list of cars, but the Rice University parking sticker was in the correct spot, and tape residue marked an area around the C and the F on the license plate. A pale blue car might look white on a grainy video, so the fact that it wasn't on their list didn't bother Noah.

He had no intention of telling Conner, not yet anyway, but

he'd recognized that high-pitched voice the minute he heard it. The red hair and glasses only confirmed his suspicions.

And having him turn up in the middle of this investigation was too big a coincidence to ignore.

Conner checked his cell phone on the way to the squad car. An unnecessary act, he knew—Jeannie had been feeling fine when he left her that morning—but one he couldn't resist. He might as well get used to it. Once their daughter was born, his worry quotient would likely double, and last the rest of his days.

He knew all too well how fragile life was. He saw it every day.

No messages. Excellent. He slipped the phone into his pocket and started the car. Something was up. He and Noah had been partners and friends for too long for that fool to think he could put anything over on him. Noah should have been more excited about finding Icky. And the questions he asked were all wrong. Playing good cop was one thing, but who cared about the kid's problems with his tutor?

Several minutes passed while he circled through twisted streets to the college parking lot. He hated to leave Noah alone for this long.

Of course Noah would take the case personally. If this was their guy, then the kid had come into his house and tried to kill him. But that wasn't what this felt like. Noah was definitely hiding something.

How am I going to watch his back when he keeps it turned away from me?

He needed to get back fast, before Noah made a mistake that could cost him his career, or worse.

CHAPTER SIXTEEN

THE EVENING SKY had turned a shade Noah couldn't quite name. Betsy could have. Her face would have come alive as the colors bathed her skin. "Oh, isn't that gorgeous?" she'd have said. "The sky's such a lovely shade of…"

And she'd have been right. The minute he heard the word, he'd have known exactly what she meant. But not him. That was a talent he didn't have. He recognized tonight's dusk was exceptionally lovely, but without a name for the color, it lost something. And without Betsy, well, it lost even more.

Ditching Conner wasn't easy. He'd left his partner with a stack of paperwork while claiming he had to check on Sweet Pea. But he'd called the vet earlier and Pea was doing fine. He planned to have her home again soon. And tonight was the first step in that direction.

Pulling into the garage gave him a chill, and he could swear remnants of exhaust fumes lingered in the air, but that only strengthened his determination. Remembering last July when that Howell kid ogled Betsy in her little white shorts and tank top as she bent over to put her cherry cobbler on the picnic table, turned it to stone.

They'd laughed about it that night and Noah had said, "At least the little nerd has good taste." Then they'd made love to the rhythm of firecrackers and he'd forgotten about the incident. Until he heard that squeaky voice and saw that head full of red hair.

Whenever he looked at the white plastic test stick hidden in his drawer, its small blue plus sign staring at him accusingly, he counted back and came to that night. He'd caught a big case the next day and hadn't come home for three nights, so that had to be the time. But was he the only one watching the joy on Betsy's face while fireworks lit the room? The belt that stretched tight across his chest and kept him from breathing properly tightened one more notch.

It didn't make sense, not yet anyway, but he'd keep plugging away until it did.

Noah stepped out of his truck and stretched, loosening his muscles. He removed his Glock and checked it over before returning it to his holster. No need to chamber a round. Not yet.

He couldn't start with the Howells. That would be too obvious. So he began three houses down, knocking on doors, asking questions, smiling, and taking useless notes.

His heart rate quickened as he reached the Howell's home. Paint was peeling on the front door, and spider webs filled one corner of their porch. The entire house had a shabby, rundown feel. A "Please Knock," sign covered the doorbell.

His hand shook slightly as he reached up, so he let it fall, cleared his throat and tried again. An annoyed, "I'm coming," sounded from inside.

What should he do with his face? His smile felt false and hurt his teeth. He'd knocked on hundreds of doors in his lifetime and never once worried about his face. Now it was the only thing he could think about.

The door flew open and an older, heaver version of Ryan glared out at him. The red hair had faded and was mixed with gray, and the glasses were bifocals, but the nose was the same, or at least it had been before broken blood vessels covered it.

"Hi, Mr. Howell. I'm Noah Daugherty, from down the street. I think we met at the Fourth of July picnic."

Howell shook his head and his jowls waved back and forth. "I'm sorry, but we don't need any cookies or wrapping paper or whatever your kid is selling, and I'm not signing any petitions for a stop sign or speed hump."

"No, sir. I'm here on official business." Noah opened his coat to reveal his badge. "There was a break-in down the street and I promised to canvass the neighborhood to see if anyone noticed a strange car or someone who didn't belong here."

Howell's eyes widened, but he never stopped shaking his head. Those jowls were going to flap right off his face if he didn't slow down. "I haven't seen anything like that."

"How do you know what date I'm asking about?"

"I'm here all the time. I would have seen." At least the man had quit shaking his head. Watching those jowls was like following a ping-pong game and Noah's eyes were beginning to cross.

"May I come in? If your wife's at home, I'd like to talk to both of you." He tried to smile, but his cheeks were frozen.

Howell twisted toward the living room and Noah squeezed

past before he had time to object. "That's very kind of you… Jerry, isn't it?"

Mrs. Howell stepped into the room with two drinks in her hands. Noah could smell the alcohol from six feet away. She took a step back when she saw him, her brown hair falling over tired eyes.

"Hi, Delores. I'm Noah from down the block. Sorry to bother you this late." What was it, six-thirty? "But I needed to question you both about last Thursday. There was a break-in and a couple of people remember hearing a car—older, needed a tune-up— but no one saw it."

Noah held his breath and waited.

Jerry took the amber drink from his wife's hand and downed a large portion, then swirled the ice cubes. "Ryan came home Thursday night. Might've been him. His car sounds like a herd of asthmatic buffalo. He's above little things like changing the oil or getting a tune up." He turned toward Delores and raised his eyebrows.

She plopped into what was obviously her chair and tucked bare feet under her, still clutching her drink like a lifeline. "That's not fair, Jerry. He probably doesn't have the money for a tune-up."

"Could be, but an oil change he could manage himself, if he was willing to get his hands dirty." Jerry's drink was almost gone and he rattled the ice cubes and looked expectantly at his wife.

Oh, he's not above it. You'd be real proud of him if you knew just how hands-on he was.

"He's at Rice now, isn't he? That's not an easy school to get into." Noah settled himself on an ancient sofa whose springs sagged and sighed under his weight. The fabric had pilled to a rough finish in spots, and strings hung from the worn armrests.

Delores' shoulders went back and she raised her chin. "He had his pick of Ivy League Schools. Jerry insisted on Rice because it was somewhat cheaper and there wasn't any travel expense." She reached over to the table beside her and added a splash of Diet Pepsi to her drink.

"Kid could have paid the difference if he'd wanted. He's paying his own way now." Jerry glared at Delores and shook his glass. She ignored him.

"Wow. That's impressive. Paying his own way. Does he have a scholarship?"

Delores beamed. "A partial. And he tutors to earn the rest."

"You say he was home Thursday night. What time did he leave? Maybe he saw something on his way out." Now they were getting somewhere. He'd find out everything he needed if Jerry didn't interrupt her. She was relishing center stage, probably hadn't been talked to like an equal in years.

She took a healthy slug from her glass and savored it for a moment before answering. "He spent the night. He was sound asleep when I left for work."

Sure he was. He wore himself out scouting my house.

Jerry pushed out of his chair and stomped into the kitchen, giving Delores the evil eye.

"I'd love to ask him if he noticed anything. Does he come home often?"

Jerry's voice floated in from the kitchen "He only comes if he wants something. Thursday he came home for his electric blanket because his room is cold."

This is it. Will Jerry bite or is he sharp enough to keep his mouth closed?

"I think I remember him from that picnic on the Fourth. Was he still living here then?"

Jerry returned with a fresh drink for himself, but not one for his wife. "No, he'd moved out by then. I remember the Fourth because I was all dressed for the picnic and he waltzes in expecting me to work on his damn car. He had to drive to Galveston for some school-sponsored thing and wanted me to check his oil and tires. He brought his friend Derrick and they stuffed their faces at the picnic while I worked. They were on the road well before dark."

The dummy probably thinks he's shut me down by giving his kid an alibi, but he's told me more than he thinks. Mamma doesn't know what she's dealing with, but Papa does.

Would the school sponsor something in Galveston? And on the Fourth of July? Maybe some club would. That should be easy to check. Noah let out a breath. The kid might not have been watching that night. But what about another time? He seemed to know the layout of his house.

"By the way, do you know the people that used to own my house? I think their name is Yates. My water heater is acting up and I wanted to see if they had a warranty. I was told it was new."

Delores gave her first real smile. "Sure, Ralph and Beebe. They used to come over all the time. After a while, we drifted apart. Beebe is sort of loud and..." She glanced at Jerry as if searching for a word or maybe permission.

"Vulgar," Jerry muttered and went back to his drink.

"And Ralph, he was just rough and ill-mannered. But Ryan was great friends with their son, Kenny. They played together all the time when they were young. Then Ryan skipped a couple of grades, and Kenny was... Well, Kenny was slow and what didn't seem to matter when they were kids, mattered more as they got older."

Bingo. He was closing in on the little turd. He knew the house, and he'd been in the area the night someone tried to kill him. That was means and opportunity. But what was his motive? Could that geeky little pervert actually have anything to do with Crystal Hudson's death? Hard to believe, but why else try to kill him and Sweet Pea? Did he think that would shut down Crystal's murder investigation? The HPD was capable of investigating two cases at once, even if one of them was a cop.

As Delores lifted her drink, a glint of silver caught his eye. Noah waited until she lowered her drink again. Yes, definitely a silver band set with gemstones. He'd give his eye teeth to see what the stones were.

"That's a lovely bracelet, Delores. Is it an antique?"

"No, it's just costume jewelry. But Ryan gave it to me for my birthday and one of the stones is purple, like an amethyst, so I love it."

Yeah, I know what an amethyst is. Betsy was born in February also. If the other stones are pale green and dark blue, we'll have a peridot and a sapphire for our wedding and my birthday. But she didn't move her hand again, and he couldn't see them.

Time to talk to Kenny Yates and get the real scoop on Ryan Howell. One piece of good news. It seemed unlikely that he'd been spying on Betsy if he'd moved out by the time they moved in. It was possible he wouldn't have to kill the kid after all.

Of course, Ryan *had* tried to kill him and Sweet Pea. And if he got home and Betsy's bracelet was missing, then just killing the thieving, peeping, murdering cocksucker might not be enough.

~

Streetlights punched perfect circles in the darkness, and Noah tried to keep his pace to a brisk walk. A large man running in a suit and dress shoes on a cold night would attract too much attention. He gripped the piece of paper containing the Yates' address and phone number in one hand while checking his watch.

Seven o'clock. He should be able to make it to their new condo by seven-twenty. Not late in the summer when dusk still lit the sky, but borderline late in the winter when the night had been full dark for over an hour.

I could telephone. It's not too late for a phone call. No, this needs to be a face-to-face meeting. I want to see their reactions when they talk about Ryan.

Rush hour traffic was ebbing, and he made the drive easily. The Yates' condo was in the third building, toward the back, facing the swimming pool and hot tub.

The entire complex screamed "singles." Hot young things, or those who thought they were hot, or those who just wished to be near someone who was hot, lingered outside, drinking beer and chatting despite the cool weather. At the far end, someone was grilling steaks and the aroma wafted across the pool and reminded Noah he hadn't eaten since breakfast.

Not far from the Yates front door, two bikini clad hotties lingered in the Jacuzzi while guys fawned and offered to bring them drinks. He dreaded to think of his nieces at that age. Thank goodness they were Rachelle's problem. He wouldn't be able to handle it.

The brunette with the diamond stud in her navel called out

as Noah passed. "Hey, big guy. I haven't seen you around here before. Why don't you ditch that suit and join us?"

Noah couldn't think of anything worse than living with that many hormones floating in the air, although, he had to admit, he'd noticed the diamond stud.

Ralph Yates opened the door after Noah's first knock. "Yeah, what is it?" he growled over the sound of the TV.

A car chase continued to roar in the background as Noah put on his most congenial smile. "Hi, Mr. Yates. I'm Noah Daugherty. We never got a chance to meet, but my wife and I bought your house on Shannon Drive."

Ralph's eyes narrowed. "That sale's all finished. I can't be responsible if anything breaks now. It's been what, six or eight months since we moved out."

"There's no problem with the house. We love it. I just found something that probably belongs to your son and I wanted to see about returning it." Noah waited to be invited in, but Ralph didn't budge.

"Okay, I'll hold it for him till next time he comes by." Ralph stuck out his hand.

"I don't have it with me. I was on my way home from work and thought I'd get his address and mail it."

"Who is it, Ralphie?" Beebe Yates called from inside.

Noah took a step forward and Ralph backed up until he had to let Noah in. "The guy what bought our old house," he called, still backing away.

In the light, Ralph looked every bit of the thirty years he had on the prowling herd outside his door. He sported an elaborate comb-over, but the hair he'd lost on top now sprouted out of his nose and ears. His shirt was undone at least one button too far and gray hair spilled out in every direction. A heavy gold chain nestled in the pelt. He looked, sounded, dressed, and acted like a mob wannabe. If they'd been in New York or New Jersey instead of Houston, it would have been funny. Instead, it was ludicrous, or maybe sad. Noah couldn't decide which.

Beebe had obviously used surgery in an attempt to remain youthful. Her skin was tight enough to bounce a quarter off and her lips puffed out in a permanent pout. Boobs the size of cantaloupes spilled out of a skin tight jumpsuit with enough sequins to read by. Gaudy, oversized jewelry decorated every finger and competed with fingernails so long and red, she'd need help picking her nose. If asked her favorite color, she'd have undoubtedly said, "Glitter."

"Hi, Mrs. Yates. I'm Noah. We spoke on the phone a couple of times."

"Well, of course you are. I'd recognize that voice anywhere," she purred. "Come in and have a seat." She scooted over a half inch and patted the sofa next to her.

"Ralphie, do turn that awful TV down so we can hear." She wiggled those fingernails in the general direction of her husband.

Ralph glared and turned the TV down one decibel.

"I was talking to your old friends the Howells the other day and they said Kenny and Ryan were great friends." Noah's heart hammered as he waited to see if she would take the bait.

A look of distaste passed between the Yates and Ralph turned the TV down to a reasonable level as he nodded to his wife.

Beebe leaned forward as if to pass on a great secret and those melons threatened to tumble out completely. "We tried to be nice to Ryan for his parents' sake, but he was completely socially inept. Kenny hated playing with him. We used to have dinner with Jerry and Delores every week or two. We'd alternate houses, and leave the kids at the house we weren't using. Kenny had so many friends, we thought he'd be a good influence on Ryan, and Ryan was some sort of prodigy while our Kenny was a little slow so we hoped Ryan would help him."

Ralph snorted. "Say it, kid's dumb as a rock. How he got into college I'll never understand, but it's a good thing he got a scholarship, cuz I'd never have wasted the money on him. But at least he's normal. Ryan, well, he's a little creep. Used to watch Beebe and spy on her when he thought no one was looking. Always trying to look up her dress or down it."

"Oh, Ralphie. He was just a kid. All boys that age try to sneak a peek when they can, isn't that right, Noah?" She leaned back and put her hand on Noah's thigh. Those melons quivered from the aftershock.

Noah's skin crawled from her touch, and he tried to think of a reason to stand. "How can I get in touch with Kenny? I found several comic books that I think are his. Some of those old ones are valuable now."

"Comic books. I should have known." Ralph snorted. "If it wasn't for the pictures, he probably couldn't have read them." He snapped his fingers at his wife and pointed to the back room.

"I'll get you his address. He doesn't come around here much." Beebe let her fingertips trail to the inside of Noah's thigh as she stood.

The hairs on the back of his neck bristled as she pranced into the bedroom, her buttocks fighting to escape the tight fabric. Was this woman for real? How would she like it if he made a move like that on her? Scratch that. She'd probably love it.

Betsy never had to dress provocatively or act like a slut. One look at her and he just knew. Laurel was the same way. It wasn't a matter of money or fine schools, it was class. Betsy had it, so did Laurel. This woman probably couldn't even spell it.

He'd learned all he could from the Yates and wanted out before Beebe sat down again. But he had to keep things friendly in case he needed to ask more questions later. He glanced around the condo. "How do you like it here? It must be nice not to have to worry about yard work or upkeep. And that hot tub looked inviting." *If you didn't worry about catching some unpleasant disease from the water.*

"Huh," Ralph glanced in the direction his wife had disappeared and lowered his voice. "It's not as much fun as we'd expected. Those young people aren't so friendly to guys our age." He nudged Noah's arm.

Our age? You've got twenty years on me. Not to mention thirty pounds. Ten of it in unwanted hair.

"Those gals just want the young studs with the six-pack abs. They don't think to the future, when a little extra money might be important. And the guys all but laugh at Beebe when she goes out to sunbathe. We'll probably move on when our lease is up."

If they laughed at Beebe, Noah didn't want to think what they did when Ralph put on a bathing suit.

He couldn't wait to get out of there and wash his hands. No, take a shower. If only he could wash out his eyes. He didn't blame Kenny for staying away. He didn't plan to come back either, at least not without a chaperone.

CHAPTER SEVENTEEN

INTERMITTENT VOICES ECHOED down the hallway. Ryan ignored them. He entered his room, his sanctuary. Every surface clean and orderly. No clothing littered the floor. No sweaty shoes waited to be tripped over. The scent of old textbooks and printer ink made him smile. Even his window appeared a perfect square of black, never tempting his eyes away from his work.

After seeing that cop, alive and well, in Icky's room, he needed the serenity of this space. He hadn't been able to concentrate on a word his professor said all afternoon. His heart rate had only now come back to normal.

What was the guy made of that poisonous gas didn't faze him, and what would it take to kill him, a stake through the heart? A silver bullet?

He settled at his desk and opened his computer to Wednesday's physics paper. Within minutes, he sank deep into the lesson. When an insistent ringtone filled the air, he grabbed for his cell phone and answered immediately, never taking his eyes off the computer screen.

"Yeah?"

"What have you been up to this time, you little piece of shit?" his father hissed, hardly above a whisper.

Ryan jerked back, his spine digging into the wooden slats of the school issued desk chair. "I don't know what you're talking about. I haven't left campus since I saw you last week."

"That's what I'm worried about. What fool thing did you do while you were here that sent the police to my door?"

"Police?" His heart stopped and he couldn't catch his breath. "What'd they want? Were they looking for me?"

"There was no 'they.' Just the one guy. The same one from down the street that you oh-so-casually asked your mother about on Thursday."

Even worse. Could the cop have recognized him? Why not? He'd recognized the cop. That still didn't explain how he'd followed the trail to Icky.

All thoughts of his physics paper disappeared. "Did he ask for me specifically?"

"Only in the most round-about way. His face didn't give away a thing. Not like yours, jumping all over the place. He said there'd been a break-in somewhere in the neighborhood, had we seen anything? What about you? Had you come around lately? Maybe you saw something."

Ryan sighed. If Pops had kept his mouth shut, it might be all right after all. "You didn't tell him I'd been home, did you?"

"Hey, I warned you last time I'd finished covering for you. Even if I'd been willing to lie, which I wasn't, your mother would have corrected me. She actually believes you're the innocent choirboy you pretend to be. And that's not all. You ever drug me again, you better sleep with one eye open for the rest of your life."

This time Ryan's heart jumped all the way to his throat. Cold sweat pooled under his arms and trickled down his back. Things were starting to get serious. That cop was interfering with his GPA.

The time for finesse had passed. He glanced at the last sentence he'd written and hit the delete key. That's what was in store for mister meddling cop.

Silence greeted Noah when he opened his back door. No yapping or barking, no toenails scrabbling on the floor. The house even smelled different. Instead of Pea pooh, he recognized the sour smell of spoiled milk. His eyes quickly found the forgotten carton, still sitting on the kitchen table.

Shit, no cereal for breakfast. And no toast. He'd never made it to the store over the weekend.

One way or another, Pea would be home soon. He had thought the house was quiet before. Now it felt like a tomb. Even his breathing echoed around the empty room. If he couldn't even protect a dog, he deserved to die.

The refrigerator started to hum, but instead of filling the house, it accentuated the emptiness.

"Enough of this feeling sorry for myself," he muttered. He stormed out of the room, yanking off his tie.

He stripped off his suit and hung it on the back of the closet door. Maybe he *should* give some thought to clearing out a few of Betsy's things. His clothes looked like they'd been slept in after being crammed into the small space that was available. He could store some of her blouses in one of those containers made to slide under the bed.

No, I'll buy the container all right, but it's my own shirts that'll go in it.

Five minutes later, he had on sweats and tennis shoes. He flipped on the light in his office and a reflection from the closet's folding doors caught his eye. One door hung slightly ajar. Inside, nothing seemed disturbed and he lifted his father's violin off the top shelf.

The wood still gleamed and felt smooth under his fingers. He ran the bow experimentally over the strings, then adjusted the tuning and tried again. Even when he got the instrument properly tuned, he couldn't replicate the flowing sounds his father had produced with so little effort.

The one thing he'd hoped would keep his father's memory alive, only reminded him how long the man had been gone. He'd love to kick his teenage-self's ass for slacking off on his lessons. Had his voice gotten as rusty as his bow?

He eased himself into his favorite spot—the Henry Miller chair Betsy had bought him as a housewarming gift—and called Conner.

"How's the murder book coming? Is the Lieutenant going to be satisfied?" Noah leaned back and propped his feet on the desk. One of the perks of being the senior partner, probably the only perk, was that Conner had to keep up with the paperwork.

"Satisfied is up to his wife and the mood she's in tonight. But from the phone call he got before he headed home in a hurry, I'd guess not so much. Now pleased with our work is another story. Every T is crossed and every I is dotted. That book is a work of art. I dare some defense lawyer to question it."

"Anybody else there tonight?"

"Earl the Pearl and Alonzo the Giant, doing the same thing I was while their partners were home sitting on their lazy butts."

"You better watch it. If Alonzo or his partner hears you call him that, I won't be able to protect you." Some nicknames were accepted, but others were best left outside the office. He didn't even want to know what he and Conner were called behind their backs.

"True, he's the only person in the department bigger than you are."

"I was thinking of his partner. He could bench-press you without breaking a sweat. Did you ask Alonzo if icky meant something in Spanish?"

"He couldn't think of anything, unless she comes from Argentina or Chili. The dialect changes the farther south you go. Otherwise, nothing."

"Of course not. It wouldn't be that easy." That left Ignacio and his friend Ryan. No more questions about another meaning.

Conner chuckled. "How's the dog? Did the vet let her come home?"

"I sat with her for a few minutes, but her blood count is still too low. Maybe tomorrow. Speaking of which, that's why I called you. I want you to start running down everything you can on our friend, Ignacio."

Noah paused and took a steadying breath. Lying to his partner stuck in his throat, but he couldn't put Conner's life or career at risk. "I'm going to follow up with Rosaria. Make sure she told me everything she knows. Maybe she forgot something, anything that will help. I'll ask if she's sure Hudson used the word icky. I'll be in about noon, maybe earlier. Depending on what you find, we'll decide on our next step."

"Whatever you say, Boss." Conner's words may have said yes, but his voice said he didn't approve.

Continuing to work behind his partner's back was about to get harder.

One more chore before that torture chamber called a bed. Going to sleep was bad enough—strenuous exercise usually knocked him out, although many nights he sat on the edge of the bed and watched the red glow of the digital clock as it counted down the minutes and hours until daylight.

Waking up was the real kick-in-the-gut. His eyes would fly open minutes before the alarm was set to go off and, out of habit, he'd roll over to see if Betsy was awake. Occasionally the covers were mussed, or her pillow had been moved, and his breath would catch before he realized the bed was empty.

Disgusted with his thoughts, he began working on the elliptical machine. He challenged himself at a punishing rate and stayed with it until he was drenched with sweat and his legs trembled. Then he worked with the free weights until his arms were as tired as his legs.

That should do it. If I can't sleep now, nothing short of a general anesthetic will knock me out. The little turd wouldn't dare come back tonight, and if he does, he'll have saved me the trouble.

Conner glared at the phone. He'd barely resisted the urge to slam the receiver down, knowing if he did that, Jeannie would be all over him, asking questions he didn't want to answer. Damn, Noah was starting to aggravate him. This one man crusade had to stop now.

If that Ignacio kid turned up dead and his fingerprints were found in Noah's house, they'd both be up shit creek. They might joke about their Lieutenant, but he hadn't gotten where he was without knowing when smoke was being blown up his ass.

"There's only one person who'd call this late. Make that two people, but my mother's on a cruise. What did Noah want?" Jeannie stood in the doorway. Her skin glowed, but the slight slump to her shoulders showed how tired she was. One hand supported the ever growing swell of her belly.

He crossed the room in two steps and wrapped his arms around her. When he leaned down to kiss the top of her head, he breathed in the fragrance of her shampoo, with only the slightest hint of paste and Crayolas. "Just laying out the plan for tomorrow."

That much was true, anyway. "How were the little darlings today? Any of them give you trouble? They do know your husband's a cop, don't they? If that doesn't keep them in line, I'll come up to the school tomorrow and show them my handcuffs."

"They weren't angels, but they weren't devils either, and that's the best I can hope for."

"I've got a couple of hour's work I'd like to do here. Why don't I run you a warm bath and then you can watch that hospital show you like. I should be finished by then and I'll give you a backrub or a foot massage before we go to bed."

He hadn't lied, he just hadn't been forthcoming about why he needed to work tonight, and the words tasted foul on his tongue.

She smiled and his heart reminded him there were more important things than Noah and his problems.

"Umm, that's a tough choice. Do I have to decide now?"

"Both, it is. I'll get the water started and you find your robe and those flannel pajamas. In the morning, I want you to take my car. I'll get the oil changed in yours on my way home."

He could do the research on Ignacio from his home computer, and if his test kit showed the same fingerprints were on Ignacio's license plate and in Noah's house, then he planned to be parked outside Noah's in the morning and see where that slippery son-of-a-bitch went.

He wanted this case over and done with. When he was home with Jeannie, that's where his mind should be. Not worrying about what kind of trouble his partner was getting them into.

CHAPTER
EIGHTEEN

NOAH COULDN'T WAIT to get started the next morning. The sooner he had this case solved, the sooner he could get back to his real life, such as it was. Traffic was moderate heading north on I-45. All the tie-ups were heading the other way, into downtown. Poor suckers. The worst of the traffic should be clear by the time he started back to the office.

Sam Houston State University was the poor second cousin to Rice. Located far enough north of Houston to edge into the piney woods, it had plenty of trees in the background, but not enough on campus. The atmosphere screamed, "College," while Rice discreetly murmured, "Higher Learning." But it offered two things Rice didn't: affordable tuition and a degree in Criminal Justice. That made it the winner in Noah's mind.

The sun flashed in his eyes as he cruised the parking lot, looking for a space. He flipped the visor down, then back up when it blocked his view. A space big enough for his truck instead of one made for some little compact opened and he pulled in and switched off the engine.

He took a last swallow of cold, travel-mug coffee as he stepped out of the truck. His stomach growled and he vowed to find something to eat before the hour and a half drive back to town. No supper and now no breakfast. His mind didn't care, but his body objected.

If the kid had an eight o'clock class, Noah had missed him. But what kid didn't know how to avoid an eight o'clock by his sophomore year?

"If you'd drive something a little smaller, it wouldn't take you so long to park."

Noah's head snapped around to find Conner leaning against a brick wall. "What the fuck? Don't you have a job you're supposed to be doing in the office?"

Conner tapped a folder against his thigh. "I know everything there is to know about our boy. Even things he hasn't told his parents. And this *is* my job. Unless Rosaria is working on an undergraduate degree, you're the one who has some 'splaining to do."

"Okay, you caught me." He should have known better than to think Conner would let it slide. "Let's talk while we walk. What did you find out about Ignacio?"

He started down the sidewalk without giving Conner another glance.

Conner fell into step beside him. "Top of his class, but with only forty-seven graduating, that might not be too hard. Of course, he worked in his father's auto repair shop all through school, plus equipment manager for the football and baseball teams, and on the debate team. Voted most likely to succeed, but not to any class office or popular position. Even in a class of forty-seven, he was the class nerd. He has an IQ of 130. Not quite Mensa level, but pretty damn close."

"It's the things he hasn't told his father that I'm more interested in."

"There's a rumor, unproven, that some of the popular guys invited him to a party, got him drunk and left him naked on a turtle-trap in the middle of a lake. No one can figure out how he got home without causing a scandal. But by the time one of the boys got back to the party, his truck was missing. It turned up a block from Ignacio's house and the boy's gym shorts and shirt were gone.

Noah chuckled. He could almost like the kid. *If it didn't turn out he was a murderer.* "That's where the 130 IQ comes in. He did work in an auto shop, so he'd know how to hot-wire a truck."

"Which doesn't help him in this case."

"Why? His own car was used when Crystal Hudson was killed. If anything, it makes him less likely to be the one." Noah consulted a slip of paper and turned toward one of the dorms.

Students swarmed past them, giving the two men a quick glance and hurrying on. Some of the girls had on shorts and belly-baring T-shirts. The weather had warmed up, but not that much.

"Your turn, oh sly one. What are we doing, taking a tour of all the colleges in the area? Is St. Thomas next? What about University of Houston? Texas Southern? At least they're closer."

Noah ignored him and increased his speed. "What did you find out about the money? How broke is he?"

"Not overly as long as he keeps his grades up. His scholarship covers tuition, room, books, food. Everything except spending money. His family's not rich by a long shot, and they have three other kids, but his father's business is sound and in the black. Even then, his church sends him a couple of hundred dollars a semester. Did I mention he was an altar boy?"

They had reached the steps of a modern brick dorm. Noah spoke over his shoulder as he took the stairs, two at a time. "No, and you didn't mention what you discovered about his fingerprints."

Noah stopped abruptly at the top of the stairs and Conner almost plowed into him.

Standing one step below him made Conner at least a head shorter, but that didn't seem to intimidate him. He held Noah's gaze without flinching. "The prints on the license plate matched the ones I took from inside your house. He was definitely the one who broke in. Sorry."

"The person who handled Ignacio's license plate was the one who broke into my house. Not necessarily Icky. Do we have a copy of his prints?" Noah gave in and blinked first. Conner might have looked relieved, but he wasn't sure.

"No, he's clean. Never had his prints taken that I know of." Conner sidestepped Noah and climbed the last step.

Noah took a deep breath. Conner was about to give him trouble. "Okay, here's what I need you to do. And no fooling around this time. Head back to the office and get to work on Hudson's files. We have to find the connection. He and the shooter hooked up some way, somehow. Rosaria said it was through Craig's List. When I get back, we'll head over to the Taj Mahal and show Hudson what we've got. Then we'll explain to him the wisdom of rolling over on his accomplice."

Conner didn't disappoint him. He was shaking his head before Noah got the words out. "No way, partner. I'm glued to your side, night and day if necessary. You're too slippery to trust on your own. So who are we visiting here, and how does," he glanced around. "He? She? Figure into this case?"

Noah stabbed his finger into Conner's chest, something he'd never done before and, from the look in Conner's eye, shouldn't try again. "This case has gone on long enough. We need to close it before someone else gets hurt. Now head back to the office and find me that information or go home and take a nap—I know you had to wake up early to be waiting outside my house—because you are not following me another step."

Conner lowered his voice. "You're gonna get yourself killed before this is over."

"Maybe, but I'm sure as hell not going to get you killed. I don't mind driving Jeannie to the hospital if you're too drunk, but if you get yourself shot, I'll kill you myself. Now get back to work and I'll see you in a couple of hours. Then we'll put *somebody* in jail."

Noah spun on his heels and pushed through the heavy glass doors without a backward glance. Inside, he breathed in the industrial air of a hermetically sealed building and counted to ten. When he didn't hear Conner's footsteps, he waited another few seconds before looking over his shoulder. No sign of Conner.

He moved to the side where he had a good view out the door without being visible himself. Conner's back was all he could see. He must have been furious. Kids were swerving around him like avoiding a mad dog.

When he got into what must have been Jeannie's new car, Noah laughed. "Call *me* sly, will you? You've obviously paid attention to everything I taught you."

Noah pushed out the heavy door and started down the steps.

When he reached the bottom, he turned left, toward one of the older dorms.

Of course, I didn't teach you everything I know.

"Go away," the muffled voice on the other side of the door called.

Noah knocked again, harder.

"Beat it," the voice answered.

"Kenny Yates." Noah used his most authoritative tone. "Open the door."

"Open it yourself, you want in so badly."

Noah turned the knob and the door swung open to total darkness. He felt along the side of the wall until he found a switch. Light flooded the room and the mound under the pillow moaned.

"I was up till three finishing my paper. I sent it in electronically. I even got a reply email that it was received. I. Don't. Have. To. Be. In. Class. Leave me alone."

Noah pulled a desk chair beside the bed and straddled it. "Not until you take that pillow off your head and talk to me." He lifted a corner of the pillow and held his badge in front of Kenny's face.

Bloodshot eyes, matted hair, and several days worth of unshaven beard stared up at him. The poor kid took after his father. "What the…Who the hell are you, and what do you want with me?"

"Detective Noah Daugherty. And I want you to get up, go to the bathroom, take a piss, wash your face, and, please God, brush your teeth. Then come out here, sit in a chair and talk to me like a gentleman. Combing your hair wouldn't be out of line, either," he called to Kenny's retreating back.

Two minutes later, Kenny grabbed a bottled water from the mini fridge and sat opposite Noah. "Yes, sir. What can I do for you, sir?"

Noah relaxed. The kid wasn't in on it. He was too sarcastic to have a guilty conscience. "You can turn that brain of yours back a few years and tell me everything you know about Ryan Howell."

He hadn't expected laughter. Kenny got a case of the giggles so bad tears were running down his face. The bottled water splashed onto Kenny's jeans as he tried to wipe his eyes.

"Thank you, Jesus," Kenny cried as he lifted his arms to the ceiling.

Kenny looked at Noah, a grin splitting his face. "I knew this day would come if I waited long enough."

"You want to tell me what's so funny?" Noah felt a smile forming, but forced it back.

"That sick fuck. That perfect darling, child protégé could keep his true nature hidden for only so long. I just wasn't sure I'd be around to see him fall. What's he done?" Kenny rubbed his hands together. "Tell. Tell."

Noah couldn't help but chuckle. "That's not the way these things work. You tell me. I understand that you and Ryan were friends when you were young."

"Oh, no, Mr. Detective. We were never friends. His parents thought I could teach him to be sociable, and my parents thought he could teach me to work harder at school. They were both wrong. He is, in my humble opinion, a psychopath. The only thing I ever taught him was how to be a better one."

Kenny had quit laughing. His voice took on a hard edge. "And I'm severely dyslexic. No one—not Ryan, my parents, or any teacher—ever made any attempt to help me. They just called me stupid or lazy."

Bitterness shown in Kenny's eyes, but he kept talking. "Junior year, my drama teacher realized my problem when I couldn't tell stage right from stage left. He stayed after school to work with me. If not for him, I'd be flipping burgers. If I didn't get fired for messing up the orders. I'll always have problems, but I've learned to cope."

The room fell silent as Kenny took a long gulp of water and wiped his mouth with the back of his hand. His eyes seemed to stare off into the distance and Noah tried to bring him back to the present.

"This is just background information, so I'll know how to deal with him. Still, I need specifics if you're going to be any help. What *exactly* did the sick fuck do to you?"

"He tormented me every way he knew how. Homework took me forever. Any kind of paper was agony. Even math problems. I wouldn't finish 'till after midnight. I'd set my papers on the desk and they'd be gone in the morning. I'd look everywhere—in drawers, under the bed—they'd just be gone. I still don't know how he did it, but I know he took them because he made jokes about it. My parents or teachers never believed me. I can't tell you how many beatings I took for not doing my homework. Finally I quit doing it altogether."

Kenny got up and paced around the tiny room. Noah's heart went out to him. Betsy had taught dyslexic kids. She'd told him how important it was to start working with them early. *How did this kid manage with no help from his parents?* But having met the parents, he believed it.

"You know his parents and my parents had a wife-swap thing going for a while? I think my father blew it by treating Mrs. Howell too rough. I never told Ryan. Even with everything he did, I couldn't hurt him that way and he was too naive to understand what all the little winks and nudges meant. That didn't keep him from making comments about my mother. He ogled her and drooled over her. It was sick. He had to have watched through the window or something. My folks didn't believe in closing the blinds. They'd have gotten a kick out of it if they knew."

Not through the window, kid. He had his own private viewing platform.

Noah shook his head. It was about what he'd imagined had gone down, but hearing it from Kenny turned his stomach. Maybe it was a good thing he'd never be a parent. Nothing messed up a good kid like bad parents. Yet Kenny's were ten times worse than Ryan's and he turned out okay. It wouldn't have mattered if he'd been lousy at the job. Betsy would have nailed it.

If she'd had a chance.

"You know about his finger, don't you?"

Kenny's voice brought him back to the cramped room. "I couldn't see his hand. He was holding a stack of books."

"Most of his first finger and part of his second are missing on his right hand. I'd say that's what screwed him up, but he was well down that road when it happened. The thing is, he won't admit it's gone. Pretends there's nothing wrong, because it doesn't fit with his belief that he's perfect in every way."

What the fuck? Noah had known experts who adapted to shooting with the top portion of their trigger finger missing, but not with most of it gone. And with part of his second missing, he wasn't using that one instead.

If the kid was right-handed—and he was from the way he picked up his books—the case was shot to hell. And if he was left-handed, he'd need to fire across his body. A more difficult shot and one that was likely to result in a burned right arm. Either way, he'd fucked up. Ryan wasn't the guy.

CHAPTER
NINETEEN

A DOUBLE MEAT WHOPPER and fries, eaten while driving, was a poor substitute for three meals, but the large, chocolate milkshake refreshed Noah and he was ready to get back to work. He'd wasted too much time on a dead end, and worse, he'd wasted his partner's good opinion.

First things first. Figure out who killed Crystal Hudson, then make amends with Conner.

Or should it be the other way around? He had to work with Conner on more than just this one case. He didn't have so many friends in his life that he could afford to piss one off. But if Conner was a real friend, he should cut him some slack.

Noah circled two floors of the parking garage before he found an empty spot. He eyed the trashcan beside the elevator and leaned over to gather up his empty food wrappers. No sense letting them smell up his truck or he'd have to drive home with the windows open to air out the onion stink.

He shook his head as he approached the elevator. Conner

had already cut him plenty of slack. All the times he'd been short-tempered, snapped, hadn't returned phone calls. Conner didn't owe him any more slack. He owed Conner. And it was time he quit racking up debts he couldn't pay with cash.

But he owed Crystal Hudson his attention also. How could he have screwed up so completely? If he alienated his best friend *and* couldn't solve a simple case, what would Laurel think of him? His hand froze above the trash can. He meant Betsy. What would Betsy think of him?

Laurel was Crystal's friend and wanted the case solved, that's all. He didn't believe in Freudian Slips.

Conner hit send with a flourish. Finally, the last report was finished. He could get some real work done.

The scorched smell of vending-machine coffee caught his attention. On the corner of his desk sat a steaming Styrofoam cup and a Baby Ruth candy bar.

"They were out of M&Ms," Noah's voice came from above him.

Conner glanced to his half-open drawer where the last two bags of M&Ms the break room had to offer sat within easy reach. "Too bad you didn't get here earlier."

"You're not going to make this easy for me, are you?"

"Nope. Don't plan to."

"I'm an ass."

Conner felt a smile struggling to break through, but he pushed it back. If he laughed now, Noah would pull the same shit again. "That's a well-known fact. Even uniformed officers working traffic try to avoid you whenever possible. I've watched

Records Clerks duck into the bathroom when they see you coming down the hall. The question is, what are you going to do about it?"

Noah opened his mouth and closed it again. "One time. One time I raised my voice *slightly* to a Records Clerk, and they all act like I'll eat them for breakfast."

"Are you sure it was just once? And what about the traffic cop who tried to give you a ticket? Did he deserve to be reported? You *were* speeding."

"I was headed to a scene."

"No, you weren't. You needed to go home and feed that dog of yours before you went to the scene. You were embarrassed to be caught in your own neighborhood."

Noah's face flushed. "It was still work. I would have been at the scene for half the night."

Conner's voice dropped to a near whisper. "What about lying to your partner and blowing him off? What's your excuse for that?"

"I told you. I'm an ass." Noah's voice matched Conner's. "But, before you ask, I plan to be less of an ass tomorrow, and even less of one the day after that."

Conner reached past the M&Ms and pulled out a sheet of paper. He held it up so that Noah could see the Request For Transfer heading. "That's good, because I'd hate to think this was the last case we'd ever work together."

The professor droned on and on, but it was all white noise to Ryan, the words never imprinting on his brain. His mind jumped from one scenario to another as he shifted uncomfortably in the hard chair.

The cop had to go first; he was the one leading the investigation. No, the client. Without him, the proof would disappear. But what about the witness he'd read about in the warrant? Only the client would have a clue who that might be. Besides, with Derrick out of money, the client couldn't be touched.

Maybe Derrick should go first. Or would that bring down more attention? This wasn't getting him anywhere. He drummed his fingers on the table.

"Mr. Howell, are you with us today? I'm waiting for an answer." The professor glared at him from under Andy Rooney eyebrows.

His mouth went dry, and his tongue had trouble forming the words. "Sorry, sir. I don't know the answer." Shit! Never in his life, not one time, had he ever been unprepared.

Heat crept up the back of his neck as students twisted to gape at him. A soft buzz filled the room. That was it, the cop was done for. They were all done for. But the one he would enjoy most was that sorry excuse for a dog.

He could creep in any day while the cop was at work. He'd put his hands around that little throat and squeeze, maybe letting up for a few seconds before squeezing again. His fingers tingled in anticipation.

No one, no...*thing*, made him look like a fool and lived.

This all started because he couldn't shoot a gun. A stupid, insignificant talent. He couldn't tap dance or juggle either, but did that make him less valuable? What about singing or playing some silly instrument? That was no different than being born with brown eyes or blue. He remembered the piano and violin in the cop's house, could almost feel the wood under his fingers, and the excitement of touching his private belongings.

Think of all the time wasted learning to master those instruments. Time that could have been spent expanding the mind.

Shooting was different. It was a useful skill and he intended to learn it. And that wouldn't happen until he faced the fact that his right hand would never be strong enough to pull a trigger.

He glanced down at his paper. He switched his pen from his right hand to his left and resumed taking notes.

No need for Derrick now.

Laurel searched frantically through her jewelry box. Where were her good jade earrings? She upended the box on her bed and pawed through the tangled pile of earrings and bracelets.

She hadn't worn them in months. Hadn't worn any jewelry in months. They could be anywhere. She glanced around at the mess that was her bedroom. Clothes littered the floor and every flat surface was two inches deep in debris. The room even smelled musty. Rosaria had changed her sheets and put a load of underwear in the wash, but she could only do so much.

Okay, she'd clean up the minute she got back from her interview. Meanwhile, what about the small gold and diamond earrings? They weren't too ostentatious for daytime.

Missing. So were the pearls, and the opal set. What about the dangly onyx and diamond ones in white gold? Her heart beat faster. That broach set with gemstones? Nope.

She emptied the box on her bed and pawed through the contents.

Her grandmother's silver and turquoise pendant was there,

so was the bracelet her father had given her as a wedding gift.

She sat back, each breath a struggle. Every piece of jewelry she had left came into the marriage with her, or cost less than a hundred dollars. Her eyes shot to the secret compartment in the bottom of the box. She put a hand out, but it shook so that she dropped it back into her lap.

Do it. You already know the answer.

Holding her breath, she slid the small compartment open. Empty. No safe deposit box key. The major pieces would be long gone by now.

"You son-of-a-*bitch*," she yelled and threw the box across the room. A lot of good that did. Now she had spare earring backs spread throughout her dirty clothes. Heat rose up the back of her neck, but no tears came.

Only an hour until her appointment. *There has to be a matching pair in here somewhere. Something silver will work just fine.*

Peter could keep his trinkets. They weren't the expressions of love he'd always claimed. They were chains that weighted her down and kept her from seeing his real character. Bribes, payments to keep her quiet and docile.

Knowing him like she did now, they would feel like lye against her skin. She'd rather go without than wear his brand.

CHAPTER TWENTY

NOAH HELD HIS breath as Conner leaned back in his chair and rested one foot on the open drawer. If Conner didn't accept his apology, he might lose the best friend he'd ever had. The only person left in his life willing to put up with his crazy, see-sawing moods. Well, Rachelle, but she was his sister and had to love him, right?

"So prove you're now willing to act like a real partner," Conner said. "Tell me exactly what you've been up to and why you believed whatever it is you believed."

Noah glanced around the noisy squad room. Was anyone listening? Earl Sparks was taking a statement from a less-than-cooperative witness and Alonzo, his partner, was standing in the Lieutenant's door discussing either a case or golf. It was hard to tell which, but the Lieutenant laughed, so it was probably golf. Everyone else was on the phone or out on a call.

The printer coughed and wheezed as it came to life. That did it. They might as well be sitting in a cone of silence.

He scooted his chair closer to Conner and sighed. This was going to be hard. Could he get by with the condensed version? No, he needed to tell Conner everything. If he found out later that Noah had held back, it would be bad. He flashed back to lying in the attic, waiting to ambush whoever stuck their head up and realized he might have to leave a few things out.

"Whoever came into my house on Saturday night had to have been there before and knew their way around. That could have happened on Friday, when he poisoned Sweet Pea, but climbing around in the attic felt too familiar. At first, I thought it was the kid who used to live there."

"And that was the reason for the trip out to Sam Houston?" Conner didn't move, but his eyes bored holes through Noah.

"Just wait, I'll get to that. When we were interviewing Icky, I recognized that red-headed kid the minute I saw him, even his voice was familiar. And from the way he reacted, he recognized me, too. While you were bringing the car around, I checked his plates also. They had the same sticky substance around a couple of numbers that Icky's did, indicating he'd tried to disguise them."

Conner's voice got tight. "Yet you didn't see fit to mention this to me."

Noah squirmed. His chair was beginning to feel like an Inquisition rack. "I thought he might be a kid that lived down the street from me. I'd only seen him once, briefly, and I wasn't sure." *Okay, lie number one.* He'd been sure. Sweat formed behind his ears and on the back of his neck.

"I made up a bullshit reason to talk to his parents, and, yes, that was Ryan. He'd been friends with Kenny, the kid that lived in my house, and had spent a lot of time there. It was just too big a coincidence. Whoever broke into my house had been there before, I could feel it. Ryan had and Icky hadn't. Besides, that attic is too tight for a dough-ball like Icky. I had to back out. There wasn't room to turn around."

Shit, he hadn't meant to say that. Now Conner would wonder exactly what he'd been doing up there. He hurried on with the story before Conner had time to question him.

"But Ryan was off at college by the time we moved in so he didn't know me or where I lived." *Lie number two. He'd obviously noticed Betsy, and could have asked about me or which house we lived in. But he'd definitely left for Galveston before the picnic was over.*

"Then I talked to Kenny's folks, got my first hint what a creep Ryan was, and got an address for Kenny. *That* was the reason for the trip out to Sam Houston." Finally, a whole sentence that was truthful.

"Uh huh, so what changed your mind? You would never have come in here and apologized if you hadn't found out you were wrong." Conner hadn't touched his peace-offering coffee, but Noah couldn't blame him. The smell alone would put off the most dedicated caffeine addict.

"I never wrote off Icky completely. That's why I had you checking him out. Ryan's an even bigger pervert than I thought. He spent his time spying on Kenny and his family from the attic. But just because he's a creep, doesn't mean he's a murderer. He couldn't be the shooter. He's missing most of his trigger finger and part of his index finger."

Conner tapped his pen on the desk, for the first time showing more interest than anger. "How'd the kid lose his finger?"

"You're gonna love this. The Howell's had a bird feeder, and rats got into the birdseed. Ryan tried to invent a better rat trap and set up a tiny guillotine. He chopped off his own two fingers trying it out." Noah felt a smirk build. "After that, small animals started to disappear around the neighborhood. A cat was found mutilated in a wooded area where the drug store is now."

Noah sat back, relieved. He'd told the story and was done. One glance at Conner said he wasn't finished.

Conner leaned forward, his eyes still hard. "So far, so good. Now tell me the things you left out."

If telling the story the first time was hard. Going back and filling in the details he'd omitted was agony. He skimmed over the part about waiting in the attic, but from the look in Conner's eyes, he'd already guessed that. When he described the trip to visit Kenny's parents, Conner actually laughed.

"Two things." Conner swiveled his chair in front of his desk and started making a list. "Having more than one person involved in a murder is rare, but not unheard of. Let's check out that weird kid who was behind Ryan in the dorm. If not him, we'll investigate Kenny further."

"I hate to say this, but the only suspicious thing about Kenny is that he seems to have turned out normal despite having such screwed up parents. The idea of a partner goes a long way toward explaining that bull's-eye shot out of a moving car during a sleet storm. I suspect Ryan doesn't have many friends, so that Derrick kid is a good place to start. What's your second item?"

"You said from the beginning that the perp tried to do the job in Bellaire and if we found out why, we'd be closer to finding out who. We let that slip when he tried to take you out. That might have been his reason for coming after you."

Fuck, he hated it when Conner showed him up. "Let's take an hour. You check out that Derrick kid and maybe even Kenny. I'll see what Ryan was up to in Galveston and look for any similar murders in this part of the state. Then we'll confront Hudson. He hired *someone* to kill his wife. I think we can turn him."

With all his money and power, he's still the weak link. He has the most to lose.

More than an hour had passed when Noah looked up to see Conner place a Starbucks coffee and a chicken salad sandwich on his desk.

"We're going to need all our wits to face Hudson, and vending-room food won't cut it."

Noah pulled the cup to him, inhaling the potent brew. "Thanks, partner. I didn't know how much I needed this. Did you find out anything good?"

Conner slipped the top off his own cup and took a long swallow. "I didn't bother checking Kenny. I found all I could possibly want with Derrick."

A jolt of fresh caffeine hit Noah and he sighed, his exhaustion slipping away. "So what's he been up to?"

"Derrick was a competitive shooter in high school. Not a champion, or I'd have found it sooner, but a decent shot just the same. If he hadn't listed it on his admission essay, I might have missed it. When I checked his meets, one guy kept beating him. Zack Taylor. Then guess what I found?"

Noah just grunted and started eating. He felt stronger with every bite of the sandwich.

"Zack recently purchased seven replacement barrels for

a 9 mm Glock from a gun store in Amarillo. There's only one problem. Zack's doing his junior year in Italy. And Derrick, who comes from a ranch just outside of Amarillo, got behind on his tuition payments when his parents had to sell off their herd after last summer's drought. He belongs to some weird, off-beat religious cult that preaches retribution. They believe the drought is God's punishment for all the evil in the world, and things won't improve unless good people try to wipe out sin."

Noah caught his breath and waited. Conner's pet peeve was people who did evil in the name of religion. It was a subject they had talked about at length during many long stake-outs. He wasn't disappointed. Conner's jaw clenched. "Derrick got caught up on his payments a couple of months ago, but his family's still scrambling to save the ranch."

"I found a few interesting things, also." Noah pushed his sandwich aside. It tasted good, but couldn't compare with solving a case. "No club or organization Ryan belongs to held any event in Galveston around the Fourth of July. However, a woman was killed that evening while jogging. The police questioned her husband, but the case is listed as an accidental shooting by a person unknown who was firing in the air while celebrating the holiday."

"What caliber gun?"

"A 9mm Glock. That's not all. Tomball had one in October. Wife killed in the back parking lot of her small craft store and robbed of the cash deposit she was taking to the bank. Over in Sugarland, a man was killed in a dark parking garage while leaving his office well after hours." Noah flipped a page in his notes. "Good to know they're equal opportunity killers."

"So, one in each jurisdiction. No two crimes investigated by the same outfit. Pretty smart. What about Houston? Are we so sharp they're avoiding us?"

"No, we got ours in December when a woman was supposedly followed home from Christmas shopping and killed in her driveway. All the gifts stolen. That's why they wanted the job done in Bellaire. There may be others that I haven't found, but these all used a Glock. None of the riflings matched, though. But why buy a new gun when all you have to do is swap out the barrel?"

"That's four, five with Crystal Hudson. If he bought seven, he's got two barrels left." Conner brushed a crumb from his suit.

"Maybe three. He had one on there to start with. Hard to believe Galveston was his first. Maybe the small animals were his warm up. I have one other piece of news."

Conner straightened the crease in his pants. "Yeah? What'd you find out?"

"Martin, the head techno geek, called. They found the backdoor hidden in a Craig's List add for a mechanic. It leads to a website that was set-up at a Texas City library. It can be accessed from anywhere with the right code. He'll keep searching, but the phone number's a throwaway. If Ryan suspects we're on to him, that phone's gone by now."

Noah pushed back from his desk. "Let's go see what Hudson has to say about all this. I can't wait to see his face when he opens the door."

"Good afternoon, Mr. Hudson. We wanted to return a few of your things." Noah smiled, but Hudson obviously wasn't buying it. His frown pulled his features into an unpleasant grimace.

Too bad. He didn't need Hudson to like it. He just needed Hudson to go along with it.

"A few of my things? Where are the rest? You haven't harmed anything, have you?" he growled.

The morning's bright sun had disappeared behind a wall of gray and did little to warm the air. The cardboard box Noah was holding cut into his hands, and he didn't like not having easy access to his weapon.

Conner strode up the walk with a matching box. "Everything's fine, Mr. Hudson. Nothing's harmed and I think it's all here. If you'll let us put these boxes down, there are several more in the car."

Hudson's frown may have lessened a millimeter or two as he opened the door wider.

Noah and Conner entered the same ornate hallway as on their last trip, but Noah was even less impressed with the chandeliers and furnishings. He turned toward the back office, but halted when he heard Hudson's voice.

"Stop right there. I don't want you in my house. Just set the boxes here and I'll move them myself."

Move them yourself? Not likely. You'll probably get the maid or gardener to move them. I doubt you've ever done a lick of physical work in your life.

"Sure thing, Mr. Hudson. Let me bring in the rest of your things."

Noah was on his third trip carrying boxes into Hudson's home when Laurel Bledsoe pulled onto her driveway. She smiled and waved as she climbed out of her car.

He couldn't help smiling in return. She hardly resembled the woman he'd met just a few days ago. She'd pulled her hair off her face in some type of arrangement that looked both simple and intricate at the same time. She wore make-up and jewelry, and a business-looking suit that still managed to flatter her figure. High heels showed off trim, shapely legs.

He shook his head. He wouldn't have noticed any of those things a month ago. Not even two weeks ago.

But it was her face that showed the most dramatic change. Her smile felt warm and honest and her skin glowed. If he wasn't a married man, or at least still felt like one, he'd have said she was a knock-out. What was happening to him? Had he changed as much as she had?

"I know you can't talk now, but if you have time, stop by when you finish," she called. "I have good news and I need someone to share it with. And if you can tell me you're getting closer to solving Crystal's murder, then it will be a true celebration. I'll put on a pot of coffee." She waved again and disappeared through her back door.

Hudson's voice brought him back to reality.

"Is that it? I want you fellows out of here."

Noah didn't answer until he'd set the last box on the floor. "Let's go back to the kitchen and sit for a minute. I need you to sign some papers saying we returned everything in good order."

He started for the kitchen without looking back, but he could hear Hudson muttering.

"How do I know they're in good order? I haven't looked through them yet. And what about the money? Where is it?"

"Right here." Noah pulled an envelope from his pocket. "Why don't you count it? I want you to be satisfied we returned every dollar." *But not before we recorded the serial numbers.*

Hudson grabbed the money from Noah's hand and riffled

through it. He pulled the form close and clicked open the pen Noah handed him. The scratching of the pen as Hudson signed his name seemed to echo through the silent mausoleum of a house.

He's going to leave a mark on this fancy table if he presses any harder.

"Take it." Hudson pushed the form back to Noah. "Are we done here?"

"Not quite." Noah glanced at Conner. "We found a few suspicious things on your computer."

Hudson's face froze. "What are you talking about?"

Conner grinned. "That was an interesting mechanic you found on Craig's List. It didn't take our computer guys long to find the backdoor to his real website."

"What? What? Backdoor? I don't know what you're talking about." He sputtered and spittle flew out of his mouth and onto Noah's arm. Noah reached over and lifted a cloth napkin from a stack on the counter. He wiped his arm without taking his eyes off Hudson.

Thank goodness for crime shows on TV. Now every doofus thought forensic labs were invincible. If only they knew how thin their budget was. Lying to a wife murdering scumbag didn't bother him at all.

"Come on now, Gary." Noah switched to his first name to show that all pretense of respect was gone. "The tapes you made of Crystal's phone calls prove you knew what she'd discovered, and your actions show what you planned to do about it. Our tech guys can follow every keystroke you made. We know exactly what you found, when you found it, and how many times you visited it before you made the first call."

Hudson's eyes went wide and Noah struggled to keep the smile off his face. This wasn't the time to screw up.

"You just signed a receipt for the computer you found him on and the cash you promised to pay him with. Not to mention the cell phone you used to call him. You might as well have signed your own death warrant."

Hudson's shoulders slumped and Noah thought he saw tears in the man's eyes. Now came the tricky part. Hold out a ray of hope before he had time to ask for a lawyer. He leaned closer and lowered his voice.

"You're not the one we want, Gary. You're responsible for one death. The guy you hired has killed five people we know of. And he'll go on killing if we don't catch him. Help us and it'll go easier on you. You can live a long and comfortable life."

If you call jail comfortable. Three hots and a cot, all furnished by the state of Texas.

"All right. I'll help you find him." Hudson began to cry in earnest. The sight made Noah want to puke. Killing his wife. Just to save money on a divorce.

He turned to Conner. "Call a squad car and take him in. I'll be along by the time you have him booked. I don't even want to ride in the car with him." He felt dirty sitting near him at the table.

CHAPTER
TWENTY-ONE

NOAH WAITED UNTIL Conner and Hudson left in the squad car. He locked Hudson's door securely, then tromped across the damp grass to Laurel's back door. He needed to see something fresh and innocent, to breathe in uncontaminated air.

Besides, he convinced himself, she'd been a big help on the case. She deserved an update.

He tapped twice on the glass, and saw her shadow flit across the curtain. The aroma of coffee and perfume greeted him as she opened the door. She had changed into tight jeans and a snug sweater. Her hair hung loose and silver earrings twinkled between the blonde strands as she moved her head.

"Hi, Noah. I didn't know if you'd be able to make it. I didn't mean to disturb you while you were working. Especially if it meant locking up that sorry excuse for a human."

He watched her smile and something cold inside him melted. "You didn't disturb me. I thought you deserved to know.

The case isn't completely closed, but Gary Hudson admitted to hiring someone to kill Crystal. It isn't official yet, he hasn't signed a confession, so please don't mention it until you see it in the paper." He was breaking protocol by telling her, but it helped him wash the filth of Gary Hudson from his mind.

"Don't worry, I have too much respect for Crystal's memory to spread gossip about her. I think I miss her more every day."

She led him into the kitchen and he sat in his familiar chair. A cup of coffee appeared in front of him.

He reached for the cup and she glanced at his hand. "How's your bite doing? Are you taking good care of it?"

"It's much better. I've been doctoring my hand twice a day and I can't see any sign of infection. Thanks for suggesting it. As for Sweet Pea. . . We seem to have made peace. She's forgiven me for whatever she thinks I did." *Like live when Betsy didn't.*

"I know better than to ask, I'm guessing you're still on duty, but I'm going to have a glass of wine. It feels wrong to be happy that you caught Gary when Crystal's still dead. We were an odd pair, but we were friends. I'm ten years older than she was."

She glanced at Noah and grinned. "Twelve years. She could be loud and crass and showy, but I was teaching her to be more sophisticated and she was teaching me to be freer. To love life with abandon. And I needed her lessons much more than she needed mine."

Noah took a sip of coffee and eyed her wine. He wished he could put a jolt of something stronger in his cup, but he'd broken enough rules for one day. "Her half-brother is in jail. I think the two of you are the only ones who'll miss her."

"Can I do anything to help him? I think Crystal would have wanted that."

"I'll check on it and let you know. Now, you said something about good news? A celebration?"

Her eyes sparkled. "I have a job. And I got it all on my own. It's the first interview I ever went on that my father hadn't already arranged the job before I got there. I was *so* nervous. It's only part-time to start, but that's good. I'll have time to settle in, get used to working again."

"Congratulations. What do the Aussies say? Good on ya."

"I wanted to tell you because I felt like I owe it all to you."

"I didn't do anything. You're the one who went out and found the job."

"You gave me a good kick in the butt when I needed it. I'll always be thankful for that." She reached across the table and squeezed his free hand.

He could feel his face turn red and he nearly knocked over his coffee cup, but he didn't move his hand. It was the first time he'd felt warm since. . . August?

Laurel stood back and admired her clean room. Every article of clothing had been hung up, put away, set out for the cleaners, or in the clothes hamper.

The room even smelled better. Fresher. No wonder she had been so sickly, sleeping in that damp, musty air.

She'd laughed when she found the good earrings and watch she'd been wearing the day Peter dropped the bombshell on her.

Bet he wished he had those back.

"It's not you, honey. It's me. I need some time to find myself." She remembered the smirk in his voice as if he were standing beside her.

Well, he'd found himself alright. It was undoubtedly a complete surprise when he woke up and found himself in bed with Miss Sex-Kitten.

Laurel tried to work up a good case of righteous indignation, but she didn't have the heart for it. She was tired of it all. Let him have his bimbo. He deserved her.

After all the work she'd just done, she'd earned a cup of tea. She set the handful of extra earring-backs she'd picked out of the carpet onto her dresser and headed for the kitchen.

She was as prepared as she could be to start work on Monday.

One last thing she needed to do—call a locksmith. No doubt Peter had taken her jewelry with him when he left, or before, while he was hiding all his assets, but he still had a key and she didn't want him coming in unexpectedly.

The pre-nup favored him in that he could do what he wanted, while she could lose everything. Not that she planned to do anything. She was still married, at least for another few months, and she took that seriously. Even if he didn't.

She twirled her tea cup and looked across the table at the empty chair where Noah had sat an hour earlier. His hand had engulfed hers and felt so strong when she squeezed it.

Wonder what those shoulders feel like. Or those arms.

She grabbed the phone book. She was only calling the locksmith because Peter had forfeited any right to come into her home unannounced. Not because thoughts of Noah smiling across the table from her kept dancing around in her head.

Noah leaned back in his desk chair and propped his feet on the bottom drawer. Conner was three feet away, in the same position at his own desk.

Noises floated in from down the hall, but their squad room was silent. The last detective had left twenty minutes earlier. Their lieutenant, ten minutes later.

"This feels good, but we're a long way from finished." Noah took a sip of Diet Coke and let the cold soda trickle down his throat. The caffeine might give him enough energy to make it home.

"It galls me to think that scumbag will be home safe and warm before we are." Conner hurled his empty Styrofoam cup toward the trash can, but it settled among the crumpled papers with hardly a plop.

Noah heaved out an exhausted sigh. It had been a long day, starting with an early morning trip to Sam Houston and ending in a small room with Hudson and his lawyer discussing a plea deal. Not to mention a short visit with Laurel in between. Now that part made him smile.

He was too tired to worry about Hudson. "That ankle monitor will let us know if he sets foot out of his house. And we've got his passport and all that cash locked up, so leaving the country won't be easy. Let's call it a night and work on catching his accomplice in the morning. You need to get home and remind Jeannie why she loves you, although distance might be a better way to handle that one. And I need to pick up Sweet Pea from the vet's before she forgets who I am."

And before we lose all the progress we've made so far.

"Hudson was pretty firm. His Icky had a high voice and our Icky's voice isn't exactly a bass, but it hints at his size." Conner sat up and pushed his bottom drawer closed.

Noah kicked his drawer closed a little harder than necessary.

"Still, I'd love to have one piece of solid evidence before we go after Ryan. I'd give anything for a copy of his fingerprints."

"Give it a rest, partner. We'll solve it tomorrow. Hudson fell all over himself offering to wear a wire." Conner stood and slipped on his jacket.

"True, but I don't trust him and I sure as hell don't want to give him any ammunition on his plea deal." Noah had to agree with Conner, it chapped him for Hudson to get any reduction in his sentence for helping them catch the killer. Crystal wouldn't be dead if he hadn't decided his fortune was worth more than her life.

Noah tossed his soda can into the trash and followed Conner to the elevator. By the time the bell chimed, he was already thinking about the hamburger he was going to buy for Sweet Pea.

With each tick of the clock, the twilight deepened and Ryan's visibility lessened. He had to catch Derrick before he got too close to the building or he'd want to go up to his room, but lurking behind a tree was a sure way to get himself noticed.

Derrick looked bushed when he rounded the corner toward the college. *Good, less chance he'll insist on stopping by his room.*

"Hey, just the man I was looking for." Ryan plastered a smile on his face. The grin felt unnatural. It was an expression he didn't often wear.

"What's up, man? I only have an hour 'till study group and I need to eat and get my books."

"That's why I was looking for you. I ran into that geeky blonde girl and she mentioned your physics study group was cancelled for tonight. Said she sent you an email but didn't know if you'd gotten it because her computer was acting wonky." He was in it too deep to back out now. If Derrick insisted on going to his room and ran into anyone from his group, well, even a numb nuts like shooter-boy would figure out something was up.

Derrick rolled his eyes. "Why was it cancelled? I need the study time."

"How the hell should I know? What I do know is that I have a two-for-one coupon to a new Mexican restaurant and I'll treat you. I'll even go over your study notes with you while we wait." Ryan cut across the grass toward his car. He held his breath until he heard Derrick's footsteps behind him.

Halfway to his car, he whirled around and tossed his keys to Derrick. "Wait in the car. I forgot the coupon." He didn't stay around for an answer, just sprinted back the way he'd come. He couldn't afford to have anyone see them together.

By the time he'd reached the college, counted to ten, and walked slowly back to the parking lot, dark had fallen.

"Got it," he said, sliding into the driver's seat. "Before we eat, I have one stop I need to make. I want to show you something."

"What's that?" Derrick had slumped down in his seat, barely visible to anyone passing. Perfect. About time things started going his way.

"My dead drop. I've never showed it to you before because. . . Well, I think you understand. What you don't know can't hurt you if anyone comes around asking questions."

"So why now?" Derrick sat up, excitement in his voice.

"You might need to do the pick-up sometime. We've got a new client. He contacted us yesterday. I did some preliminary research on him. He sounds solid, but I'll have to dig deeper before I accept the contract. I'm serious about that promise we made."

"Yeah, yeah. No one who doesn't deserve it."

"That's right. Remember the guy in Sugarland? He'd put his wife in the hospital half a dozen times. She was right to believe he might kill her if he lost control." *Well, the divorce settlement would kill her. Wipe out everything she'd tried to hide from him.*

"And the lady we just did? She was a real piece of work. Running around on her husband and rubbing his face in the pre-nup. Aborting his baby because she didn't want to lose her figure."

"But I thought you didn't want to take on a new client for a while."

"I know you're short on money, bro. And partners stick together." He tried to look sincere, but who knew if he managed it. Inside the car was dark enough that Derrick probably couldn't tell.

So far, this was going easier than he'd hoped. He drove for fifteen minutes before he pulled off the road and parked behind a bush. A mosquito buzzed around his head, but no other sound penetrated the deep woods. "It's only a little farther. Let me get the flashlight out of the trunk. We have to walk the last part. It's pretty dark, but we won't have to worry about being seen. No one ever comes around here. That's why I picked this spot."

They hiked down a path that was little more than a deer trail. Excitement buzzed through Ryan's veins as he tested the weight of the flashlight. When Derrick glanced over his shoulder a second time, Ryan knew they had gone far enough. It was time. "Over there, by that big rock. What I'd like to do, it's the reason I wanted you to come along, is for us to kneel and pray for the right decision before we open the package."

Noah had trouble driving with Sweet Pea wiggling and squirming and trying to lick him in the face. Good thing he'd bought the hamburger first and set it in the back. Pea definitely noticed the aroma, and had attempted to climb over the seat, but she let it go and was more interested in greeting Noah.

Pulling into the driveway with the dog in his lap felt right. Why had he resisted loving her for so long? Probably because he felt too guilty to believe he deserved any happiness at all.

Wow, wasn't he turning into some kind of a psychoanalyst? Or maybe just a psycho. Was it too late to try those grief counseling sessions his sister had enrolled him in?

No, he hadn't changed *that* much. Maybe, just maybe, he'd read the book she'd given him. After he caught Crystal Hudson's murderer.

Sweet Pea scooted around the backyard as if she was in Heaven. She smelled every tree and peed on every bush. Then she ran to the back door and jumped up and down like a yo-yo.

"Here you go, girl," Noah said as he pushed the door open.

She charged in so fast her feet flew out from under her and she skidded across the floor. Noah held his breath as he reached for her food bowl, but she wagged her tail and ran in circles.

"I'm going to give you this hamburger, but if you get sick, I'll have to find a new vet. I can't take you back to that guy. He already thinks I tried to kill you twice. Well, once he thought I tried to kill us both, but he wasn't too far off the mark, so I can't fault him for that."

Noah crumbled the burger in Sweet Pea's bowl and set it on

her mat. The dog stood by the bowl and looked at him.

"What? You want more? Eat what you have and then we'll talk."

The dog didn't move until Noah unwrapped his own meal and took a bite. She matched her pace to his, eating when he did, pausing when he stopped. When they had each finished, Noah dropped his last morsel into her bowl.

"It's not that late, old girl. Want to go for a short walk?"

Pea ran to the laundry room and pawed at the wall under her leash. Betsy had always strapped some pink puffy jacket on Pea when the weather was cold, but Noah wasn't sure where it was, and knew for a fact he wasn't walking any dog wearing a pink coat. Once around the block. She wouldn't have time to get that cold.

They were passing the Howells' house when Jerry Howell struggled out of the carport, breathing hard and sweating, dragging two bags of garbage behind him. Shoot, he'd forgotten tomorrow was garbage day. He'd have to take his out when he got home.

Might as well keep up the pretense of being friendly. "Evening, Jerry. Can I help you with that?"

"If you don't mind. I've got one more by the door. I forgot last time and the fried chicken we had when Ryan came over is getting pretty ripe," Jerry wheezed, his jowls flapping.

Noah grabbed the two bags with one hand and deposited them on the curb, bottles and cans clanking loudly inside.

Jerry reappeared with another bag and dropped it beside the first two. "Thanks, Noah. Appreciate the help. Did you ever find out anything about our neighborhood burglar?"

"Well, you didn't hear this from me, but it was the guy's own kid and his friend. You just never know, do you?"

Sweet Pea sniffed the last bag and the hairs on the back of her neck went up as she let out a low growl.

"I best get her back. This weather's too cold for her. Say hello to your wife for me." Noah scooped Sweet Pea into his arms and tried to look casual as he strolled home.

Once inside his own house, he lifted the dog to his face and planted a kiss on the top of her head. "I'm going to have to get you your own gold shield, Pea. I think you just might be a better detective than I am."

CHAPTER
TWENTY-TWO

NOAH'S ALARM SOUNDED its familiar *beep, beep* at 2:55. Sweet Pea snuggled deeper under the covers as he reached across her to switch off the irritating noise.

"I'll be right back, Pea. Keep the bed warm for me."

The dark sweats and hoodie hung over the chair where he'd left them when he crawled into bed, a couple of gallon-sized baggies, a pair of gloves, and a penlight in the pocket. The kitchen door opened soundlessly and he slipped into his backyard. Near the front of the house, he watched the street for a full five minutes before stepping out of the shadows.

The moon was a couple of days shy of full, but spotty cloud cover kept it to a muted glow as he made his way silently down the street, keeping to the darkest areas. At the Howells', he waited and studied the house for signs of life. No light showed, but a noise drew him closer to the bedroom window.

One of the Howells snored like a freight train. His money was on Jerry. With those jowls, he was a walking advertisement for sleep apnea. That meant he might wake himself at any moment and that Delores probably didn't sleep well at all.

The three trash bags rustled softly as he carried them from the curb to a sheltered spot under the carport. Holding the penlight in his teeth, he untied each one. The first two were frozen dinners and beer and wine bottles, along with used tissues and paper towels.

Good thing I remembered gloves. Now, I only hope nothing in here is broken and could cut me.

The last bag held remnants of fried chicken. Jerry was right– it was plenty ripe. More beer bottles and diet soda cans clinked against each other. Noah froze, waiting to see if anyone noticed.

A dog barked once, then was quiet.

Near the bottom of the bag was a lone Coke can. Not one other bag contained any soda except Diet Pepsi. He pulled a baggie from his pocket and used it to lift the can. A wine bottle moved, but Noah caught it and eased it back into place, then sealed the can into the baggie and slipped it in his jacket.

Just as he stood to carry the bags back to the curb, a car motor rumbled in the distance. He dropped back into the shadows and watched as a constable's car crept past, patrolling the neighborhood.

Where were you when this asshole was trying to kill me, you-son-of-a-bitch?

Would the white plastic bags be visible from the street? He didn't move, didn't breathe until the red glow from the taillights disappeared around the corner.

He glided like an ice skater, afraid to make any sudden moves and placed the three bags in the same position they were in when he found them. Then he ran like hell for home.

If anyone asked, it was the only time he could find to jog.

Conner finished the warrant and stabbed at the print button. On the far side of the room, a printer came to life, grinding and chugging and beeping before spitting out the pages. *Finally*. He grabbed them and called to Noah. "Okay, partner, I've got it. Let's run this over to the courthouse and find a judge to sign it."

It had taken two hours to confirm that the prints on the Coke can were the same as the ones in Noah's house and Conner didn't know which one of them had the hardest time waiting. He'd interrupted Jeannie at school just to ask how she was feeling even though it was awkward for her to receive calls during class. Noah had paced a hole in the floor, and chewed half a pack of gum. Neither had been capable of doing any other work.

"You go. I'll stay here and try to find Ryan's class schedule. That way we'll be ready as soon as you get the okay."

Conner took a breath. Noah wasn't going to like this, but it needed to be said. "You better come with me. The judge might have some questions about how you acquired the Coke can."

"I told you how I got it. The trash was sitting in the street. Howell told me they had fried chicken the night Ryan came over, and I could smell it when I walked the dog. It might have been risky, but it was perfectly legal for me to go through it."

Noah's shoulders tightened and Conner could see his eyes turn hard. Too bad. If Noah couldn't stand up to a judge's questioning, he'd never be able to face a defense attorney. "I never said I didn't believe you." I might have thought it, but I never said it. "I said a judge is going to want to hear it from your own lips. At this point, the warrant's only for entering your house and attempting to kill you, so he'll be extra suspicious.

Now put your coat on and let's go. We'll have to stop back by here to let the lieutenant know what we're doing anyway."

"Flip you to see whose car we take." Noah reached into his pocket.

"Are you kidding? It'll take longer to find a parking spot than to just walk over there. I've never yet found a space without circling three times. Come on, it'll be good for you. Some fresh air and exercise. We're both too tense to question Ryan without blowing it big time."

It's the same argument every time. To get a car out of the garage, drive eight blocks, circle the Criminal Courts Building garage, and park again is a good fifteen minutes. To walk it is fifteen minutes and half the stress.

Noah frowned, but put the quarter back in his pocket. "I don't suppose you're planning to take the tunnels?"

"That would increase the walk by five minutes, worth it in the summer for the air conditioning, but only for wimps in the winter."

They stepped out of the Travis Street headquarters, and the wind hit them. Their hair whipped back and forth, and invisible specks of debris stung their faces. The street was almost empty. Other pedestrians had retired to the tunnel system.

Conner pulled his jacket tighter and ducked his head.

He heard Noah mutter, "Wimp," as he trotted down the steps, head held high.

"Showoff," Conner said, under his breath. He knew better than to let Noah hear him.

Noah's favorite judge was out of the building, and he had to settle for a visiting judge he'd had a run in with before.

The judge held the papers at arm's length. "And how are you so sure the prints belong to this Ryan Howell person if there's no copy of them on file?"

"As I stated in the application, there was only one can of Coke in the three bags, and it was in the bag containing remnants of the meal served when Ryan was at home. All the other cans were Diet Pepsi. And I personally saw the Howells' drink Diet Pepsi and Ryan drink Coke. The first thing we'll do when we pick him up is check his fingerprints. If they don't match, he'll be out the door and home before I finish apologizing."

"Can anyone verify your story that the evidence was obtained legally, Detective Daugherty?" The judge pressed together lips already so thin and pale they seemed to disappear.

"No, Your Honor. While sifting through someone's trash is permissible, it isn't popular with the homeowner. Especially if you're trying to put one of their family members in jail. It's generally a good idea to avoid confrontation whenever possible."

The judge grunted and studied the warrant as if new words might magically appear on the page. "It's always best to have a witness. Primarily when there is a personal connection. I'm not happy about this, Detective Daugherty. Not happy at all."

"I wasn't real happy to wake up to carbon monoxide pouring into my bedroom."

"Exactly. That's why I'd prefer to see another name on this application." The judge glared at Noah through watery blue eyes. Noah stared back. Two could play that game.

Finally the judge scrawled his signature on the warrant, but held it tight for another moment. "Next time, bring me something more solid, Detective. I'll be watching you."

Noah grabbed the warrant and sprinted down the hall. He

called over his shoulder, "Yes, sir." *You old fart.*

Conner stayed long enough to say, "Thank you, Your Honor," before jogging after Noah.

Noah was already coaxing a patrol officer to give them a ride back to headquarters when Conner caught up with him. "Ass kisser," Noah said, grinning at his partner.

"Brownnoser," Conner answered.

"About time you dead beats got back." Lieutenant Nate Jansen stood at the door of his office, glaring at Noah and Conner. "I've got a job for you."

"We're on a job, Loo. It's called a murder." Noah held his breath. They'd been on it for several days, but they were making progress. It was too early to shut them down and move them to another case. Not with a freshly signed warrant in their hands.

"That's your problem. This one is called a missing person, and I want you on it right away."

What was going on, drop a murder investigation for a missing person? "Are you kidding me? Homicide trumps missing any day."

"Not when it's a college kid whose name you've been running through data bases seven ways from Sunday. Once you flagged his name, anything to do with him gets kicked straight back to us."

"Ryan Howell?" If that kid had gotten away because he took off so he could pick up Sweet Pea before the vet's closed, he'd never forgive himself.

"No, some other kid. Derrick McAllister. He missed his study group last night and wasn't in class this morning. His parents have been trying to call him for hours."

Noah's breath caught in his throat. He couldn't speak. This was worse than losing Ryan. His selfishness had gotten someone killed. Again. It didn't matter if the kid was an accomplice to several murders. He still deserved his day in court. He dropped into the nearest chair, his legs unable to support him. *Then why don't I feel the same way about Ryan?*

Conner seemed unfazed. "Are you serious? A grown kid cuts class and ditches a couple of calls from his parents and you bring out the big guns? He's probably shacked up with a girl. Pull the fire alarm and he'll come running out of one of those dorms or colleges, or whatever they call them, carrying his shoes in one hand and his pants in the other."

"Not according to his parents." Jansen shook his head. "He's pledged to some girl in his church. And he speaks to his parents every night. Look, you're probably right. I hope to hell you are. But you two are going over to that school and show the colors. Talk to everyone who knows him or might have seen him. Look under the bed if you have to. Check in every hour, so I'll know you're doing what I told you to."

Jansen's phone rang, and he turned toward his office, but twisted back to look at Conner. "And don't pull any damn fire alarms or you can explain it to the guys with the funny yellow helmets."

Conner sighed. "He's not *that* much of an angel. I read his file. Come on, partner. Bring the warrant. We'll spend an hour searching for Derrick, then we'll arrest Ryan. If Derrick has any sense at all, he's hiding from his friendly neighborhood hit man."

Noah couldn't move. His voice shook. "Derrick isn't hiding or shacked up. He's dead. We might as well have killed him ourselves. We should have moved faster, it's not like Ryan had *that* many friends who would have partnered up with him. Once Ryan suspected we were on to him, he started cleaning house. Derrick was a loose end. So is Hudson. Maybe even Icky. We better warn them."

Oh crap. Rosaria. Did I use her name anywhere? It wasn't on the warrant, or even in his computer. Her phone number was on a separate page in his pocket. Would calling put her in more danger or less? If she got frightened and ran, he'd lose his best witness against Hudson. He couldn't take a chance, he had to warn her.

"You're as much of an alarmist as Jansen. The kid is fine, wherever he is. If something did happen to him, he brought it on himself. He's the one shooting people for money. Once you step into that profession, you put yourself in jeopardy. Derrick picked a psychopath for a partner. We didn't have anything to do with that. And we didn't have all the information we needed last night. The fingerprint analysis didn't come in 'till this morning. We barely conned the judge into giving us a warrant with the prints. We'd never have gotten one without them. Now, get off your ass and let's go find him."

Noah stood, his legs trembling. "We'll need to bring a shovel or dive suits if we ever expect to see him again. I'll call Hudson and Icky. You drive."

I'll keep telling myself it was too late last night to have finished investigating, get a warrant, and arrest Ryan, but I don't think it'll do any good.

Conner hated sitting on some strange kid's unmade bed, but

it was the only clear spot in the room. Books, papers, soda cans, and food wrappers littered every available space. The stench of stale food and unwashed boy permeated the entire area. If only the kid would open a window.

The contrast with Derrick's pristine room was striking.

"And you're sure it was Derrick McAllister you saw yesterday evening?"

The kid, Trevor, pointed out his window to a patch of lawn. "I was watching for Derrick. I wanted to go over his lab notes before study group. I saw him trudging across the lawn, his head down."

"Was he with anyone?" Conner glanced up from his notes. Did these kids spend all their spare time in study groups? What happened to keg parties and girls?

"Maybe, I'm not sure."

Noah spoke up for the first time. "What do you mean, maybe? How could you not know?"

Conner cleared his throat. Noah was going to scare the kid off if he didn't calm down. "Try to describe what you saw. We'll worry about what it means later."

"Derrick was about six feet behind Ryan Howell. Maybe he was following him, or maybe they were both just heading the same direction."

"Did he have his backpack with him?" Conner tried to keep the excitement from his voice.

"Sure, I think so."

Noah growled. "Sure, or I think so, which is it?"

Trevor looked like he might wet his pants at any moment. Conner got up and put his hand on the boy's shoulder. "We appreciate your help, son. If you think of anything else, give me a call." He handed the kid his card, but the boy held it like he was afraid it might bite him.

"Let's go see where he might have been headed." Conner held the door open and waited while Noah took one last glance out the window and followed him into the hallway. The musty smell was almost a relief.

Noah's face was grim. "We don't know where he went, but we sure as hell know where he didn't go. His backpack and his books aren't in his room and his study group notes are. Ryan said something to him to make him turn around."

They exited the building and started across the lawn. The air was still nippy, and students hurried past them on their way to class, or back to their rooms.

Conner glanced up, measuring the spot where Trevor had seen the two boys. Noah stood on a slight rise, his hands on his hips, staring forward.

"Come look at this," Noah said.

Directly in front of him was the parking lot where they'd seen Ryan's car the day they first interviewed Icky. The car was still there, but moved to a different row.

Noah's voice took on a hard edge. "*Now* do you think it's time to arrest Ryan?"

CHAPTER
TWENTY-THREE

NOAH OPENED THE classroom door and slipped inside. Conner followed on his heels.

The room was semi-circular, with rows of seats leading down to the floor where the professor paced in front of a blackboard covered with numbers and figures Noah didn't understand.

Two dozen eager faces twisted toward Noah and Conner when the heavy door clicked shut.

The professor pushed horn-rimmed glasses up on his nose and wiped chalk-covered hands on pants already coated in white dust. "Sorry, gentlemen, but class is in session. You'll have to wait in my office if you need to speak to me."

Noah spotted Ryan's red hair on the front row. *Of course that's where he'd sit. He's a front row, ass-kissing type of kid.*

"We won't be long, Professor," Noah called. His eyes charted the most direct path and he headed for the boy. "Let us collect young Mr. Howell and we'll be on our way."

Best to move fast, get the kid, and be gone before anyone had time to object. This was Rice University—a bunch of liberal, spoiled, rich kids. At A&M, they'd probably help him collar the little turd.

"We're reviewing for an exam, sir. And he'll need this information. You can wait outside. Class is over in twenty-five minutes." The professor crossed the room to stand near Ryan.

Ryan jerked toward Noah and his pen skittered across the floor. Innocent blue eyes turned hard in a flash.

Noah tried unsuccessfully to keep a smile off his face. "I doubt he'll have a use for it where he's going." He opened his jacket to show his badge and placed his hand loosely on his weapon.

Ryan let out a high-pitched scream. "Run for it. He has a gun."

On the far side of the room, someone took up the cry. "It's a gun. Run."

Fuck. There goes fast and neat.

Some students threw themselves on the floor, while others scattered—running, climbing over seats, plowing into each other and spilling books, cell phones, and jackets along the way.

The silent room exploded in a cacophony of yelling, crying and crashing furniture.

Ryan jumped out of his seat and yanked the professor in front of him. Ryan was a scrawny kid. Not more than five-eight, a hundred and twenty pounds. The professor was taller, heavier, older, and unprepared. He stumbled and Ryan threw him across the same aisle Noah was sprinting down.

Noah saw the professor fall and lined up to jump over him, a move he'd completed a hundred times in his football playing days, but his foot landed on Ryan's pen and his knee hit the cement floor with a crack audible over a roomful of screaming kids. He threw out an arm to keep his face from hitting the floor and felt the jar clear to his shoulder.

For one brief, blissful second, he felt nothing. Then the message center of his brain told him something bad had happened and he knew that to straighten his leg would be agony.

Behind him, he could see Conner trying to fight his way down the stairs while being buffeted on first one side and then the other by fleeing students.

Conner held out his badge and yelled, "Stop, police. Everyone stay where you are."

A few kids stopped, but others kept running. Half a dozen blocked the aisle, keeping him from Noah's side.

No help coming from that direction

Noah twisted to the spot he'd last seen Ryan, only to find empty air and a slowly closing side door.

Noah punched Conner's number into his cell phone, but it rang three times before his partner picked up.

Conner growled, "What is it this time? I'm trying to reach the lieutenant."

"Don't bother. I won't be here that long. Either look for the fucking doctor or come back in here and help me find my pants." He'd been in that curtained cubical for almost an hour, and while half a dozen people had been in doing all manner of unpleasant things to his poor, battered body, he had yet to see the one person who could set him free.

The curtain hangers screeched as Conner threw the flimsy

cloth to the side, the cell phone still in his hand. His voice assaulted Noah from two directions. "Hang up the phone and stop calling me. You don't have any pants. They were cut off while you were in the ambulance. The doctor will be in when he runs out of other things to do and not a moment before."

He reached over and snatched the phone out of Noah's hand, pressed the off button and stuck it in his own pocket. "I can't wait on you and organize a search at the same time. You're in the hospital, act like it."

"I'm not *in* the hospital, I'm in the Emergency Room. And I don't plan to stay here long. If the fucking doctor would come release me, I'd be back at work. Now give me back my phone and I'll work on the search grid."

"No way, Flying Wallenda. You were crying like a baby when they hefted you into the ambulance. The EMT's put some Demerol in your IV just to shut you up. You're off duty for twenty-four hours."

Noah flexed his foot. No waves of pain radiated up his body. "Those asswipes. I never gave permission for that."

"They were on the radio with the doctor the whole time. He gave them permission. Probably because he couldn't hear what they were saying over your sobs."

"Maybe I was yelling, a little, but it was because everyone was worrying about me instead of searching for that slippery devil."

"Either way, you're not working 'till you get the all-clear. So lean back, relax, and let me do my job. If you need someone to help you, ask the nurse to call your sister. She actually cares about your raggedy ass." Conner's voice rose with each word and his footsteps echoed down the hall.

Noah slammed his head against the pillow, frustration gnawing at his gut. If he raised the head of the bed, some monitor beeped in his ear, if he laid it back, florescent lights glared in his eyes. He needed to get out. Once home, he'd figure out his next move. How much trouble would he be in with his boss if he just walked out? What did they call it, AMA? Against medical advice.

Well, first of all, he wasn't sure he *could* walk. *And* he didn't have a car, *or pants*. Getting Conner to drive him was out of the question, but he'd seen a patrolman out front. Could he convince the guy to give him a ride?

He shifted uncomfortably on the narrow bed. His shoulders brushed the railing on each side and his feet hung off the end. He'd call Conner *again*, get him to find that doctor. He patted around on the bed, looking for his phone. *Fuck.*

Well, they couldn't take away his call button. He saw it sitting on a table, just out of reach. Apparently, they could.

Evening shadows masked Ryan's movements as he slipped through Gary Hudson's back door. He crossed the darkened room without a sound. There was only one hope of returning to the life he knew, and removing Hudson was it. All the years he'd spent training his exceptional mind, gone in a flash. He wasn't prepared for life on the run.

But just in case he had to, he'd need a bankroll.

The sound of ice falling into a glass told him where to find Hudson and he started in that direction. He'd not only researched Hudson's background, but watched the man himself while preparing for his last job. He'd know Hudson anywhere. But Hudson had never seen him.

"Hello, Gary. Having an evening cocktail?"

Hudson spun around, flinging ice and bourbon across the Italian marble floor. Now his fancy house smelled like a cheap bar.

"Who the hell are you? How'd you get in my house?"

"I'm Icky. You didn't think I'd take a job without checking out your house and learning if you're really who you say you are, did you?" He put the slight Hispanic tilt to his voice that he'd used over the phone, but it was hard to pull off with his red hair. He'd never had to worry about that before. Hudson was the only client who had ever set eyes on him. Not that he'd live long enough for it to be a problem.

"Are you fucking with me? You're nothing but a snot-nosed kid. I wouldn't trust you to mow my lawn." Hudson gestured with his now empty glass.

"And yet you hired me to kill your wife. Maybe you're the one who should learn to do research. I did my job, now it's time to pay up." Despite the difference in their economic status, the man's condescending attitude reminded him of his father, and he wanted to strangle him right then.

"I don't know what you're talking about. Get out of here before I call the cops." Hudson pulled a cell phone from his pocket.

Ryan struggled to keep his voice low and calm. "Are you sure you want to do that? Wouldn't you rather pay what you owe me and never see me again? The cops are already looking at you. If they find me, you're done for. Give me my money, and I'm gone. Then the chain is broken. If you keep your mouth shut, you're safe."

Hudson set down his glass and wiped his hands on his pants.

He was dressed as if he'd just left his office. Dress shirt, dress shoes, slacks, tie. But Ryan knew he'd been home for hours.

"Now's the time, Gary. Make your decision. Close this chapter in your life and move on. You deserve a new start. You've done the work, now reap the benefits." Ryan waited with feigned patience as Hudson's pea brain clicked through the possibilities.

"And I'll never see or hear from you again?" Hudson chewed on his lip.

"Scout's honor." Ryan placed his hand across his heart. *Like he'd ever wasted his time playing Boy Scout.* "I have to leave. This town's too hot for me. I need a bankroll."

Hudson sighed, whether with relief or resignation, Ryan wasn't sure. "Follow me to my office." He spun on his heels and marched off without looking back.

Ryan had cased the house earlier, but he kept his eyes open as he followed Hudson to his office.

All those monitors and what good had they done the old guy? He'd bypassed them with ten minutes work, then watched 'till the maid left and slipped through the yard and into the house just like he'd done three other times.

Hudson took a small key from his pocket and opened what he probably thought was a secret door and pulled out the third file drawer from the top. Ryan knew exactly what he was reaching for.

As Hudson bent to retrieve the accordion folder full of cash, Ryan slipped on a pair of gloves and reached for the baseball bat Hudson had stashed between two file cabinets.

He took one step closer and tried to remember what some middle-school baseball coach had attempted to drum into his head. Left hand here, right hand here, plant your feet, reach back and give it everything you've got.

Unused muscles strained as his back twisted. He struggled to keep a tight grip with his right hand. He'd positioned himself so that the majority of the blood splatter would be blocked by the open door. His dark clothing would disguise the rest.

Hudson must have heard a noise or sensed movement because he lifted his head and twisted toward Ryan. "What the . . .?"

Ryan had already started his swing, and tried to adjust the angle in mid-stroke. The bat grazed Hudson's shoulder, which took the brunt of the force, before landing on his jaw. Hudson went to his knees, but grabbed the file drawer with his left hand and remained semi-erect. His right arm hung useless at his side.

"Ou little ucker," he mumbled through broken teeth and blood.

Ryan stood, waiting for the man to fall. The pressure in his head pulsed with every maddening heartbeat as the anger built. Why didn't the man go down? What right did he have to interfere with his perfectly laid-out plans?

First the cop, then that damn dog. Now this useless piece of shit. Didn't anybody know how to die?

Hudson swayed slightly as he released his grip on the file drawer. His left hand groped in the accordion file and a gun appeared.

Ryan laughed as the gun in Hudson's hand wavered. Now it was getting fun. "What are you going to do, old man? You can't even hold yourself up, much less see to point that gun at me. It might as well be a water pistol." He danced from side to side, taunting Hudson.

A shot rocked the tiny room and Ryan felt the breeze as it

passed by his face. His ears rang and the smell of gun powder filled his nose. Before he had time to clear his head, another shot rang out. That one was wide of the mark and Hudson's arm dropped.

Enough was enough. The old fool might connect by accident. It had been fun, though. No one else had ever fought back. He might have to give some thought to doing the deed face to face from now on. No, that would be a foolish risk.

He watched as Hudson struggled to lift the heavy gun. He'd never had any desire to play golf, but really, how hard could it be? He switched his grip on the bat and lined up with Hudson's hand. His swing was off by several inches and he only connected with the tip end of the gun, but that was enough.

Hudson's hand slammed into the file drawer and the gun fell to the floor, but not as far away as he wanted, so Ryan kicked it to the other side of the room. Hudson spit and a wad of blood and teeth and a substance he didn't even want to think about landed near his foot.

"That does it, old man." Ryan swung again and laid the bat directly across Hudson's forehead. His head snapped back and crashed into the metal file cabinet. If it made a sound, Ryan couldn't hear it. His ears still rang from the two gunshots.

He reached across the limp body and pulled out the folder.

Empty.

"First you pull a gun on me and then you try to cheat me? Big mistake." He kicked Hudson in the stomach and the man let out a low groan.

Still with us, are you old fart? Then you should enjoy this. He pulled back his foot and kicked him again. *And this.* He kicked him twice more, the last time to the head.

Hudson's neck twisted at an unnatural angle, and his eyes stared lifelessly at nothing.

I haven't had this much fun since I used to troll for bums on Saturday night. It almost makes up for seeing that cop come back to life. Almost.

Blood covered every surface and it was impossible to walk out of the room without leaving tracks. He used the baseball bat to lever the nearest file cabinet over, and when it crashed to the floor, he crawled across it and out the door.

In the living room, he tossed the bat into the roaring fireplace. It settled on top of the fake logs and caught fire immediately.

Now what? This was supposed to be a robbery gone wrong, and without the money, I'm going to need a cushion. I'm safe here and don't have anywhere else to go. Might as well do a little treasure hunting.

Hudson's closet yielded two thousand in cash and a stack of gold Krugerrands hidden under the carpet. His wife put him to shame. She had a false bottom built into her underwear drawer with five grand in small bills.

Ho, ho, ho. So you were planning to leave him after all. Smart girl.

Her jewelry would be too easy to trace, but it would look suspicious to leave it behind. He could toss it into a lake.

Hudson was bigger than he was, but the wife was about his size. After a shower to wash off all the blood, he dressed in a pair of her sweats and tennis shoes. His clothes could go in the fire, along with the bat. In fact, maybe it would be best if the whole house burned down.

No, that would draw too much attention. Better to open a few windows and let the cold air skew the time-of-death measurements.

CHAPTER
TWENTY-FOUR

"WAKE UP."

An unpleasant hiss buzzed around Ryan's ear. He sank deeper into his pillow and ignored the sound.

Strong hands gripped his arm and shook. "I said wake up, you conniving little piece of shit."

Ryan opened his eyes and stared up into his father's face, only inches away. A face red and contorted in anger. His room was still dark. It couldn't have been much past five a.m. Only three hours of sleep on a day when he'd need all his wits. *Why was Pops up so early?*

The hissing voice started up again. "What have you been up to now? The cops came by with a warrant last night. Said you were in some kind of a riot at school. Several kids fell and were injured. No one could find you. Upset your mother so bad, she took a pill and went to bed before supper."

If Pops was keeping his voice low, that meant his mother

wasn't up yet. Good. Time to figure things out before she woke. "What about you, Pops? Were you worried about me, too?"

His father's eyes narrowed. "I was worried alright, but not about your safety. So what time do you need me to have gone to bed?"

Ryan sat up and swung his legs over the side of the bed. "With nothing on TV and no one to keep you company, I'll bet you went to sleep right after she did."

"That sounds about right. I fixed a sandwich, had a stiff drink, and was asleep by seven o'clock."

The alcohol on his father's breath, and the empty bottle he'd seen on the counter, meant he'd had several stiff drinks before stumbling into bed. "I must have just missed you. I got home around seven-thirty and you were both dead to the world. After the upsetting day I had—seeing a man with a gun break into our classroom and my friends running and screaming—I just crawled into bed myself. Did the cops say what they wanted me for? Were they just checking to see if I got out safely?"

Pops barked out a short laugh. "Yeah, right. The cops always bring a warrant when they're concerned about your safety. Apparently, you're wanted for breaking and entering the cop's house down the street. I knew that fucker was up to something when he came around here the other night, acting so friendly."

He sat on the edge of Ryan's bed, the anger gone from his face. "Listen, kid, I think we understand each other well enough that we don't have to play tag with words. I'm too old and slow to pull the kind of inside jobs I did when I was young. And I can't afford to bring any unwanted attention to myself. There're still one or two things out there that haven't reached their statutes of limitations. I've got a good set-up here. I'm working on getting disability payments, and your mother has a solid job. I'll go along with you this one last time so we can keep to the status quo, but if your mother gets so upset she can't work, all bets are off. I've filled my parental quota of covering for your sorry ass."

"You're right, Pops. We understand each other perfectly. If breaking and entering is the best they can do, I'm safe. I can beat that rap, and it's the only way I can get my life back. But I'm going to need a lawyer, and the sooner the better. You and Mom will have to hire him. I've got enough money saved to pay you back. I just can't let anyone know I have it."

The room had lightened enough for Ryan to see his father's face. One glance told him how serious his father was. "I wouldn't trust you to pay for your own condoms. Give me the cash first, we'll call it a retainer. And I *will* be charging interest. Now, let's wake your mother and see if we can keep our stories straight."

"Sure thing, Pops. But while you're in there, you might want to hide that bracelet I gave Mom for her birthday."

"Shit, boy. You're even dumber than I thought. Didn't I teach you never to take a souvenir?"

The next hours were the worst in Ryan's life. His mother cried, his father cursed, and the lawyer charged enough to make Ryan reconsider his pre-med major. He was fingerprinted, photographed, handcuffed, and led like a bull with a ring through his nose from one stinking shit hole to another.

The big cop was nowhere to be seen—maybe he'd been put out of action for good—but the skinny cop was there, watching every move he made. His lawyer kept the cop away from him, not even letting him in the same room. The cop had tried, he could tell that much, but so far, he hadn't had to answer any questions.

Every time a cell door slammed, he jumped. He told himself he'd be home in a few hours but fear gnawed at his gut. What if they had more evidence than he thought and the lawyer couldn't get him out? Should he have run when he had the chance? No, he had his life planned and hiding wasn't part of it. Best to beat this now and be more careful in the future.

Tears threatened, but he held himself together while they shackled him to a line of low class, bottom feeders and led him into the courtroom. The sight of his mother's tears freed his own. Only now, they might help him instead of threaten his safety.

He didn't have to pretend to be afraid when he stood before the judge. But the lawyer did his job and Ryan was granted bail.

His father whispered in his ear as the bailiff came to lead him away. "You better have enough stashed away to pay a bail bondsman, because I'm not risking my house as collateral that you won't run."

There went the rest of his nest egg.

Fortunately, he hadn't had time to get rid of Crystal Hudson's jewelry. He could at least have it melted down for the gold. That, or break into the bail bond office and take his money back.

Handcuffs dug into his wrists as he sat on a cold, cement bench, waiting for someone to release him. Cell doors clanged and sounds of human misery floated across the holding area. The inescapable stench of unwashed bodies had embedded itself into every surface of the room.

It was late afternoon, and he hadn't been offered any lunch, but he wouldn't have been able to eat it if he had. He needed to find a quiet place to sit and think about the rest of his life.

He couldn't spend it in a jail cell, he knew that. The noise, the smells, the lack of privacy, the general sense of…confinement. That didn't even take into consideration the type of lowlifes he'd be crammed in next to. How did people live like that? He'd heard that some criminals felt more at home in prison than on the street. Unbelievable.

Even a brief sentence would be the end of him. How would he ever be able to sleep, take a shower, pleasure himself? His mind would die of starvation. He already felt dirty. As a kid, he'd occasionally played in the dirt, gotten sweaty, but this was different. This went past his skin, into his bones.

But could he give up his secret pastime? What if he just went back to using his special skills on animals, would that be enough? Maybe occasionally spying on the unsuspecting. No, that would never satisfy him, now that he'd tasted blood.

Getting out of this situation was his only hope and removing Hudson and Derrick had been the right thing to do. Should he keep going with the big cop or the witness? He'd have to think about that.

Noah squinted at the mid-morning sun as he opened the back door and his sister pushed her way inside, her arms full. *Please God, not another casserole.*

"I brought you a casserole for later. I'll just put it on the table so you'll remember it and not stick it in the freezer." She gave him a quick kiss on the cheek.

Sweet Pea ran in and stood on her hind legs, sniffing the air. The casserole did smell pretty good. He didn't let that fool him; he'd tasted Rachelle's casseroles before. Her kids looked healthy, well fed, but they had been eating her cooking all their lives. They probably didn't know any better. And her husband—he considered pepper to be one of the major food groups, so he'd destroyed his taste buds years ago.

"Aren't you supposed to be using those crutches?" She cocked her head to the side and studied him.

After Conner called her yesterday, it had taken an act of Congress to get Rachelle and the doctor to agree to let him go home. But his knee wasn't broken, just some pulled ligaments, and he didn't intend to lie in bed, out of the action.

He was wearing sweat pants with one leg cut off above the knee. A knee that was swollen, discolored, and supported by an elastic brace. He knew he hadn't shaved, he couldn't remember if he'd brushed his hair. Not a look that was going to make her feel comfortable enough to leave him alone.

He limped across the kitchen, leaning on the counter for support. "I'm not putting any weight on my knee, and I use the crutches most of the time." He had to get her out of here, fast, and if he told her how much the crutches hurt his sore arm, she'd never go. There were things in this house he didn't want her to see.

He'd spent too many years protecting her. He didn't plan to stop now.

She set the Pyrex bowl and a bag of groceries on the table. "Right. That's why the swelling is going down so fast."

She disappeared around the corner and returned with his crutches, handing them to him without a word.

"Thanks, Sis. I appreciate the food. I know how busy you are. I'll help you put it away and you can get back to your girls. I'll be able to drive by tomorrow." *Not according to the doctor, but what did that overeducated prick know?* It was his left knee. If he could bend it enough to get behind the wheel, he was good to go.

"Not so fast. Frank took the girls to that princess movie and then they'll go to the park. You have me for the whole day, and I have plans for how we'll spend it."

And he'd thought the casserole was bad.

She reached into the sack and pulled out a box of plastic garbage bags. "Don't groan or roll your eyes at me. We're going to clean out your room. It's time. You are not responsible for Betsy's death. Whatever you did that slowed her down, that's not what killed her."

"How do you…"

"I can read you like a book, Noah. I always have. Anyone who ever met the two of you knew how much you loved her, but I've seen you deal with grief before, and this isn't grief, it's guilt, remorse. And I've seen you deal with that, too. Remember, you weren't the only one who sat up nights with Mother."

He opened his mouth, but she kept talking as if she didn't notice. "You can keep a few items that have special meaning for you. Betsy had nice things, and there're people out there that need them. Now, follow me, but *use your crutches.*"

Five minutes later, he was propped up on his bed, his bad leg stretched out in front of him and Sweet Pea by his side. Rachelle pulled out dresses and slacks and shirts, occasionally holding one up and telling about the shopping trip the two of them had taken when Betsy bought this one, or reminding him of the restaurant they'd all gone to when she wore that one.

Only once did he ask her to put something back. She looked at him questioningly, but the memory was too private to share.

"You can keep it, but I'm going to put it in your bottom

drawer. I don't want you mooning over it every time you open the closet door. What do you want me to do with her jewelry?"

"You take it. I'd love to see you wear it. Anything you can't use, let the girls play dress-up with. There's nothing special I want to keep." Well, there was one thing, but it was on the arm of a no good, thieving murderer's mother and he planned to get it back real soon.

Noah glanced at the stack of folded clothes, expecting to feel pain. Instead, he felt relief. Talking about Betsy, remembering, reliving their good times with Rachelle, had lifted a weight from his soul.

Why had he thought it so painful to say her name out loud? Why had he worked so hard to avoid his sister, the one person left in the world who cared about him? That he cared about. Well, the girls, Emma and Iris, and also Conner and Jeannie. But the list was small, and he'd done his best to push them away in case they figured out what he was planning.

Maybe it was time to reconsider the way he'd been living his life.

"This wasn't nearly as hard as I'd expected. Thanks, Sis. I truly couldn't have done it without you."

"I'm glad you thought it was easy, because what comes next is the hard part." She pivoted and left the room.

Oh, shit. Where is she going?

He heard her open the closet in his office and his heart stopped. He struggled to get off the bed, but Sweet Pea was in his lap and his leg tangled in the sheet. Rachelle's footsteps sounded in the hallway.

When she appeared in the doorway holding the violin, he couldn't breathe. She doesn't know anything, he tried to tell himself. She was only seventeen, just a kid.

"It's time to get rid of this." Her eyes weren't smiling, and her voice didn't leave any room for doubt.

"That's worth a lot of money. It'll pay for college for the girls." He tried to stall, wait for her to give away a clue.

"It's not your responsibility to pay for my kids' education. Frank and I will take care of that." Her voice took on a hard edge.

"Yeah, but Frank—"

"Frank what? Had to borrow some money when Emma was born? How long are you going to hold that over our heads? He paid it back. We were young. He has a good job now." She wasn't shouting, but it was close.

"I want to help take care of the girls. They're all I have." This was spiraling out of control. Just like he knew it would. Exactly why he kept them at arm's length.

"Then help them by being there for them. If you hang onto this, you won't be. What do you think it will do to them to have the uncle they love so much in jail for the rest of his life?"

CHAPTER
TWENTY-FIVE

TALK ABOUT SAVED by the bell, Noah had never been so glad to hear the phone ring in his life. He thought it might be Conner, but he never expected Laurel Bledsoe.

"Are you okay, Noah? I looked for you among all those people at Crystal's house, but Detective Craw... Conner said you were home ill. Your bite didn't get infected, did it?"

"No, my hand is fine. I just had a little fall and banged my knee. I'll be back at work tomorrow. So Conner was at Crystal's?" What was his partner keeping from him now, and why?

"Oh, there are dozens of people at her house. Guys in suits, guys in uniforms, people in paper jumpsuits. I don't know what all they're doing. There's a van that says CSU, squad cars, regular cars, lights flashing. I haven't seen Gary."

"How long has this been going on?" And he thought he had things to make up to Conner. All bets were off now. That promise he'd made to share all information? As far as he was concerned, Conner was the one who'd broken it.

"I'm not sure. I just drove up and they were here."

"Thanks for the update, Laurel. I better check with Conner." He hit disconnect before she had time to answer.

Rachelle stared at him, her eyes big and her mouth partly open. Had he said Laurel's name out loud? Damn, he didn't know.

"Got your keys, Sis? I need you to give me a ride."

"Don't brush me off like that. We still have things to talk about." She held the violin in one hand, and the bow in the other.

"We can talk in the car. But first, I need you to help me put my pants on. This is work and I have to go." He took the violin and bow from Rachelle's hand and slipped them under his bed.

Ten minutes later, sweat pooling at the back of his neck, he looked presentable. If he hadn't lost weight over the last few months, Rachelle would never have been able to slip his slacks over his brace. The pain when she moved his leg was almost unbearable, but he kept his face impassive. If she had any idea how much the slightest movement hurt, she'd refuse to drive him.

The aroma of her casserole greeted him as he hobbled into the kitchen. How could something that smelled so good taste so bad? Had he eaten any lunch? Too bad, he'd get something later.

Sweet Pea followed them into the kitchen, so at least he didn't have to chase her. He dropped fresh papers on the floor without bending over. "Let's go. I need to get moving before they finish whatever it is they're doing."

"Just a minute. Let me put the casserole in the fridge. You can heat it up again later. Are you sure you can get a ride home?"

He'd never be able to get rid of that casserole. It would follow him forever, like a bad debt. He wouldn't eat it, he couldn't feed it to Pea, it would probably clog the disposal. Maybe he could give it to Conner. That back-stabbing SOB deserved it. No, it might make Jeannie sick.

"I can always get a ride. A gold shield isn't worth much money, but it will buy you a ride every time."

They started for Rachelle's car and his heart sank. Her silver Kia sat in his driveway, laughing at him. He'd never be able to get his leg in that thing. "You want to take my truck?"

"No, then I'd have to get it back to you. Don't worry, I have plenty of gas."

Gas wasn't what he was worried about.

She clicked her opener, and the doors unlocked with an audible *pop*. Before moving to the driver's side, she opened the passenger door and moved the seat back. He relaxed as he saw the seat slide back farther than he would have imagined. She propped his crutches in the rear while he eased himself into the cramped area. So far, so good. If she didn't make any sudden stops, he might be okay.

"Don't think you're going to skate on this one. " Rachelle kept her eyes on the road, but he could feel her anger. "We're not through discussing this. You cannot keep that violin any longer. Get rid of it, now, today. And for Heaven's sake, don't try to sell it. I wouldn't touch that money, it's blood money. Even if it was the right thing to do."

The entrance to Hudson's cul-de-sac was cordoned off, but Noah flashed his badge and the silver Kia pulled up in front of the now teeming mansion. Squad cars, forensic vans, and unmarked cruisers waited, some with lights flashing, others dark and silent.

It was the sight of the coroner's wagon, parked discreetly to the side, that sent Noah's heart slamming against his ribs.

Conner was nowhere in sight, which suited Noah just fine. It gave Rachelle time to drive off. Made it harder for Conner to send him home.

He flashed his badge again to a couple of newbies and made his way inside. Conner had his back turned, directing a CSU tech toward the fireplace. Something nasty had burned in there. Something rubber or plastic. Shoes?

The whole room had an acrid smell that burned his eyes. The house was cold, only slightly warmer than the outside air. That door must have been open for hours.

His crutches caught on a throw rug and he cursed softly, causing Conner to twist around.

"Tell me you weren't dumb enough to drive here with your knee in that condition." Conner sighed, resignation coating his voice.

"Rachelle brought me." Crammed in that little car with a knee that didn't bend, he'd rather have walked.

"I don't suppose you'd have come inside if she hadn't already left."

Noah didn't bother to answer. "So what happened here? Our little friend still cleaning up?"

"Or a robbery gone bad. Lots of stuff missing." Conner motioned around the room. A decorative shelf sat empty. Noah didn't remember what had been on it, just that it was something gaudy and expensive looking.

Heat rose up the back of Noah's neck and he struggled to keep his voice in check. "Where the fuck was his protection?"

"Two officers patrolled the grounds, then did a complete

walk-through, checking every door and window. After that, they did a drive-by once an hour. That's all somebody upstairs would allow. Nothing looked amiss until the maid came running out and flagged them down."

Noah remembered the woman from the night she served them coffee. At least she hadn't been hurt. "Where was she when the shit hit the fan?"

Conner pointed with his chin toward the garage. "She lives out back, but it was her night off and she spent it with her kids. Then she had a dentist appointment this morning. Didn't get back till after lunch. And yes, I've already checked with her family and the dentist."

"You can tell the lieutenant about this one. I wasn't here." Would the outcome have been any different if he hadn't been laid up? Probably not, but he'd never know for sure.

"Jansen already knows. He came by earlier."

"What'd he say?"

Conner drew out his words in imitation of Jansen's East Texas drawl. "You better hope the press doesn't get wind of this or you'll spend the next hurricane standing outside directing traffic."

"Yeah, I'll bet that's all he said. My ears were on fire just riding over here. He doesn't look like much, but he has an impressive vocabulary. Don't sweat it. He knows that decision was made higher up. He may fuss, but he'll have your back."

"That doesn't bring Hudson back." Conner's shoulders slumped slightly and he didn't look Noah in the eyes.

Yup, that's exactly how I felt about Derrick. They were murdering scum, but being responsible for another person's death stings like hell.

Noah balanced on one foot and raked a hand across his chin. He still hadn't shaved and his face was starting to itch. "Why didn't the fool leave town, or at least go to a hotel? It's not like he couldn't afford it and the judge would have given permission in a case like this."

"I suggested that. He didn't want to leave his house. Said he'd invested in the best security available. That it was better than having ten cops sitting beside him. Then someone disconnected the alarm and substituted an innocuous feed in a continuous loop. The same moth flits by the security light every three minutes."

Conner kicked a numbered forensic marker across the room where it hit the leg of a bar stool and spun around. "Fuck. I can't believe I let this happen."

"What do you mean, you let it happen? You warned him, arranged as much security as our budget allowed, even suggested he go to a hotel. Short of locking him in a holding cell, he was as safe as you could make him."

Heat built in Noah's blood and he wished he could kick something, but couldn't figure out how to manage it on crutches. "He did this to himself the minute he started searching the Internet for someone to kill his wife. You lay down with dogs, you get up with fleas. Only in this case, I'm assuming he didn't get up at all."

"He didn't get up, but he sure as hell fought back. Several bullets struck the wall. Probably too much to ask that any hit Ryan. Anyway, isn't that what I told you about Derrick?"

Noah blinked twice as Conner's words sunk in. He tried in vain to think of a logical argument, but none came to him. "In that case, we were both right. Now, show me where this confrontation took place."

Conner led, the slap of his shoes echoing through the protective paper booties onto the marble floor. Noah followed, his crutches making a muffled "thump," while his feet swooshed a half second later. His mind swirled, leaving him too deep in thought to speak.

Noah paused outside the door to Hudson's inner office as his gaze wandered over the scene. His mind filed away bits of information. There'd be plenty of crime scene photos for him to study later, but they would be cold and dry. Antiseptic.

In person, he could judge how long the blood had been pooled on the floor by its color and texture. If its scent still filled the air. If the smell of gunpowder still burned his nose.

Noah leaned in to study the room, but the overturned file cabinets blocked his view. He sat on one cabinet and swung his legs over, then did the same to the second. This was getting old. It was one thing when his bum knee gave him trouble at home, but now it was interfering with his investigation.

The room was small, with little ventilation. He took a deep breath but caught only the faintest whiff of gunpowder. The coppery smell of blood was present, but not overwhelming. The blood splatters and the smaller drops were dry. Only the one under Hudson's head remained damp.

"What's the doc say about time of death?"

"He doesn't know bupkus. This cold air screwed up his measurements. It might have been right after the maid left at seven, or a couple of hours ago."

"Not a couple of hours. Blood's too dry. Closer to seven last night, eight at the latest." Noah lifted his head and looked around. "What's with this cold air anyway? If the front door was standing open, shouldn't the patrol car have seen it?"

"Back door and windows are open and the AC is on. Gas in the fireplace was going full blast, but the heat went right up the chimney."

"Any sign of a break in?" Noah still hadn't moved, his eyes studying every corner of the room.

"Nope. Killer waltzed in here smooth as a silk dress. Unless Hudson opened the door for him. But why would he do that? We warned him Ryan was cleaning up."

Noah peered at the empty accordion folder, half out of an open file drawer. "Because he thought he'd have plenty of warning with all his fancy security. He decided to set a trap. Had a gun hidden in the folder instead of the money. He made the biggest mistake of his life; he thought he was smart enough to take on a professional killer."

He gazed around the room, taking in the blood spatter on the walls. "Killer had to be covered in blood. If that stink I smelled in the fireplace was his clothes, what'd you suppose he went home in?"

CHAPTER
TWENTY-SIX

A N HOUR PASSED before the forensics team finished documenting the scene and the coroner's office could move the body. File cabinets were shifted and Noah got his first good look at Hudson's body. Some mortician was going to earn his money with this job.

It killed Noah to admit weakness in front of not only Conner and the whole forensics team, but he couldn't stand up any longer. If he rested his body on his crutches, his underarms felt like boils. If he held himself up, his hands, especially the still tender one, ached. He could only balance on one foot for so long before he began to sway dangerously.

He sank into the soft leather of Hudson's expensive desk chair, its fragrance wafting up as he leaned back. Conner glanced at him but didn't say anything. Shit. He might not comment, but he'd definitely noticed.

The chair had a familiar feel. Noah twisted his head to study the back and arm rests. It was the same chair Betsy had bought for him, only adjusted for a shorter man. Damn. How much had she paid for that thing?

She claimed to have bought the chair with her signing bonus when she started at the new school. Music teachers for special ed kids were both rare and disposable. Hard to find, but the first ones to be cut during a budget crisis. A shame too, because music helped them in so many ways.

"You still with me, partner?"

Noah glanced up to find Conner standing over him. The tips of his ears felt hot. Conner had caught him not only resting, but also daydreaming. He needed to get his act together, fast.

"Right behind you. Shall we head upstairs and see if we can follow our visitor's trail?"

"Can you manage those stairs?" Conner asked.

Noah glared at him but didn't answer. Hell, he didn't know the answer.

He experimented with several methods, but eventually placed both crutches under one arm, grabbed the railing, and gritted his teeth. Sweat had beaded on his forehead and down his back by the time he reached the top.

Conner was already surveying the master bedroom. "Looks like both the Hudsons had cash or valuables stashed in their own secret hidey-hole." He pointed to the ripped-up carpet and overturned drawers. "No telling how much he got away with."

"Look in here." Noah nodded toward an elaborate bathroom with gold fixtures and plush rugs. Embroidered hand cloths lay next to the sink, but the towel rods by the glass enclosed shower hung empty. An empty bleach container lay on its side. "Do you think he showered?"

"Shit, probably took the towels with him or tossed them

in the fireplace. No forensics left behind in here. Both closets are such a mess, it'd be impossible to know if any clothes are missing."

"If we find anything suspicious, maybe the maid could identify them. Okay, I've had enough. I'm through pretending we don't know who did this. Let's get busy and see if we can find him. How long can a nineteen-year-old kid with bright red hair and a voice like a squeaking door stay hidden? Somebody knows where he is." He'd had enough. Crystal was dead, Derrick was undoubtedly dead, now Hudson was dead. Time to stop playing around and put this guy away.

"I know exactly where he is: home with Mama."

"What the fuck are you talking about? You know where he is and we're just standing here?" Blood pounded in Noah's ears and his chest felt tight.

Conner shook his head. "Cool it. We can't touch him. He turned himself in early this morning and he's already out on bail. We're not allowed to talk to him without his lawyer present."

"Then let him get his fucking lawyer, because I plan to talk to him." Noah's heart raced and his teeth hurt from clenching them so hard.

"Not today, you won't. You're off duty."

Noah sputtered, but Conner held up his hand. "I won't be talking to him today either. I'm under direct orders. You're going home and I'm headed back to the office to start a new murder book on Hudson."

"Shit, at the rate this guy's going, he'll soon have his own wing at the library." Noah wanted to pace, but it was unsatisfying on crutches.

"That's why it's so important that we do this thing by the

book. Jansen's waiting for me back at headquarters. He doesn't want some defense attorney to find room for any questions. One thing I did right, maybe the only thing, was word the warrant for Ryan's arrest so that I could confiscate anything suspicious I saw in plain sight. His mother had a bottle of sleeping pills on her bedside table. By late tomorrow afternoon, we'll know if they match the powder found on your shoe."

"I'll be in first thing in the morning." This was *his* case. Just let them try to keep him out of it.

"If you show up on crutches, Jansen will send you home. Or at least restrict you to the office." Conner's voice held a note or warning.

"I won't be on crutches. And you did plenty of things right."

One of the forensic techs offered to drive Noah home, but needed to finish cataloging the evidence first. Noah decided to wait at Laurel's house. She deserved to know what was going on. That was the only reason he hobbled across the lawn in her direction.

He tapped on the back door and was rewarded with her familiar smile. Exactly what he needed to wash the ugliness of the day away.

"Hi, Noah, I hoped you'd stop by." Her eyes took in his crutches and grew bigger. "Are you okay? I though you said it was only a little fall. Don't just stand there. Come in and sit down. Does it hurt? Is there anything I can do?"

He grinned. Hearing her rattle on felt like home. "I'm fine. Trying to keep my weight off my knee so the swelling will go down. It doesn't hurt."

It hurt like a son-of-a-bitch, but no reason to tell her that. "Thanks for calling to let me know about the trouble next door. I'm supposed to be off duty, so no one bothered to notify me."

"So you're off duty?" She stopped in the act of pouring coffee.

"That's what I've been told. Several times today."

"In that case, how about a shot of Bailey's in your coffee?" She set the cup down and stood on her toes to reach an upper cabinet.

Noah smiled as her sweater rode up several inches to expose pale skin. "That ought to warm me up. It was almost freezing at Hudson's house."

"Can you tell me what's going on over there, or is it confidential? I don't want to get you in trouble." She placed a cup of coffee and the bottle of Bailey's in front of him and he poured a shot in both their cups.

He was already in trouble and he'd told her too much from the beginning. No point in stopping now. "I guess you've already figured out that Gary Hudson was killed sometime last night or early this morning."

She played absently with her coffee cup. "Poor Gary. Despite what happened to Crystal, I hope he didn't suffer."

He suffered. Probably not for as long as he deserved. "No. It was quick. He didn't see it coming."

A tear glistened at the corner of her eye. "What about Crystal's brother? I want to go see him. She was going to get him into one of those lockdown treatment centers. Is there any way I can help him?"

How could she and Betsy be so different yet so much alike?

Betsy had been tall, with dark hair in a mass of curls that she hated and he loved. Laurel was short, almost tiny, with blonde hair that fell past her shoulders. The color might have a few highlights, but it matched her skin and eyes, so was undoubtedly natural.

Betsy had come from nothing and had scrambled all her life to make something of herself. Laurel had come from money and never wanted for anything. Yet both cared about other people and did their best to be a good friend. And both women could smile at him and make him feel whole again. Almost, but not quite, clean.

"I'll check into it and let you know. You don't want to go to the jail by yourself. I'll take you after I talk to the Assistant DA. She's a friend of mine. She might be willing to cut him some slack." Noah felt himself flush. She used to be a friend of his. He wasn't sure now.

That relationship was already dying out when he met Betsy at Conner and Jeannie's wedding. As best man and maid of honor, they'd spent a lot of time together. They were married long before Conner's first anniversary.

Had Laurel noticed his stutter? Oh yeah, she'd noticed, but why did he care?

"Is she the one who drove you over here? I saw your friend let you out and drive away. I guess I ruined your day off."

"My friend?" He hadn't set eyes on that Assistant DA in over a year. "You mean Rachelle? She's my sister. She'd stopped by with a get-well casserole when you called, so I asked her to give me a ride."

The corners of Laurel's mouth twitched slightly. "Sure, I could see the resemblance from here."

Resemblance? Not likely. Rachelle was beautiful, inside and out.

The forensic tech tapped on the door. "We're all finished over there, Detective. Whenever you're ready."

Noah stood and reached for his crutches when Laurel's eyes grew wide. "I didn't think to ask how Gary died. Was it the same guy who killed Crystal? I was here last night. Asleep. Am I in danger?"

All the ugliness of Hudson's death swept over him. "I can't imagine why he'd be interested in you, but if you see a short, butt-ugly, red-headed kid with thick glasses and a squeaky voice, keep your door locked and call me right away. In fact, don't stay here at all, please. Stay with your mother, or a friend, for a couple of nights. Just until I can get him put away." *Or put him down.*

This reckless fool didn't care who he hurt. Look at Crystal, Derrick, even Hudson. All the others he'd taken out for a few bucks and the thrill.

If he hurt Laurel, he'd go after the guy with his bare hands.

The tech looked like he hadn't been out of school more than fifteen minutes. He drove a big SUV, with plenty of room in the back for his supplies, and room in the front for Noah's leg. The drive would have been pleasant if the kid hadn't kept trying to chat about the case. But Noah remained silent, his mind going back over every piece of evidence.

Without Hudson to testify, did they have enough to convict Ryan? Rosaria's testimony suddenly became crucial, but she was in hiding and might be afraid to come out when she learned what happened to Hudson.

He'd tried to keep her name a secret, but Ryan seemed to stay one step ahead of him on everything.

The tech hit a speed hump and Noah grunted. Without twisting his head, he cut the kid a dirty look and went back into his trance. Even the proof that Ryan had been in his house didn't count for much when the Yates admitted he'd visited them many times.

He thought about his vow to take Ryan out by himself. He'd been down that road before. Could something be both right and wrong at the same time? No, wrong was wrong, no matter what Rachelle claimed. And he knew it. That's why his conscience had never let him forget.

Noah had the car door open before the kid had rolled to a complete stop. "Thanks for the ride. I owe you one."

He hurried out of the car before the tech could offer to come in and help him get settled. Too many people had been in his house lately. His sanctuary was beginning to feel like a public coffee shop.

He hadn't eaten since a piece of toast for breakfast, and Laurel's coffee with a splash of Bailey's hadn't been a good idea on an empty stomach. He opened the refrigerator and Rachelle's casserole stared back at him. No, not that, anything but that.

Why hadn't he gone to the store while he was still mobile? He scooped a small serving of the casserole onto a paper plate and warmed it in the microwave. He had to admit it smelled good. Maybe her cooking was improving.

One bite confirmed it was the same tofu and unknown ingredients she always made; still convinced that red meat played a part in their mother's cancer. At least it stuck to his ribs. It would probably still be sticking to his ribs the day he died.

Sweet Pea whined and scratched on his leg. "No way, Pea. I

like you too much to give you this stuff."

The rest of the evening he sat with his leg propped up and an ice pack on his knee. That swelling *would* be down by morning.

CHAPTER TWENTY-SEVEN

NOAH USED HIS mother's cane when he hobbled into work the next day. He'd discovered it in a back closet. Most likely an antique, it was made of polished rosewood with a brass handle in the shape of a miniature dog. Long, sharp muzzle, ears that hung down, and wide set eyes. Easy to grip. Cool against his sore hand. Walking with the cane was bad enough, but the general fussiness of something so obviously made for a woman drove him over the edge. He might as well be wearing one of her dresses.

She had been a tall woman before illness shrunk her, a commanding stage presence with the voice of an angel, but she hadn't been nearly as tall as Noah. He hunched slightly to one side, unable to put all his weight on that leg. His hand, almost well before his fall, protested with every step. He tried switching the cane to the other side, but couldn't get the rhythm right, each step awkward and out of balance.

If he could reach his desk before Jansen saw him, he'd have

it made.

"Look who we have here," Earl the Pearl said, his velvet voice echoing in the almost empty room. "If it isn't Hopalong Daugherty."

Jansen came to the door of his office and groaned audibly. "Turn around and go home, Daugherty. We *are* capable of running an investigation without you."

"I'm fine, Loo. Knee's almost back to normal. I won't be in anyone's way." *Liar, liar, pants on fire.*

He'd just lied to his boss with a straight face and not a twinge of conscience. What did that say about him? Nothing he was proud of.

Jansen stared at him and Noah could almost see the wheels turning while the lieutenant decided whether to call his bluff. Finally, he shrugged. "Okay, you can stay, but you're on office duty only. Don't go cowboying off somewhere. If you do anything to screw up this case, it'll be your ass that's fried." With that, the lieutenant spun on his heels and slammed his office door.

The squad judged the depth of Jansen's anger by how loud the blinds on his door rattled when he shut it. On a one to five scale, this was a solid four.

Noah reached his desk and sank into his chair with a heavy sigh. He'd give anything for a cup of coffee, but he didn't have the strength to make it to the break room or a free hand to carry it back to his desk.

He closed his eyes and tried to get his breathing under control. *Man, I swear I can smell coffee. I must want it bad. I know I'm dreaming because it smells like the good stuff.*

One eye opened and he saw Conner setting a Starbucks cup on his desk. He might consider forgiving Conner for leaving him in the hospital with no pants and no cell phone.

"I figured you'd be in early. Hoping to get to your desk before Jansen saw you. Did you make it?"

"I would have, if Earl had kept his mouth shut. I'm on desk duty, but I haven't been sent home." Someday, he'd get back at Earl, but not till this case was just a bad memory.

"Don't worry, you aren't going to miss anything. This'll be an inside day. The ME won't do the post before tomorrow morning and if the lab has those reports back to us before they close tonight, I'll eat that cardboard cup."

Noah held the cup to his nose and inhaled deeply. *Heaven.* "Even this cardboard would taste better than the vending machine coffee."

Conner slammed his hand on his desk. "If only we could have kept that weasel in jail. He was the most miserable looking thing I've ever seen. He even cried in front of the judge at his bail hearing. One night behind bars and we'd have broken him. But now, home with mama or back in school, his mind will never stop spinning, coming up with new plans to cover his ass."

"Wait." Noah sat his cup down so hard coffee splashed on his shirt sleeve. "You were there? You saw him at his bail hearing? Did he see you?"

"See me? I tried to interview him, but he kept his lips locked tight. His lawyer was the only one doing any talking. I came on as strong as I could without giving away any information, but his lawyer wasn't fooled. Without Hudson to testify, we've got nothing but entering your home. Even that counts for zip because the only prints we could positively identify were on the ceiling panel and your back door. They could have been there for years."

Noah's heart lurched. *Fuck, why didn't I paint the kitchen before we moved in like Betsy suggested?*

"Conner, think about this for a minute." Noah tried to keep his voice calm. "He's already tried to take me out, he got rid of Derrick, and now Hudson. Before yesterday, you weren't even a blip on his radar screen. Now he knows you. You aren't safe. Jeannie isn't safe."

Conner could feel the blood drain from his face. *Shit, Jeannie.* He grabbed his cell phone. Man, he hated to call her at school. He had to go through the switchboard and that snooty secretary acted as if he'd asked to speak to the Dalai Lama.

He usually timed his calls for her off period, although she'd assured him that if he needed her, he should call anytime. He glanced at the time icon on his phone. Ten minutes until her next break. Could he wait?

Hell, no.

His hands shook and he had to set the phone down while he wiped them on his pants. The secretary must have heard something in his voice because she connected him without her usual caustic comment.

"Hi, honey, something's come up, and I'm going to pick you up from school in fifteen minutes. Tell them you won't be back for the rest of the week. Can you call your folks and say you're coming for a visit? Maybe just say you want to spend some time with them before the baby comes?"

The silence on the other end of the phone stretched longer than was comfortable. If his heart didn't slow down soon, he'd have to ask the ambulance driver to swing by and pick her up.

When Jeannie finally answered, her voice had a hard edge. "The answer is no on so many levels. If there's some kind of danger, we're not putting my parents in harm's way without a warning. And I'm not running off to hide and leaving you to face it alone. We'll check into a hotel. But before we do that, we need to have a long talk about what's going on. Pull up in front of the door to the school. I'll run out. Once I'm in the car, don't even bother to say hello until you've explained *exactly* what's happening."

He closed the phone and slipped it back into his pocket. How could all the things he loved about her be the same ones that drove him crazy?

"How'd it go?" Noah didn't even pretend not to eavesdrop.

"About like you'd expect. Think what Betsy would have said, then double it." Ah, fuck. Now he'd done it. He'd said the B word. How could he have let that slip out? He stole a glance at Noah, but his partner was smiling. Chuckling even.

"That bad, huh? Do you want me to come with you for protection?"

"From Jeannie or Ryan?" He still didn't trust the change in Noah. It felt like waiting for the other shoe to drop.

"Jeannie. You could handle Ryan in your sleep."

A year ago, he'd have made some sarcastic remark about how well Noah had handled Ryan while he was sleeping, but an improved Noah still wasn't the old Noah, so Conner bit back the comment.

"It'll end up costing me big bucks, but I'll try to talk her into staying in the hotel tomorrow, enjoying a massage, getting her hair done. I'll have her convinced by the time I get back. Damn, I wish I'd kissed that Blarney Stone when we were in Ireland."

Conner dropped his head into his hands.

"Don't worry, one of your ancestors did and that was enough to do the job. I've seen you talk a squirrel out of his nuts, though Jeannie might be a harder sell. Tell her you think it's a bunch of hooey, but I insisted. Or better yet, tell her Jansen insisted. Hey, let's go talk to the old fart. He *will* insist and then you won't be lying. I know what a piss poor job you do of it when it comes to Jeannie."

Noah jumped out of his chair and headed for the lieutenant's office before Conner had time to stand. He didn't make it halfway through his report before Jansen insisted Conner move Jeannie somewhere safe.

"I'll be back as soon as I can. I want to go over every scrap of evidence we have, be ready to move when the reports come back from the lab in the morning." Conner grabbed his coat and headed for the elevator, already planning the fastest route to Jeannie's school.

Noah snatched up his cane and hobbled behind him. "Stay with Jeannie tonight. You can go over the nonresident cases on your laptop. Warn me first if you find something. I'd hate like hell for some other jurisdiction to snatch him from under our noses. I'll stay here and examine everything we've got. Maybe I'll get lucky, find something new."

At the elevator, Conner stopped, his hand on the down button. "What about Rachelle and her family? He wouldn't go after them, would he?"

Like a bad case of déjà vu, Conner watched Noah as the blood drained from his face and he fumbled for his cell phone, his hands shaking.

Finally, Ryan's mother had quit fussing over him and left for the grocery store. She might even lower herself to cook tonight. Pops was in his usual spot; parked in front of the TV.

Ryan closed his bedroom door softly, no sense alerting his father, and booted up his laptop. Time to troll the cop's computer. See if he could learn anything new.

His keyboard clicked rapidly as he typed in the cop's password, but Pops would never hear it over the television. He had the volume so high, Ryan could feel the vibration each time Han Solo shot down another Empire Star Ship.

Damn. No new information on the case. Just the same draft of a warrant listing an unknown witness. If he could find that fucking witness, he could make this all go away.

Could he have hidden the information in some innocent sounding folder? Might as well check. This was more fun than window peeping.

Fuck, where'd all that money come from? Cops were supposed to be broke, he *was* broke last June. Must have been when he bought the house. So where did it all come from? Ah, insurance.

Ryan scrolled forward. Damn, the man had never touched a penny of it. He ought to at least buy himself a decent suit. *Well, if he doesn't want it, I do. All I need to do is figure out where to transfer it so it can't be followed.*

He had just finished setting up an account in the Cayman's when he felt his father's hot beer breath on his neck.

"Don't be stingy, send a little of that my way."

Ryan jumped, almost knocking his chair over. Shit, Pops had planned this from the beginning, turning the TV up so high, he couldn't hear him come in. There went half his profit. The old man might be past his prime, but he still had a mind like a bank vault door. He'd try, but he didn't see his father falling for it.

"We'll leave it here till the heat dies down. If you start spending now, bells will go off all over town." Ryan hit enter and watched the money magically move from Houston to the Caribbean in less time than it took Pops to send another beer laden breath into his face.

"Good one, son. I'd have been disappointed if you didn't try." The hand that had been resting gently on his shoulder began to squeeze, gradually tighter and tighter until pain shot down one arm and up his neck into his head. Acid rose in his mouth and Ryan cried out. His father loosened his grip.

"Now, let's set me up one of those nifty accounts and move half that total over to my name, or whatever identity I choose. Go slow. I want to learn how you do that."

Ryan's arm hung limp at his side. The army of hungry caterpillars eating his brain receded, millimeter by millimeter.

"Take your time. Whenever you feel up to it." Pops patted him on the shoulder and stinging ants crawled the length of his arm.

Ryan cleared his throat and struggled to raise his arm to the keyboard. "Here Pops, let me show you how to do it."

Pops leaned over his shoulder, grunting occasionally and asking him to repeat a step once, but otherwise silent. When the transfer was complete, Pops gave what might pass for a smile and left the room.

If he was lucky, Pops would leave one or two hundred in the account to keep it open while he moved the rest to the new account he'd undoubtedly open immediately.

He wouldn't be able to follow the money to the new account unless he was sitting at Pops' computer. And that would never happen while Pops was still alive. The cop might be fool enough to use the same password for everything, but Pops wasn't.

Wait, wait, wait. The cop. The same password. Why hadn't he thought of that? The guy probably used the same password at his office. It might be possible to find the witness after all. Then he wouldn't have to run. Leave his comfortable life behind.

A hard hour working with an arm that was only now beginning to respond, and he'd broken through HPD's firewall and into the cop's office computer. Bingo. The same string of numbers he'd used at home. A date of some kind. A birthday? Anniversary? Who cared? He had it. A chuckle escaped before he clamped his lips together. He couldn't afford to alert his father.

He learned plenty about how the cop built a case with painstaking work and meticulous records, but no witness name. In a file marked 'Little Turd,' he found a new warrant for his arrest. *Cute, Detective Dickhead. Your turn will come.*

The warrant listed other cases he was suspected of; Galveston, Fort Bend, Sugarland. How had the flatfoot figured that out? Those jobs were clean.

Derrick. They were all the jobs he'd used Derrick on. None of the ones he'd done alone. Good, a decent lawyer could put all the blame on Derrick, who had obviously run when he felt the heat.

He scrolled down to the last page and his heart stopped. The Houston job. They'd found something on it. He couldn't tell what. And a lab report, connecting his mom's sleeping pills to a substance found in the cop's house.

He slammed his hand on his desk and the ants returned to

remind him of his mistake in trying to put one over on Pops. That fucking cop. He could trace all his troubles back to him.

He had to be ready to run in case he couldn't find that missing witness. There were things he couldn't bear to leave behind.

He snatched up his keys and backpack and started toward the front door. "Hey, Pops. I've got an errand to run. I'll be back in twenty minutes. You need me to do anything for you while I'm out?"

"You're not old enough to buy beer, so what good are you?"

Good enough to set you up so you can afford your own beer.

His hand rested on the doorknob when he heard Pops mutter, "Try not to get caught this time. You've done such an outstanding job of that so far."

All his treasures, his beautiful mementos. Ryan sat on his bed, caressing each item as he watched the door, making sure Pops hadn't seen him come home. Could he bear to part with them? He'd have to if he was going to run.

Maybe he could pare them down. Just keep the ones that meant the most to him. But which ones? He loved them all.

He fingered a tiny cat collar, listening to the bell tinkle. Certainly not this one. His first. He could still feel the silky fur, and the heart beating so fast. . . until it didn't beat at all.

No, he'd have to take them all. He'd save a small piece of Crystal Hudson's jewelry and sell the rest. With the money he'd saved, and now the cop's insurance, he'd be fine. He'd be even finer if Pops hadn't helped himself to half of it.

Shit. Thirty minutes with the old man's landline, and he'd have it back where it belonged. He glanced toward his open bedroom door and rolled his shoulder. Better not risk it.

He didn't need it anyway. Running was only a last option. Once he took care of the witness and that nosy cop, he'd be golden. They couldn't prove a thing.

That little dog would just be icing on the cake.

CHAPTER
TWENTY-EIGHT

SWEET PEA SCRAMBLED across the kitchen to meet Noah, her tail wagging. He bent over and scooped her up with one hand.

"How you doing, Pea? You miss me?" He set the take-out bag on the counter. "No hamburger for you tonight. You remember what the vet said." Sweet Pea cocked her head to one side. "So I got you chicken instead. Will that satisfy your majesty?"

The dog wiggled excitedly as the aroma of grilled chicken filled the room.

Noah carefully mixed the chicken breast with dog food and set her bowl on the mat, before unwrapping his own meal. "Want to tell me about your day, Pea? Any door-to-door salesmen come by? No cat prissed across our yard, did they? You must have done a good job of keeping them out."

The grilled chicken didn't taste too bad. He hadn't wanted to order a hamburger if Sweet Pea couldn't have one, and watching that pudgy teenager had reminded him that he'd better improve his own eating habits before criticizing others.

He leaned back and stretched out his leg. "My day wasn't so great. Our friendly neighborhood murderer is out on bail and living down the street from us. I had to talk Rachelle and her family into bunking in with Frank's folks for a few days. You can guess how that went over."

Sweet Pea finished eating and tried to wipe her face on the mat.

"Conner and Jeannie are in seclusion. Even Laurel and Rosaria are hiding. One psychotic little twerp and half the city moved out of their homes. What do you think of that, Pea? We're the only ones dumb enough to stay home. I called two motels, but they wouldn't take dogs. We should be safe. He wouldn't dare try us again."

Sweet Pea belched.

"Yeah, I agree with you." This whole mess made him want to puke. Good people in hiding while that murderer sat at home, eating his mother's cooking.

Maybe I should call Laurel, check that she got to her mother's okay. He had her cell phone number. Now why did that make him smile? It was only conscientious police work. She had still been at home when he left.

He would change his clothes, get comfortable, then make the call. But only to be certain that the last of the little chicks he'd put in harm's way was now tucked away safely.

Noah hobbled to his feet. He'd leaned his cane against the table when he lifted Sweet Pea and now used it to cross the kitchen toward his crutches, waiting in the corner. His knee had held up fairly well for most of the day, but by afternoon it had started to swell. The skin felt tight and bending it was a bitch.

He slid the cane between the counter and the refrigerator, hooking the brass dog's snout over the countertop. Man, he hated going back to the crutches—they hurt his pride almost as much as his sore hand and arm—but he had to be able to walk without help tomorrow if he wanted to be in on the arrest. And the only way to accomplish that was to rest his knee tonight. Absolutely no weight on it until he reached the office tomorrow.

He maneuvered his way down the hall to his bedroom where he sat on the edge of the bed to change into sweats. When he stood to put his gun and badge away in the nightstand, he caught a glimmer of light reflecting from under the bed.

That damn violin. What was he going to do with it?

He remembered his mother's pleading as if it was yesterday instead of fifteen years ago. When the police notified them that someone had tried to hock his father's violin, they'd both assumed his murder was solved. But the evidence disappeared and no charges were filed.

She began to obsess about getting the instrument back. It had been in his father's family for several generations. She wanted Noah to have it, to hand it down to his kids.

Noah didn't care about the sentimental value—he was only twenty, and it was years before he met Betsy or considered having children of his own—but he needed the money it would bring to help pay for his mother's care.

Her health had declined rapidly and she seemed to lose the will to live. The pills the doctor had given her couldn't control the breakthrough pain that overcame her at night. He'd pleaded with the doctor for something stronger. The doctor had refused, claiming she might become addicted.

Addicted, who cared? She'd been dying and in pain.

He would sit up with her while she begged him to retrieve the violin, her voice that had thrilled millions, now only a hoarse whisper.

He hadn't been able to ease her pain, so he tried to ease her mind.

He'd gathered every penny he could scrape together—$1,178.00—and headed for the dump the guy lived in. Naively thinking he could buy the instrument back.

What a joke. Expecting the guy to hand over a violin worth a quarter of a million dollars, not to mention evidence of his part in a murder.

Noah shook his head. What a fool he'd been. Rachelle was right. Betsy had been right. That violin had brought his family nothing but sorrow. He could never bring the man back, but he could get rid of that evil talisman.

Grabbing his crutches, he hobbled into the living room. At Betsy's insistence, he'd laid out wood for a fire the day they'd moved in, ready for the first cold day of winter. She hadn't lived to see it and he hadn't had the heart to light it.

He used the butane lighter and the fire caught right away. All those years of scouting finally good for something. He watched as the blaze grew, filling the room with warmth.

Holding the violin between his knees, he removed the strings. His heart hammered against his ribs as he laid the bow on top of the burning logs. Then, holding his breath and closing his eyes, he smashed the violin across his good knee and tossed it in the fire.

The smell of burning rosin filled the room. The fire crackled, and snapped, and spit embers, but the violin disappeared as if it never existed. His throat tightened as he watched the flames.

He didn't need the daily reminder. If he couldn't remember that a man's life was worth more than a musical instrument, he was no better than the doped-up scum who murdered his father.

Ryan stowed each trinket in a zippered compartment inside his backpack. They didn't add much weight or volume and what else did he need, really?

He'd wasted an hour on his father's computer. The old man was sharper than he appeared, more twists and turns and name changes than Ryan would have thought possible. The money was now back in his account where it belonged. Add the cash Pops had stashed in an old shoe, and he could run in comfort for quite some time.

But he shouldn't have to run. He'd had a comfortable life here. Until his mother walked in on him, all his treasures spread out before him. She immediately spotted her bracelet, then she noticed Crystal Hudson's diamonds and gold. She started asking questions, her voice rising each time he didn't answer. When his father came in, he'd had no choice, he had to take steps. Could he have shut her up if he'd offered her a piece of jewelry? Too late to think of that now.

The one person who actually loved him, who believed every word he told her. Pops had been easy, but his mother, that had been hard.

It was all that fucking cop's fault. His life had started to fall apart the minute that big cop opened his mouth on TV. If he'd kept his nose in Houston where it belonged, Bellaire would still have their heads up their asses, and he'd be studying for his chemistry exam.

Pops would have said everything unraveled when he hit that patch of ice and fishtailed, losing the target but deciding to make the hit anyway without proper planning. But Pops didn't understand what it felt like when that itch came over him, the need that only one thing satisfied.

Anyway, Pops wasn't saying much of anything now, was he?

He left his backpack inside the front door. Fifteen minutes, twenty, and he'd be back for it. He glanced around the shabby room. Not much to look at, but it had been home. He might as well take Pops' car when he left. It was more dependable than his. No, the cop's big truck. He could almost feel the power that engine offered. Not like he'd be needing it any longer.

After the way Detective Dickhead screwed up his carefully planned life, he deserved whatever happened to him. And plenty was about to happen.

The back door creaked as he slid it open far enough to slip out. Cold night air caught his breath and turned it into fog. The moon hid behind thick clouds. His tennis shoes made no sound on the empty sidewalk.

Lights were still on in the house next door, but most of the neighborhood was dark. The cop had gone to bed at eleven-thirty last time he was there, so he should be about ready to turn in. Relaxed and with his guard down.

Ryan hugged the shadows as he made his way down the block to the cop's house, his excitement building as he reached the familiar yard. Good, lights were still on in some rooms. He slipped around to the side door. Did it matter if he left prints on the knob? Probably not at this point, but he covered his hand with the sleeve of his sweat shirt out of habit.

What the fuck? The garage door wouldn't budge. The SOB

had nailed it shut.

Like that would save him. Or that sorry excuse for a dog.

Ryan let himself through the gate and into the backyard, the soft ground almost silent beneath his feet. Winter bare trees allowed light to seep through the branches and he waited behind a large oak for the cop to open the door. Within five minutes, the back door swung wide, spilling light across a three-foot area of yard as the little mutt scooted out.

"Hurry it up, Sweet Pea. Don't let the cold air in." The cop yawned and stretched, standing on the back stoop. No sign that he had heard the gate open or that he was expecting anything.

Sweet Pea cocked her head as if waiting for him to join her.

"Not tonight. You're on your own. Managing even two stairs on crutches might as well be Everest."

Finally, back in fortune's good graces. About time his luck turned. The cop must have hurt himself when he fell over Professor Morgan. His biggest fear—the cop's size and strength—now abated. He could face him head on. So much more satisfying.

Pops would have called him a coward, but knowing your capabilities and acting within them was a sign of intelligence.

The dog squatted three feet from the door and rushed back inside, shivering.

Ryan grinned as the cop tried to turn on the small porch, hopping on one foot, the other held in the air.

He stepped out of the shadows, already feeling a tightness in his jeans. "Take your time," he said, pointing a pistol at the cop's head. "I'm in no hurry."

This was going to be fun.

CHAPTER
TWENTY-NINE

NOAH GLANCED OVER his shoulder at the sound of the high-pitched voice. Ah fuck. Why had he let his guard down? He took a deep breath, pulling in the night air. He needed to keep his head clear if he was going to get out of this alive.

The porch light reflected off the barrel of a gun—most likely a Glock, but it was hard to be sure with so little illumination.

Glocks were dependable in the right hands, but heavier than most revolvers and hard to rack with only one good hand. But the kid was no dummy. He'd probably chambered a round before he got here.

Sweet Pea squealed at the sound of that familiar voice and ran into the bedroom. *Hiding under the bed if past experience with thunderstorms is any indicator.* Good, she was one thing he didn't have to worry about.

The kid moved closer, the gun held steady in his left hand, never taking his eyes off Noah.

"I'm moving as fast as I can. Don't do anything foolish. Those things have a hair trigger. They go off if you breathe funny." Not necessarily true, but if Derrick had been the shooter, Ryan might not know that.

Noah fumbled with the door, hoping to slam it in the kid's face. No such luck. Ryan never gave him a chance to close it between them.

"Drop the crutches and move to the far side of the room." The gun sagged in Ryan's hand as he used it to motion toward the back of the kitchen.

"Which is it, move or drop the crutches? I can't do both." Noah used the time to hobble across the room. He swung around and leaned against the counter, his left foot raised slightly and both crutches in one hand.

He tried to prop the crutches against the counter beside him, but Ryan shook his head and laughed. "Toss them over here. Gently."

Noah eyed the distance between them and played along. He'd find an opportunity. If the kid didn't shoot him first. It wasn't so much that he minded dying—there were days when he looked forward to it—but he needed to kill this douchebag first. "So what now, kid, do you have a plan?"

"That's Mr. Howell to you, dickhead. I'm the one with the gun. Lace your fingers together at the back of your neck."

He placed his hands behind his head, but not at the back of his neck, and he unlaced his fingers immediately. "You may have a gun, but you don't know how to use it. Besides, you don't want to shoot me. All hell would rain down on you if you shot a cop."

"Wrong again. I know how to use it just fine, and what else could happen to me? You've already managed to screw up my life. Now it's my turn to screw up yours."

He needed to get the kid to come closer. "Plenty worse can happen to you. Let's see if we can work this out. Maybe I can help you."

"Cut the crap. You can't help me. But I will tell you what I want. Pull your sweat shirt off. I want to see that scar on your chest. How'd you get it anyway, a knife? A gun? Have you been shot before?" Ryan chuckled. "Remember what it felt like before you consider crossing me."

Noah didn't move. What the fuck was the kid talking about? He didn't have a scar. There was only one thing on his chest; the date of Betsy's death. As far as he knew, the only person to ever see it was the guy who'd tattooed it on him five months ago. And this creep certainly wasn't going to be the second.

Ryan waved the gun in his direction. "In fact, take it all off. I want to make sure you don't have a weapon hidden."

Noah couldn't afford for that to happen. He only had one chance. He needed to distract the kid's attention. "Jeez, kid, I knew you had a hard on for me, but I didn't know you had a *hard-on*. What is this, get your jollies day? With that squeaky voice, I'll bet you're still a virgin."

Ryan bristled, but didn't step closer. "Shut your mouth, cop. I can come three, four times a night, no problem. You're past your prime, probably lucky to get it up once a week."

He reached for one of the crutches and whacked Noah on his sore knee. "Those were orders, not suggestions."

Noah's howl of pain was only slightly exaggerated. Had something broken in there? If he took a step after this guy, would he fall on his face? He eased his foot down and placed a little weight on it. The pain was excruciating, but the knee held him up.

He pulled the legs up on his sweat pants. "There. You can see. No back-up piece." He fumbled as he turned his pockets inside out, then lowered the waistband on his pants several inches and turned in a circle, using the counter for support. Was the kid watching? "Nothing hidden. Hell, I was on my way to bed."

The kid wouldn't be able to hold the gun up with one hand and swing that crutch around with the other for long. He needed to stall as long as possible. "It's just the two of us in here now, kid. Truth or dare time. No woman's ever come near that thing, right? The only one who's touched it is you, and with a three and a half finger grip at that. Not getting the full experience that way, are you?"

Oh yeah, guessed it in one. Why can't I ever find anyone with an open face like that to play poker with?

Ryan took a step forward and shoved the tip of the crutch in Noah's mid-section. Noah let out an *oooff,* and doubled over. Ryan jerked the crutch up and rapped him under the chin. It hurt, but the rubber tip on the crutch kept it from doing any real damage, although he could taste a thin trickle of blood where he'd bitten his lip.

"Stand up, and shut up. I'll do the talking here." The smile that crossed Ryan's face at the sight of his blood sent a shiver down Noah's spine.

The kid's shaking already. Five more minutes, that's all I need.

"That's right, I forgot about Derrick. What was he, your little butt buddy? Was blowing you the price he paid for having you as a friend?"

Ryan moved closer and pointed the gun at Noah's right knee. "Keep it up. Your bad knee is about to become your good knee. After that, I'll start on your arms. I'll save your eyes for last, so you can see what's happening to your little dog. When I finish with you, I think I'll look up that sister of yours."

Keep coming, kid. Another couple of feet should do it. "What makes you think you can manage that? You've already tried to kill me once. That didn't work out so well, did it? And you've tried to kill the dog twice and screwed it up both times. That little dog brain outsmarted you two times. Well you've got us now, a cripple and a sick dog. Think you're capable of pulling it off this time, or do you need help? Too bad you got rid of Derrick just when you needed him the most."

Ryan's face turned an unhealthy shade of red. Spittle flew from his mouth and the hand holding the gun shook like a flag on a windy day.

Now we're getting somewhere. Make a move, asshole. Come on, you know you want to hit me.

"I'll tell you what I'm capable of. I've been killing since I was fourteen years old."

"Little defenseless animals. I doubt you have what it takes to kill a human. You needed to trick Derrick into doing that for you." Noah's leg ached and the blows he'd received were starting to take a toll on his already bruised body, but he couldn't afford to lean against the counter. He had to be ready to spring at the first opening.

Ryan's eyes got hard, and he took a step back, not closer. *Shit. Wrong way, kid. Move my direction.*

"Yeah, I started with animals. They're a good warm up, and they make such pitiful sounds. Always good for a laugh. It didn't take me long to move up to bigger prey."

"What'd you do, beat up drunks?" *Bingo. If that face gets any redder, he'll pop an artery and I won't have to do a thing.*

The crutch smacked against his hip. Not fun, but no real damage done. The kid's swings were getting wilder.

"The day I got my license, I took my mom's car; threw mud on the plates to cover the numbers. I told her I was going to the library." Ryan's face paled. "She always believed everything I told her. Not like my father."

What the hell was that look when he talked about his parents? Maybe it's something I can work with.

"Yeah, I saw how proud your mother looked when she told me how you were working your way through school. Wish I could have seen her face the day she had to bail you out of jail. Now *that* would have been good for a real laugh."

Whack. That blow wasn't as hard, but it hit the same spot. Noah shifted slightly, lowering his hip a few inches. If Ryan kept hitting him in the same spot, he wouldn't be able to move in a few minutes, but if he turned away, that left his family jewels exposed and one good blow there could put him on the floor.

"Those bums laughed too, when they saw me. But they didn't laugh for long. You know, it's risky to drive around with a gun in the car, but no one thinks twice about a baseball bat. Especially if you throw a glove in the back seat."

"So you beat up a few drunks. Big deal. Men too old or too wasted to fight back. You think that makes you a killer? It only makes you a little weasel." Noah gritted his teeth as Ryan swung the crutch again.

Son of a bitch. That blow came way to close to his 'nads for comfort. Not that he'd needed them lately, but he wasn't ready to give them up. Time to get this wrapped up before it was too late.

"I always watched to make sure they got up afterwards. Didn't want the cops looking too closely. Until one guy got up and looked fine, but died the next day. I must have hit him on the head. The paper said his brain swelled from a blow. He was my first, but there've been others since. I'm not like you, too chicken-shit to actually complete the deed."

Noah's breath caught in his throat. He was well aware what a subdural hematoma could do. When he'd gone after his father's violin, the guy had tried to yank the money from his hand. He'd shoved him and the guy tripped, hitting his head on a chair. The guy was already on his feet when Noah slapped the money down and grabbed the violin and a couple of bottles of Oxycodone for his mother.

When his body was found two days later, the police considered it a drug deal gone bad. And in a way, it was.

If he'd stayed, gotten the guy some help, it would have been nothing. Self-defense. But taking the drugs put it in a different class.

At least his mother had died in peace, his father's violin beside her and agonizing pain a distant memory. Unfortunately, the memory of the guy's death had never left Noah in peace.

Ryan jabbed him again and Noah cursed himself for letting his mind wander when he needed to be at his sharpest.

"What have you ever accomplished, cop? You dropped out of Juilliard. You quit music. You'll never succeed because you never finish what you start." Ryan lowered the crutch, but kept the gun pointed at his mid-section.

"What would you call success in the music business? Singing at Carnegie Hall? Winning a Grammy? I had both of those before I was your age."

Ryan took a step back and blinked several times.

That got him. He never expected that answer.

"With your little teenage choir? Big whoop. All the parents came."

"What'd you do, Google me? Shows your research is not very thorough. It was albums in those days, not CDs, but my picture was on the cover and I was listed as soloist. I still get a couple of calls a year from opera companies asking if I'd like to join them. But hunting down slime balls like you gives me much more satisfaction than standing in front of an audience singing."

"I don't believe you. Sing something for me."

"Sing? Now? Are you kidding me?" This kid was fricking unbelievable. Didn't they teach him in hit man school to do the job and get out of there? That was fine with him. He'd learned in cop school to keep the perp talking until help came or you saw an opportunity to take him out. Whichever happened first.

Noah swallowed and cleared his throat. How long since he'd sung a note? Funny thing, he'd kind of missed it lately. He almost chuckled. Hard to believe, but the kid was actually doing him a favor.

He pulled in a deep breath and let the notes of *Ave Maria* roll out, his voice rusty at first, but picking up depth as he went on. Damn, he'd totally missed that note, and hadn't held the next one long enough. The kid didn't seem to notice. A definite low-brow.

His mom had been right when she nagged him about practice—Use it or lose it. *I sure hope that doesn't apply to other things I haven't been using.*

This wasn't working. He was tiring while Ryan was resting. "You don't look like you're enjoying this. Do you want me to sing something else? Rock? Country? Anything but Rap."

"I want you to tell me the name of that fucking witness." Ryan's eyes bored into him and Noah could almost taste the hatred rolling off his body.

If he couldn't get the kid to move closer soon, he was in trouble. *I don't want to die,* he thought with a start, surprised at the realization. *Besides, it wouldn't be only me. He'll keep killing, just for the fun of it.* And he'd start with Sweet Pea. That was not going to happen. "You can try to beat it out of me, if you think you're man enough."

Ryan shifted his grip on the crutch and his gun hand wavered. That was all the opening Noah needed. He grabbed his mother's cane from between the counter and the refrigerator and swung it with all his force, burying the brass dog's snout into Ryan's gun hand. A satisfying crunch told him bones were broken. The weapon flew across the room and hit Sweet Pea's water bowl, making it ring like a bell and splashing water over the floor.

Ryan raised the crutch in the air and swung it at his head, but with fingers missing on one hand and broken bones in the other, his aim was off. The blow hit Noah on the shoulder that had been dislocated when he fell over the professor and painful tingles ran down the length of his arm.

Noah gritted his teeth and watched as Ryan tried to swing the crutch again. He held the cane up with both hands and blocked most of the blow. The cane broke with a resounding *crack*.

A strangled bellow came from Ryan as he threw the crutch at Noah. With Ryan's strange, squeaky voice, the sound would have been laughable at any other time.

Noah raised an arm to deflect the blow and took two steps forward, his hip protesting more than his sore knee. He drew back his fist and socked Ryan solidly on the jaw. Pain from his sore hand shot up his arm, but so what? It was the most satisfying thing he'd done in months.

Ryan went down like a puppet with the strings cut.

"You've got to be kidding me. I pulled my punch. Big scary killer, put down with a little tap like that." He nudged the kid with his toe, but he didn't move. Pathetic.

Noah retrieved his back-up weapon from the top of the fridge and stuffed it into the waistband of his pants. He grabbed his handcuffs and slapped them on the still unconscious felon.

"Okay, Sweet Pea," he called. "It's safe to come out."

CHAPTER THIRTY

SWEET PEA DANCED circles around Ryan's prone body. Then she stopped to pee near his head.

"That's okay, girl. I wanted to do the same thing myself." Noah sat on a chair, catching his breath. He scooped Sweet Pea into his lap. "I'm not going to tell you what he wanted to do to you, but he could never have caught you. I've spent too many mornings trying to round you up to think an amateur could corral you."

He set the little dog back on the floor. "I need you to watch him for me for just a few minutes. Can you do that? Bark if he wakes up, but *don't bite him.*"

Noah eased to his feet. Everything hurt—his chin, his solar plexus, his bad knee that had been almost well, his good knee, his hip, and other parts that he hadn't identified yet. Was it possible to limp on both sides?

He pulled his cell phone from the pocket where it had remained hidden when Ryan thought his pockets were empty.

"You still there, partner?"

"I'm here. Already on my way to the car. Couldn't figure out what was going on at first, but the minute I heard that kid's obnoxious voice, I had Jeannie call 9-1-1 from the hotel phone. They should be there any second. You all right?"

Noah hobbled into the living room, the phone still pressed to his ear. "I will be after a long soak in Epsom Salts."

"How's our little friend? You didn't kill him, did you? I don't want to have to do the paperwork."

"Nah. I sure wanted to, but I thought better of it." He stopped. No, he hadn't even really wanted to. Not anymore. It didn't seem important enough to go through that anguish again. Maybe he'd finally come to grips with what he'd done. Learned a lesson. Even forgiven himself.

Noah stirred the embers in the fireplace and added a couple of pieces of kindling. The fire blazed up, destroying any last traces of the violin. His heart lifted as it disappeared. "You need to send an ambulance though. He's out cold."

"A bus is already on the way. I knew one of you would need it. Where'd you have the phone hidden? Everything was muffled."

"In my rear pocket, except when I had my back to him. Then it was in my front pocket and I was blindly trying to find you on speed dial. Just get here as fast as you can. I don't want to face the lieutenant on my own."

Sweet Pea barked and Noah flipped the phone closed before rushing back to the kitchen.

Ryan was sitting up, trying to shake the cobwebs from his head. He kicked at the dog and she darted away.

"You hurt my dog again, and I still might shoot you." It felt distasteful even to talk to the guy.

Ryan looked up, his eyes pleading. "Do it. Shoot me. I can't spend the rest of my life in jail. I couldn't stand it. I'll go crazy."

A smile crossed Noah's face. "I know. That's why I won't."

Noah watched the pathetic lump sitting on his kitchen floor. "Heck, kid, I'll give you one break. You put my money back in my bank account and I won't tell the DA how you stole it."

Ryan's eyes widened and Noah laughed. "You think the bank didn't send me a notice the minute it disappeared?"

"You weren't using it. All this time and it was just sitting there. I needed it to start a new life."

"Well, you're sure as hell not going to use it to pay for your defense. And if the DA finds out you took it, you'll have trouble playing the crazy card."

"You'll never have a moment's peace. I'll haunt your dreams. You'll be afraid to sleep in your own bed." Ryan spoke faster and faster, hysteria tinting his voice.

"Now you're the one who's all wet. You're nothing to me. I'll never give you another thought. You're no more than a bug on the wall, just one more two-bit psychopathic egomaniac. And not even a good one at that."

Sirens wailed in the distance. "Have fun, kid. What's left of your life will be spent in a cell the size of my laundry room. Everywhere you look will be gray concrete and steel bars. You'll long for any color, any glimpse of sky. You think college food is bad, wait till you try prison chow. The only thing worse than the taste is the smell. Oh, they'll have books, but not anything you'd want to read. And even those will have chunks of pages ripped out."

Red and blue lights flashed through the windows and reflected off the pale yellow walls. Ryan's eyes filled with tears as the sirens stopped in front of Noah's house.

Conner twisted in a slow circle, taking in every detail of the crime scene. The woman's bowels had let loose, adding that stink to the stench of blood and gunpowder. She might not have known what was coming, but the man had. He'd tried to flee into the hall, and it had taken more than one shot to bring him down. Even then he'd lived for a few minutes.

How could a kid do that to his own parents? Was he born that way or were his parents to blame? Nature or nurture? The lawyers and doctors could argue that one for months to come. Years probably.

He thought of Jeannie, safe and warm in the hotel bed, and their daughter, growing bigger every day. A shiver went down his spine. So many things could go wrong. Up till now, he'd only worried about their physical health.

"You seen enough, Detective?" The pimply-faced techie stood waiting, paper suit on and evidence box at the ready.

"Yeah, I'm done. Detectives Cortez and Sparks—you know, the great big guy and his partner with the velvet voice?—are on their way. They'll be the ones in charge here. I just had to see it with my own eyes."

Conner stepped past the bodies, careful not to leave tracks in the blood, and left the house. The cold night air helped clear the smell of death from his nose, but even if he could scrub his eyes with peroxide, he'd never erase the sight of those two bodies.

He'd seen worse murder scenes, much worse, but he'd met these people while they were still alive. At the courthouse, the mother had yelled at him and cried. She obviously believed her son was innocent. The father had talked about lawyers and legal technicalities. He might not have known the extent of his son's crimes, but he'd suspected something wasn't right. Now their own flesh and blood had murdered them.

He trudged back to Noah's, taking deep breaths and trying to clear his head before he had to deal with their lieutenant. There'd be questions about why Noah hadn't left or called for protection, but in the end, they'd both come out okay.

He passed Noah sitting in a lawn chair in the far corner of his backyard. The little dog sat in his lap.

Conner nodded and went into the house. So far, Noah seemed to be holding up well, but even in the dark, the strain was evident from the slump of his shoulders.

Soon, a patrolman would drive him downtown and they'd take pictures of every cut and bruise. Noah would hate that. Would they allow him to come home to sleep tonight? Conner wasn't sure.

Lieutenant Jansen stood in the kitchen, rubbing a hand across his face. "Man, I hate this. Poking through the life of one of my men. It can't be helped, but having a wacko killer break into your home is bad enough without watching the people you work with going through your things."

A voice called from the front room. "Lieutenant, I found something I can't identify."

Conner stepped to the back door and motioned to Noah. He heard a soft groan as Noah pushed out of the chair. The cane and crutches were now sealed away as evidence and Noah limped slightly as he headed toward the door.

Conner placed his hand on his partner's shoulder and they walked into the living room together. There wasn't much he could do to help, but he could be there for support. That's what friends did for each other.

One of the techies held out a wadded mass of wires.

"Guitar strings," Noah said. "My Seagull got busted when we moved in and I thought I might get a new one. I was checking to see if I needed to buy strings. Those are too old and used to be any good."

He held out his hand and the tech handed him the wad. He stuffed them in his pocket and limped back outside.

Conner watched him go, well aware that something he didn't understand had just happened.

CHAPTER THIRTY-ONE

NOAH HADN'T SEEN Laurel for two weeks and he'd forgotten how much he enjoyed her company. Their drive to the jail to visit Crystal's brother had been easy. They'd talked. They'd laughed. As if they'd know each other for years, instead of only through this case.

The trip home was another story. She'd been silent, staring out the window.

Yeah, jail visits did that to even the most hardened soul.

He should have done more to prepare her. Or taken care of it himself.

He parked in her driveway, crossed to the passenger side of his truck and opened her door. She was so short, she had to use his arm for support as she stepped out. And he didn't mind that one bit.

Her eyes lifted and she studied the sky. "Look at that beautiful shade of azure. Makes you think this awful winter might finally end."

Noah wasn't sure what azure was, except maybe the same color as her eyes. He unzipped his jacket. "I think I can feel spring coming on."

"Well, it's not here yet." She pulled her coat tighter. "Let's get inside and have some tea."

She started for the back door and he followed, enjoying the view. When he reached the kitchen, she was standing by the sink, a strand of hair held under her nose.

"I don't know which I want to do more; wash my hands or wash my hair. I swear the stink of that awful place has soaked into my skin. How do they stand it? How do you stand it? You were obviously familiar with it. You must have to go there to conduct interviews."

Noah sat in his usual chair, unsure what to say, unsure what to do. Unsure about everything. In the days since Ryan Howell had tried to kill him, his body had healed. The bruises had faded away. Even his mind seemed clearer than it had since… Before. He could concentrate better, but the loneliness sometimes caught him unaware.

He rubbed a hand through his hair. *I should have gotten a haircut.* "They tell me the noise is worse than the smell. It's never quiet, it's never dark, you're never alone. But long-timers get so used to the life, sometimes they can't adjust to the outside."

"Sitting in that horrid room looking at him—those rotten teeth, those hate-filled tattoos—I couldn't believe he was Crystal's brother."

"That's called meth mouth. He inherited enough money to have his teeth fixed. Don't know what he'll want to do about the tattoos. Having you stand up for him in court is going to make the difference in his life."

Laurel set a mug of coffee in front of him. "I couldn't have done it without you. Convincing the DA to drop the charges, driving me to the jail, guiding me through security, even warning me not to wear anything tight." She glanced down at her dirty jeans. "Do you think he'll be alright? Arizona is far from anyone he knows." She stood so close, he could feel the heat from her body.

"That's the best thing that could happen to him. He's there because he wants to be. He agreed to be locked down for a full year and live in a halfway house for almost as long. He can't touch his money unless he completes the program, so he has a million good reasons to try."

"None of this would have happened if you hadn't set it in motion. I hope he realizes how much you did for him." She rested her hand on his shoulder. The warmth seeped through his shirt and thawed that nugget of ice hiding in his heart.

Noah pushed his chair back and stood facing her, inches apart. His voice felt rough, ragged. As if he hadn't used it in weeks, months. He hadn't been this nervous since he was a teenager. There was a time when he knew how to do this. "I didn't do it for him. I did it for you. So you could let go of any guilt you felt over Crystal. I know guilt can eat away at you worse than a cancer."

He put his hand on her waist and she melted into him. He kissed her gently at first and when she returned the pressure, he pressed harder, hungrier, drinking her in greedily. His tongue met hers and he tasted sweetness.

She slid her arms up his back. His hands tangled in her hair. She rose on tiptoes and the kiss deepened. Time stood still and every smell, sound, sight, except her, disappeared. He felt himself grow tight against her.

"Noah?" she murmured against his lips.

"Yes?"

"I can't do this." She pulled away, breaking the current of electricity between them. "I'm still a married woman, and that means something to me even if it doesn't to Paul. But that's not all. I just don't think I'm ready. Not yet."

Oh, thank God. I wasn't sure I could manage it.

"I understand. I don't think I can, either. I'm still a married man. Or at least it feels that way sometimes. Not all the time. I'm getting there, but not quite yet." He took a step back, but didn't release her. "It's not that I don't want to."

"I can feel that," she said, laughing. "So what do we do now?"

"We can be friends. You call me any time you need something, and I'll be here before you set the phone down. You finalize your divorce. I'll work on learning how to find the joy in life. Maybe sometime down the road we can try this again."

She reached up and stroked his face. "That sounds like a plan."

Noah's backyard warmed under a weak March sun. The azaleas were covered in buds. Another two weeks and they would be a riot of color.

Not quite spring, but close enough to see her shadow.

Emma tugged at his shirttail. "I don't like mine with blood running out, Uncle Noah." She put her hands on her hips and watched him flip her burger.

"Duly noted. No blood in Emma's burger. What about Iris, does she like hers charred as well?" He pressed the spatula against the burger and a few drops of blood escaped.

"What's charred? I don't know what that means. But Iris won't eat it anyway. She doesn't eat anything. Mommy says she's going to dry up and blow away. Good. Then I'll be the only little girl at our house."

He watched Iris playing tug-of-war over an old sock with Sweet Pea. Maybe if she got more hamburgers instead of tofu casseroles, she might be willing to eat.

Or maybe it wasn't the tofu. Maybe it was just his sister's cooking.

Everything she cooked tasted like pink gum erasures and smelled like a wet dog.

He'd have to pick the kids up every week or so. Take them out for some real food.

Rachelle stepped out of the house carrying a bowl of baked beans. *Please don't let her have put tofu in them.*

"There's a big empty spot in your living room. What happened to the piano? Did you send it out to get that key repaired?" She set the bowl on the picnic table and came to stand beside him.

Her salmon steak looked about done, and he didn't want it to dry out. He moved it gently away from the fire. "A guy came to the house to fix the key. Then I donated the piano to Betsy's school. She always said how much they needed one. They put a brass plaque on it with her name engraved." His eyes stung— probably smoke from the grill—and his voice caught on the last words.

He grabbed the beer sitting next to the grill and gulped down several swallows, trying to push back the lump starting in his throat.

Maybe her friends and family weren't the only ones who'd remember her. Kids not yet born would sit at that piano and read her name, passing the love of music to another generation

Rachelle squeezed his shoulder.

Enough of this emotional bullshit. He cleared his throat. "Wait till you see what I got." He waved to his brother-in-law. "Frank, can you come over and watch the fire?"

There went his steak. It would be as charred as the girl's burgers. At least he'd left the pepper in the cabinet where Frank couldn't find it. "Wait here. I'll show you."

He rushed into the house and was back in less than two minutes, carrying a new guitar. The warm, honey-blond wood gleamed under his fingers. "It's a Taylor 300 series acoustic."

Rachelle's eyes lit up and she reached for it. She ran her hand over the wood and pulled it to her nose, breathing deeply. "What is this, spruce?"

"No, it's Hawaiian Koa."

"The heck you say. You went all out."

He could afford it since his money was safely back in his own bank account, thanks to the department computer wizards.

"How's it sound?" she asked

He reached out but she pulled it away and sat on the picnic bench, strumming. "Sweet. Dad would be proud of your choice."

Hardly. Dad didn't approve of anything that wasn't classical, but he did appreciate fine workmanship.

"What are you going to do with it? Hide in your house and play for Sweet Pea?"

"I've joined a band." He laughed when he saw Rachelle's jaw drop. "Not a real band. A group of cops that go to local hospitals and play for sick kids. Do you remember Earl Sparks? You met him at that Christmas thing a couple of years ago."

"Skinny black guy that thinks he sounds like Barry White?"

"That's the one. He put this thing together and asked me to join them."

"He probably thinks he's going to sing lead. I'll bet that lasts about one song after they hear you."

"Maybe, we'll see. But I can be happy just playing back-up." Noah went back to the grill and rescued what was left of the steaks from his brother-in-law.

The side gate creaked and he glanced over to see Conner and Jeannie approaching. Jeannie carried a bowl of potato salad. *Well, there'll be something to eat if Frank burned the steaks and Rachelle ruined the beans.*

"Hey, partner, I heard a rumor you were pretending it was spring and had fired up the grill." Conner slapped him on the back and shook hands with Frank. "Rachelle, you're looking as lovely as ever. It's hard to believe you're any relation to this big, ugly guy."

Jeannie gave Rachelle an awkward hug around her growing baby bump and pointed to the guitar in her hands. "What's this?"

"Noah's new toy." She grinned at her brother. "He claims he's actually going to play and sing in public. Hard to believe. No one, and I mean no one, has heard him sing in years."

Betsy heard me sing plenty of times, whenever she asked.

The girls rushed over and Conner picked up Emma, swinging her around until she squealed.

"Mommy, Mommy, sing for us." Iris tugged on her mother's skirt.

Rachelle strummed a few cords and began to sing *I Hope You Dance,* her voice a cross between their mother and Sarah McLachlan.

Noah breathed in the aroma of grass, cooking meat, and

little girls. Sweet Pea ran in circles around his leg, waiting for a taste of steak.

A sense of peace washed over him. A new case would be waiting for him on Monday morning, and he'd work it hard, but it would be his job, not his life. This was his family. He was home.

ACKNOWLEDGEMENTS

How do you say thank you to the many people who pass through your life every day, bringing joy and encouragement?

Ron and Karen, Angela and Jason you are my anchor. I depend on you. Andrew, Sam, and Caroline, I am so proud of the people you have grown to be. Bode, you light up my heart and make me smile. I love you all.

Thank you Jan and Shawnna and the CC group. You gave me a push when I needed it and suggestions when I needed them. You made me laugh while challenging me to do my best.

To the Lethal Ladies of KOD, your help was invaluable.

Christie, Steve, I thank you both for more things than I can mention in one line

Kimberly, thanks for all your help. I couldn't have done it without you.

Did you enjoy *Winter Song?* Follow the *Seasons Pass* series with Detective Noah Daugherty and his partner Conner Crawford as they solve more cases and face new problems throughout the year.

SPRING
SHADOW

Homicide detective Noah Daugherty finds purpose in solving the most horrendous of crimes. The last thing he wants is to babysit some spoiled country singer, but that's exactly what his lieutenant demands.

Posing undercover as a member of the singer's band, he makes it his mission to protect her from a stalker whose ominous threats have become increasingly personal.

As things heat up, she hides a piece of her past that is key to solving the case, ashamed of the part she plays.

Can Noah unearth the painful truth before spring casts its dark shadow?

SUMMER STORM

It's a scorching Houston summer, and homicide detective Noah Daugherty's only consolation is his life's work: solving crimes to atone for the sins of his past.

When the high-powered CEO of Beneficial Products, a company dedicated to the production of healthy foods, is discovered drowned in her hot tub, what appears to be either an accident or suicide, quickly escalates into something much more sinister. As the body count rises, the link between victims becomes all too clear.

Can Noah find a killer bent on vigilante justice before the storms of summer strike?

AUTUMN
SECRETS

The harvest moon has arrived and homicide detective Noah Daugherty is drawn into one final, harrowing case when the search for clues leads him to the middle of a killing field. Desperate, he enlists the help of a woman from his past. Together they discover a serial killer, hell bent on reaping his own depraved version of social sanitation.

As Noah continues his urgent search for justice, the demented madman seems to stay one step ahead, taunting him and threatening everyone he holds dear.

Can Noah put a stop to the killing, or will he be buried along with autumn's secrets?